THE RICH DIE HARD

BY BEVERLEY NICHOLS

Prelude
Patchwork
Self
Twenty-Five
Crazy Pavements
Are They the Same at Home?
The Star-Spangled Manner
Women and Children Last
Oxford-London-Hollywood
Evensong
For Adults Only
Failures
Cry Havoc!
Down the Garden Path
A Thatched Roof
A Village in a Valley
The Fool Hath Said
No Place Like Home
Mesmer
News of England
Revue
Green Grows the City
Men Do Not Weep
Verdict on India
The Tree That Sat Down
The Stream That Stood Still
The Mountain of Magic
All I Could Never Be
Uncle Samson
Merry Hall
A Pilgrim's Progress
Laughter on the Stairs
No Man's Street
The Moonflower
Sunlight on the Lawn
Death to Slow Music

BEVERLEY NICHOLS

THE RICH DIE HARD

HUTCHINSON OF LONDON

HUTCHINSON & CO. (*Publishers*) LTD
178-202 Great Portland Street, London, W 1

London Melbourne Sydney
Auckland Bombay Toronto
Johannesburg New York

First published 1957

*Set in eleven point Garamond one point leaded
and printed in Great Britain by
Taylor Garnett Evans & Co. Ltd
Watford, Hertfordshire*

CONTENTS

I

THE SHOT IS FIRED

HOWEVER hotly the other facts may have been argued, in the tense and testing weeks that followed the night of October the thirteenth, on one point, at least, there was no conflict of opinion . . . Miss Larue had taken too much to drink.

There were, of course, individual variations of opinion as to the precise degree of intoxication which she had attained. John, the young footman who had served the champagne, seemed merely to think she was a little "merry"; as far as he could remember, he had only filled her glass three times. This evidence was weakened by the testimony of Miss Sally Kane who—because the party was a man short—was sitting on her right. As soon as her head was turned, Miss Kane protested, Miss Larue had purloined her glass in the most blatant manner, and swallowed its contents before she could be prevented. Lady Coniston had also noticed this unladylike conduct—which, she was at pains to add—had not really surprised her. She had also noticed that Miss Larue had consumed three dry Martinis before dinner, that she had caught her dress on the edge of a Chippendale commode as they were walking down the long gallery to the panelled music room, and that after dinner she had helped herself to an inordinate quantity of yellow Chartreuse. All of which goes to show that Lady Coniston was a very observant woman.

The other members of the house party testified according to their temperaments. Mr Cecil Gower-Jones, the brilliant young musical critic of *The New Era*, was reluctant to discuss the matter at all; drunkenness bored and disgusted him; when he saw Miss Larue's condition he looked the other way. ("Dear Cecil," as Lady Coniston was later to remark, "seems always to have been looking the other way at the crucial moment"). However, on the few occasions when he had been compelled to turn in her direction he had observed that she was extremely flushed, that she was breathing heavily, and that the corsage of her dress was disarranged. These symptoms had also been remarked by Palmer, the highly intelligent young butler, but without, apparently, arousing the same feelings of distaste. 'Fair smashing she looked,' he remarked, in the servants' hall, 'with her hair all mussed up, lolling back in her chair without giving a damn. Like that angel in the Rubens on the staircase.' An intelligent observation. Miss Larue, though scarcely angelic, had the lines, the colour, and the texture of a Rubens of the very best period.

The testimony of the others was much as would be expected. Sir Luke Coniston at first remarked tersely that he was too preoccupied with the eruption of the stock market to pay attention to the antics of a fuddled woman. So she was fuddled? Yes, he supposed so. Now he came to think of it, she had spilt some brandy over his dinner jacket. Not that he was worried by that. He had plenty of other dinner jackets.

Andrew Lloyd, the host, told roughly the same story. He too was preoccupied with the stock market . . . a good deal more heavily, indeed, than Sir Luke, and on the other side of the fence. Yes, he had noticed Miss Larue's condition. However, he had not been greatly concerned by it; he had seen that she was in the capable hands of his wife Nancy, who had tactfully conducted her to bed, an hour before it had all happened.

It remained for Nancy Lloyd to supply the only evidence that shed a rather more kindly light on the conduct of the unfortunate woman—though perhaps her gentle suggestions could hardly rank as "evidence". She agreed that Miss Larue had taken a good deal to drink, but she was a gay, carefree creature, and perhaps she had not realized what she was doing. Perhaps, too, she was not well . . . had they not noticed how pale she was looking before dinner?

Again, was it not possible that she might have taken her usual sleeping draught before dinner, instead of afterwards? Miss Larue was by no means incapable when she reached her room. She had lain down on the bed, and stared up to the ceiling, and said . . . quite sensibly . . . that she would wait a while before undressing, and that then she would have a bath, and perhaps read a little before going to sleep. She had looked so beautiful as she lay there, so tragically different from . . . from afterwards.

2

Every story, whether of tragedy or of comedy, stretches its tendrils deep into the past, but at first it is only that final hour that need concern us. And though, later on, we shall be moving closer to the characters, so closely that we can see every shadow that flits across their faces, for the moment we can content ourselves with a theatrical view of the whole affair—a seat, as it were, in the stalls.

The hour is a quarter to ten on the night of Saturday October 13th, and the time is very near to the present. The scene is Broome Place, a Queen Anne mansion standing high on the Sussex hills, the property of Andrew Lloyd, financier. The *dramatis personae* have briefly made themselves known to us.

The curtain rises to the music of a gramophone. Like every other object in Broome Place, this gramophone is luxurious and exceptional. Luxurious because it has been made by hand, by master craftsmen; exceptional because, though it is encased in linenfold panelling, of the Tudor period, and though a piece of faded crimson velvet— probably cut from an altar-cloth—is laid across the top, it does not look nearly as vulgar as it sounds. "Though of course," Nancy Lloyd had once remarked, "everybody will *say* it is vulgar, simply because Andrew is a stockbroker. When one is a stockbroker, one is vulgar even if one buys a Rembrandt."

A*

The men had just joined the ladies. Cecil Gower-Jones was the first to enter. As soon as he heard the music he clasped his hands in ecstasy and tripped up to his hostess.

'Darling!' he exclaimed. 'How did you know? How did you guess that Blue Joseph was the one man in the world I needed tonight?'

She gave him a quizzical smile. 'Perhaps I read your articles, Cecil.'

'You always say the right thing.' He kissed the tips of his fingers towards the gramophone. 'Blue Joseph—bless him!'

'Blue who?' The question, staccato and abrupt, came from a girl who was standing by the chimney-piece, holding her hands towards the log fire. She was about twenty-one, fair, with a poor complexion, but pretty in a turn-up-nose sort of way. But she looked sulky.

'Blue who d'you say?' she snapped again, before he could answer.

He stared at her in mock astonishment. 'That, coming from an American, and a Southerner into the bargain, is a most extraordinary question.'

Sally Kane shrugged her shoulders. And yet, the animal rhythm of the music began to sway her. Cecil noticed that she was flicking her fingers softly. 'You see?' he said, 'you can't resist it. Let's dance.' He saw her glance at the clock. 'Your tiresome Richard won't be coming down for another hour.'

She turned towards Palmer who was passing with a heavy silver tray, loaded with drinks. 'You're quite sure his lordship said he wouldn't be down till eleven?'

'Quite sure, miss.'

She nodded thoughtfully. Her expression indicated that Lord Richard might not receive too warm a welcome. Then she gave her hand to Cecil, and they danced.

Sir Luke came up to Nancy Lloyd and bent over her. Everything about Sir Luke was glossy, and as he lowered his head the light from the chandelier sparkled on his thick black hair.

'I always understood that you loathed this sort of music,' he said.

How strange it is, she thought to herself, that though Luke went to Harrow and Cambridge his voice still had the faint echo of an Eastern bazaar.

Aloud she said: 'I do. It gives me the creeps.'

'Then why have it?'

'Because it's the thing, of course.' She smiled up at him. 'One isn't considered intelligent nowadays unless one can go into ecstasies over a noise which—to me—sounds like a collection of negro neurotics in the last stages of epilepsy.'

'Then why have it?' he repeated.

How persistent he is, she thought, with a flicker of irritation. The Eastern bazaar touch again!

'Cecil adores it. And one has to consider one's guests.' She glanced over at Lady Coniston, who was flicking the pages of a glossy magazine. 'I expect Sybil would like to dance.'

'Why not Andrew?'

'Because Andrew never dances. And because Sybil's your wife. And because you've hardly spoken a word to her all the evening. And because—oh dear!—because if we have to listen to this horror, we might at least get some exercise while we're doing it.'

He sighed, bowed, and clicked his heels. Then he went across to his wife. She greeted him eagerly, and they rose to dance.

3

'Turn off that thing . . . turn't off!'

It was five minutes later, and the cry came from the ill-fated Miss Larue. She was lying back in a chair of crimson velvet, in the furthest corner of the room. Her eyes were half closed and—as Palmer, the butler, had observed—her corsage was disarranged. Because of the din of the music the dancing couples did not hear her, nor apparently did Mrs. Lloyd. But Andrew Lloyd heard her. He turned to his wife and said something in a low voice.

Before she could reply, Miss Larue had spoken again, this time very much louder. Pointing her finger at Cecil Gower-Jones, whom she evidently regarded as the instigator of the music, she screamed: 'Turn off that bloody thing . . . turn't off, I tell you!'

The couples stopped in their tracks and stared at her. Everything happened very quickly in the next few moments. Cecil, after a scared glance at Miss Larue, who was making efforts to rise from her chair, turned towards the gramophone with the intention of stopping it. Sally, his partner, stepped back to the fireplace with a gesture of disgust. The Conistons stood and stared. Andrew Lloyd took a pace towards her, and hesitated . . .

It was Nancy Lloyd who saved the situation. She walked quickly across to the Conistons, took Sir Luke's arm, returned it to his wife's waist, and with a deft twirl of the hand set them dancing again. She beckoned Cecil from the gramophone and brought him back to Sally. Then she went up to Miss Larue and—miracle of miracles—whispered something to her that made her laugh. Miss Larue laughed so loudly that her giggles rose above the roar of the gramophone; and it was to the sound of this laughter that she left the room on Nancy's arm.

When she returned, a couple of minutes later, Cecil turned off the gramophone and they gathered round her.

'My dear,' exclaimed Lady Coniston, 'you deserve a medal. *What* an exhibition!'

'Is she all right?' It was Andrew who spoke. There was a note of anxiety in his voice which made Lady Coniston give him one of her shrewd glances.

Nancy nodded calmly. 'Perfectly all right. She's lying down on the bed. She's probably asleep already.'

Cecil gave a stage shudder. 'I hope she *stays* asleep. If she comes down again I shall *scream*. She looked as if she were going to *spring* on me!'

'What was the joke?' asked Sally.

'Something idiotic. I forget.' Nancy turned to Sir Luke. 'Do let's talk about something else. Or do you want to go on dancing?' Nobody showed any inclination to do so.

'In that case' suggested Andrew, 'let's go and look at my new Van Goyen.'

Sir Luke scowled at him. 'You've bought another Van Goyen?'

'Certainly. Any objection?'

Sir Luke merely snorted, and followed him out of the room.

As he did so, the little Louis Seize clock on the chimney-piece tinkled the hour of ten.

4

The next half hour was an interlude of comparative peace. Indeed, if this were a play, and we were sitting in the stalls, we might feel inclined to complain of inaction. There is nothing very exciting in the movements of a number of people, wandering at random through the galleries and rooms of a great house, pausing in front of pictures and staring up at them.

It was not until just after half past ten that things began to happen. Nancy Lloyd was in the library, showing Lady Coniston an exquisite little sketch of a child's head, by Romney. Suddenly there was the sound of voices raised in heated argument.

She put down the sketch with a sigh. 'Sybil darling,' she said, 'they're at it again.'

'Who?'

'Andrew and Luke. Can't you hear them?'

'Of course I can hear them.' She tapped her foot impatiently. 'It's because of that wretched Van Goyen. Andrew ought never to have mentioned it. Is it a good one?'

'Yes. It's superb.'

'That makes it all the worse. Luke feels absolutely murderous whenever Andrew buys anything important.'

The voices grew louder. 'Somebody ought to stop them.'

'I think I've done enough peace-making for one evening.'

'But darling, you're so good at it.'

Nancy hesitated. At that moment Cecil walked into the room. He gave a start when he saw the two women. 'I thought you'd gone upstairs,' he murmured. He looked over his shoulder. 'There's the *most* awful row going on.'

'Then it's a good thing you came,' snapped Lady Coniston. 'You're the only other *man* in the house.' She gave a malicious intonation to the word. 'You can go and stop them.'

Cecil merely flashed his long eyelashes at her. Without deigning to reply he flounced through the other door.

Lady Coniston sniffed. 'Nasty little creature. I can't think why you ask him. Darling, *do* go out and pour oil over things.'

Nancy still hesitated. Then she shrugged her shoulders. 'Very well,' she said.

She walked out. The two men were in the long gallery, standing in front of a picture that had been lifted from the floor and placed on a Sheraton settee. They were arguing so hotly that they did not hear her approach.

'If you'd got the faintest knowledge of Van Goyen . . .' Andrew was saying.

'If *you'd* got the faintest knowledge of Van Goyen you wouldn't have bought it without a signature.'

'I've told you forty times, there are three periods of Van Goyen . . . the green, the grey and the brown . . . and in the green period he didn't sign his pictures and . . .'

'And you can tell me forty times more, you damned fool . . . green, grey, brown—what's that got to do with it?' Sir Luke's face was twitching, and an ugly vein was standing out on his forehead.

It was at this moment that Nancy intervened. 'Listen darlings!' she cried, in such ringing tones that they were obliged to pay attention. 'I won't have my house turned into a bear garden.'

Neither of the men replied. There was the sound of heavy breathing.

'Andrew, it's very naughty of you. You've been teasing Luke. Take him off and give him a drink.'

'If Luke wants a drink, he knows where they are.'

'Thank you' said Sir Luke curtly. Without another word he turned on his heel and walked away.

Nancy stared after him. 'Where's he gone?'

'To the loo, I should think. And as far as I'm concerned he can stay there.'

'Andrew, you're being beastly. Why?'

'I don't know. I feel upset.' He sat down on the settee, and flung his arm round the frame of the picture.

'About the Van Goyen?'

'Naturally. Luke talked a lot of nonsense about it, and I don't take kindly to fools.'

She gave him an affectionate smile. 'I seem to have heard that before. But it wasn't only the Van Goyen, was it?'

As she spoke, she heard a voice from the other end of the gallery. It was Lady Coniston. She was standing on the bottom of the staircase, clutching a bundle of magazines in her arm.

'Good night, darlings!' She spoke in a stage whisper. 'I'm off to bed!' She put a finger to her lips and pointed in the direction where her husband had disappeared. Then she blew them a kiss and started to walk up the staircase.

'Silly old trollop' muttered Andrew.

'It wasn't only the Van Goyen, was it?'

'Well, Margot didn't exactly add to the gaiety of the evening.' He sighed. Then he stretched out his hand to hers. 'I thought you managed that rather awkward interlude quite perfectly.'

'Thank you. I hope I always shall.' Her voice was cold and formal. But she gripped his hand tightly.

There was silence in the long gallery. Silence is an elastic word; it can echo an eternity in a split second, it can record a mere moment of boredom in a month. This was a strange silence, that seemed to go on and on. Yet it was not a pure silence, for outside the wind was rising, rising fast, and there were many tiny moans and rattles and sighs and protests from the old house.

It was now twenty minutes to eleven.

Nancy withdrew her hand. She was not a sentimentalist, and she had her guests to think about.

'Where *is* everybody?'

'Does it matter?'

'Of course it matters. We can't all go to bed in a ridiculous huff like this. We really must do something about it. Where's Cecil, for example?' As she spoke, the butler came through the door of the study, switching out the lights behind him. 'Do you know where Mr. Gower-Jones is, Palmer?'

'He went upstairs a couple of minutes ago, madam.'

She raised her eyebrows. 'Was he going to bed?'

'I couldn't say, madam.'

She turned to her husband. 'Surely Cecil wouldn't go to bed without saying good-night?'

'He probably only went up to powder his nose.'

'That is all, Palmer.' She frowned impatiently as the butler walked away. 'Then there's Sally. What's happened to Sally?'

'She was here a minute ago.'

'She can't have been. I've been here at least three minutes myself.'

'Don't be so meticulous. I've no idea how many minutes it was, but she was here when Luke started to get so obstreperous. So I sent her away.'

'Where to?'

'I told her to go and look at your new Hondecoeter.'

'But that's still standing against the wall in the flower-room, and she'll never be able to light it properly. It looks terrible if it's not properly lit.'

Lloyd glanced inquiringly at his wife. 'You seem strangely anxious that Sally should have a good impression of your Hondecoeter.'

'I am.' She gave him a gentle smile. 'You see, darling,

I'm not quite sure if it is a Hondecoeter at all. And if it isn't . . . well, I might be able to persuade Sally that it's just what her dear father needs for his collection.'

He took her hand and kissed it. 'I adore you when you're a crook.'

'Am I being a crook? It's a very pretty picture, Hondecoeter or no Hondecoeter. And Mr. Kane's a very silly man, millionaire or no millionaire.' Suddenly she looked over to the window. 'What was that?'

'What was what?'

'I thought I heard something.' She walked swiftly across, parted the curtains and peered out. 'No. Nothing.'

'Darling. You're getting jumpy.'

'No. Merely bored.' She let the curtains fall back again. 'Really, I do think one's guests have the most extraordinary manners nowadays. Disappearing like this. Luke was going to play me at backgammon. Where has *he* got to?'

She stepped forward, and cupped her lips between her hands. 'Luke!' she cried. 'Luke!'

Her voice . . . which was trembling, doubtless with annoyance . . . echoed and re-echoed down the long, dimly-lit gallery. It was answered by silence.

But the silence was short-lived. A moment later, there came the sound of a shot . . . the shot that really starts our story.

THE LETTER AND THE LAW

YOUNG Ronald Bates should never have been a policeman. He was altogether too gentle, too amiable, and too diffident about interfering in other people's affairs. Unless he encountered some instance of actual cruelty—when he was inclined to lose his head and take the law almost too violently into his own hands—he would much rather have let people go their own way, parking their cars on the wrong side of the road, leaving their lights off, and having illegal nips of whiskey at the awful hour of one minute past ten.

But what could one do when one had a brilliant big brother at the Yard? As soon as Arthur had been made assistant to the great superintendent Waller, young Ron had known he was doomed. "*You* may do as well one day" they had assured him. "*You* may step into his shoes." It was useless to assure them that this was the last place where he wanted to step. Into the Force he had to go. As a result here he was, on this stormy night of October 13th, sitting entirely alone in the office of the little police station at West Greenstead, praying most earnestly that nothing would happen.

He had a special reason for apprehension. Only a few hours before, his superior, who should normally have been at hand to deal with any emergency, had suddenly collapsed in agony over his desk, and was at this very moment in the local hospital having an operation for appendicitis. As if that were not enough, a telephone call had come through ten minutes later from the night duty officer of the South Sussex police, informing him that four officers from that station had been involved in a motor accident, and warning him to "stand by", in case anything happened in the neighbourhood. "Stand by." It had a most sinister sound.

He glanced at the clock. It was eleven-fifteen. Forty-five more minutes to go. At midnight, thank heavens, he would be relieved by young Simpson, who had no inhibitions, no sort of doubts as to his own ability to deal with any situation, and no sort of hesitation in informing him how much better he would deal with it than anybody else. Well . . . he was welcome to his "situations".

Then the telephone rang.

The call came from Broome Place; Andrew Lloyd was speaking. As he listened, young Bates' face assumed an expression of misery. The worst had happened. A young lady, Miss Larue, had committed suicide. There were "circumstances that seemed to call for investigation". His presence was urgently requested.

As he hung up, Ron felt near to tears. He had only two consolations—one was faint, the other not so faint. Firstly, he could not help feeling a slight gratification at the thought of young Simpson's chagrin when he heard that he had missed this chance of proving his genius. Secondly, he had a strong suspicion—half fear, half hope—that his own incompetence as a policeman would be so obvious that he would shortly be compelled—big brother or no big brother—to seek alternative employment.

2

The great house was ablaze with lights when, at precisely half past eleven, Bates junior drew up outside the porch and parked his motor-bicycle. Even as he did so the front door opened, and he saw the familiar face of Palmer. He felt vaguely comforted. He had often seen Palmer in the local pub; sometimes they had played a game of darts together. Perhaps Palmer would be able to give him a few tips.

But before he could even say hello, other figures appeared and his heart sank again. There was Andrew Lloyd, in a dinner jacket, and a lady in black velvet with diamonds round her throat, and another lady in the strangest costume —a sort of dressing-gown—and a pretty girl in green, and a couple more gentlemen. They were all staring at him.

'Good evening, officer,' said Lloyd. 'Will you come in?'

'Thank you, sir.' The very sound of the word "officer" alarmed him. As he stepped inside, and caught his first glimpse of the long gallery, he could scarcely believe his eyes. It seemed to stretch into infinity. It was like something out of a movie. No—it was better. There was a glow and a sparkle and a richness about it that you wouldn't find in any movie. Especially a richness. Young Ron might not be a good policeman but he was a sensitive human being, and for a moment he felt overwhelmed with richness. He stood on richness, as he saw the soft Bokhara rugs that stretched the whole length of the gallery. He was blinded by richness, as he saw the long series of cunningly-lit masterpieces stretching into the distance—Madonnas and saints and Holy Families, starkly painted, but glittering with gold and primitive blue and blood-scarlet. He was stifled by richness; the very air was heavy with it.

At the foot of the staircase Lloyd paused. 'Nancy,' he said, 'you might take everybody into the music-room. We may be wanted afterwards. I'll take the officer straight upstairs.'

Bates followed him up the long staircase and down another gallery, at the end of which they turned to the right. As they did so, a door opened and an elderly man stepped out. He was wearing a black coat and carrying a small leather bag. Bates recognized him as one of the doctors from the local hospital.

'I was just coming to find you,' he said to Lloyd. His voice was weak and querulous. It was long past Dr. Cartwright's bed-time.

'Perhaps you would stay and have a word with Mr....' Andrew gave Bates a sudden smile. 'I can't go on calling you officer,' he said.

'Bates, sir.'

'With Mr. Bates.'

The doctor shrugged his shoulders. 'If you wish. Though there is nothing much that I can tell him.' He stepped back into the bedroom. He turned towards Bates. 'It is not a very pretty sight' he observed curtly.

Bates merely nodded. They went inside.

3

No. The late Miss Margot Larue was not a pretty sight. But young Bates, in his brief career, had seen worse. His stomach turned once. Then he gulped, took a deep breath, and got on with the job.

He found, rather to his surprise, that the entries he was jotting in his notebook were being written in a firm hand, and they seemed to be making sense. As these entries formed an important link in the subsequent investigations, a *précis* of them is attached.

MARGOT LARUE

Cause of death. Shot through right ear at point blank range. Considerable disfigurement. Doctor confirms death instantaneous.

Position of body. Lying on bed. Right arm hanging over side. Revolver on floor about six inches from hand.

Revolver. Service Colt, mark II. Only one bullet fired.

Signs of violence. None in bedroom. Counterpane unruffled. Glass of water by side of bed, also plate of grapes. However, a broken bottle on floor of bathroom, probably of some toilet preparation. Contents retained for analysis.

Means of entering bedroom. Four doors.

1. Main door on to corridor. This was locked from inside. Key in lock.

2. Bathroom door on to corridor. This was also locked

from inside. However, key of this door was lying on bathroom floor.

These facts attested by several witnesses.

3. There is also a door from the bathroom connecting with the next bedroom. This room occupied by Miss Kane, who states that she was unaware of the connexion. Door locked. No key in lock.

4. Fire Escape. It was by this that Mr. Lloyd gained access to the room, after discovering that all doors were locked. Here again, door locked on inside, but windows partially open. Key in lock.

Special Notes. It would seem—at the present stage of investigation—that a number of people entered the room immediately Mr. Lloyd unlocked the doors. According to Mr. Lloyd, his wife was first. He states that she only stayed for a moment. But he also remembers the entry of Mr. Gower-Jones and Sir Luke Coniston. Apparently neither Miss Kane nor Lord Richard entered.

Here the *précis* stops. For it was at this point that Andrew Lloyd handed him a letter.

And it was at this point that Bates junior lost his head.

4

'I would like you to read this,' said Lloyd.

Bates, who was standing by the window, peering down the fire-escape, turned round.

'What is it, sir?'

'It's a letter that I found on Miss Larue's desk. It was lying face downwards. I don't know why I picked it up and read it. But I did. And I'm glad I did, because . . . well . . . it has an ugly sound.'

Bates stepped forward. Lloyd lifted the letter, holding it between the extreme tips of his fingers. But for the moment he did not hand it to him. He said: 'You may wonder why I did not show you this before. I had a very simple reason. I did not want to prejudice your investigations. I wanted you to proceed as though it were an ordinary suicide. As of course it may be . . . as indeed I hope it *is*.'

'You had already mentioned that there were what you described as special circumstances, sir.'

Lloyd nodded. 'So I had.' This young man, he thought, is not such a fool as he looks.

'Well, here are the—special circumstances.'

He handed him the letter. It was written in block capitals on a plain sheet of cheap cream notepaper, torn off a pad.

DEAR MARGOT,

SO YOU ARE DETERMINED TO PLAY THE SPHINX. VERY WELL. IF IT ISN'T IN MY HANDS BY SATURDAY NIGHT THERE WILL BE A SHOWDOWN. AND I DON'T MEAN MERELY A LITTLE MATTER OF SOCIAL EMBARRASSMENT.

X X X

Bates junior stared at the letter, and the words suddenly seemed to grow dim before him. Up till this moment he had been surprised at his own sang-froid. Like a well-trained puppet he had gone through all the right motions; he had asked the right questions, made the right notes. He had not allowed himself to be intimidated by the richness of the surroundings; he had not even been overcome by the gruesome appearance of the late Miss Larue. But now . . .

Andrew Lloyd was staring at him. 'What do you make of it?' he said.

Bates looked up. Perhaps Lloyd sensed something of the dumb appeal in his eyes. "Not a fool" he may have said to himself, "but perhaps not a very good policeman."

Aloud he said: 'Perhaps you will agree that we might be justified in calling in Scotland Yard?'

'I'm afraid we couldn't do that, sir. Not yet, sir.'

'Why not?'

'It wouldn't be the right procedure, sir.' At all costs, thought Bates, he must stick to the "right procedure".

Nothing would have given him greater pleasure than to get through to the Yard, and to throw himself on his big brother's mercy, but such conduct was unheard of.

'May I use the telephone, sir?'

'Certainly. It's over there on the desk. Who are you ringing up?'

'The night duty officer of the South Sussex Police.'

'That's the right procedure, is it?' There was a mocking note in Lloyd's voice.

'Yes, sir.'

'And then?'

'He'll probably get on to the Chief Constable or his deputy.'

'And then?'

'Well, sir, the Chief Constable *might* get on to the Yard. You see, the forces are independent of each other, and . . .'

Lloyd cut him short. 'It sounds as though it might be a long business. I'll wait outside.'

Normally, indeed, it would have been a long business. But the gods, that night, were on the side of Bates junior. His call to the night duty officer of the South Sussex Police revealed a state of crisis in that usually tranquil establishment. The four officers involved in the motor accident had been detained in hospital. As if that were not enough, there had been no less than three armed hold-ups in the district within the past hour. The Chief Constable was in a pretty state, so the night duty officer grimly hinted, having his week-end mucked up like this, and he wouldn't thank young Mr. Bates for putting any more on his plate. It had better be something pretty big.

'It's something pretty big all right,' said young Bates.

He took a deep breath and waited to be put through to the Chief Constable's deputy. Half a minute later he was speaking to him. He spoke to such effect that the Chief Constable had taken over the line before he had finished his story. He made it a good story. After all, he had the ingredients. Death and blackmail, against a background of millions.

And so it happened that at twenty-nine minutes past twelve precisely, the telephone rang in Room 333 at Scotland Yard.

5

Ten minutes later Chief Superintendent Waller came out of the office of the Assistant Commissioner, closing the door softly behind him.

There was a grim smile on his face. It was remarkable, he thought, what money could do. He had a shrewd suspicion that if this Miss Larue, whoever she might be, had expired in less luxurious surroundings, the Chief Constable of the South Sussex Police might not have attached so much importance to her. He also wondered if the Assistant Commissioner would have deputed himself to take over the case. However, even Assistant Commissioners read the glossy magazines, and Andrew Lloyd was the favourite financier of those journals. He behaved as social editors always hoped millionaires would behave, but seldom did.

Waller glanced at his watch. Twenty to one. Bates should have contacted Broome Place by now. Sergeant Bates was his favourite assistant—a cheerful young giant with fair hair and blue eyes. Bates's only drawback was his obvious impatience to take every case exclusively into his own large and not very experienced hands. Well, Bates's day would come, sooner or later. In the meantime, Waller was glad to have him around.

He walked to the end of the passage and pushed open a door numbered 334. Bates was on the telephone.

'Any luck?'

The sergeant looked up. 'Hold on a minute,' he barked into the receiver. He laid the instrument on his desk and put his hand over it.

'It's Ron, sir—my kid brother.'

'What about him?'

'He's speaking from Broome Place. You'll remember that he's stationed at West Greenstead.'

'Good Lord, so he is!' Waller chuckled. 'Quite a family affair! Is he making any sense?'

'Pretty good, sir, considering it's Ron.'

'Who else is down there?'

'Meaning the guests, sir?' Waller nodded. Bates put the question over the wire, and made some notes on his pad. Then he turned to Waller. 'Miss Sally Kane, Mr. Cecil Gower-Jones, Lady Coniston, Sir Luke Coniston . . .'

'That's enough.' Waller strode over to the desk. 'Give me that telephone!' Even as he said the words he regretted them. The expression on Bates's face was like that of a child from whom one threatens to snatch a toy. "This is my case," he seemed to be protesting. "It's my brother. He found the corpse."

A slow grin crept over Waller's face. Very well. It was time Bates had a break. He'd let him do the spade-work.

'On second thoughts,' he said, 'you'd better carry on. How long will it take you to get down to Broome Place?'

Bates caught his breath. 'You mean . . . you think . . .' he began.

Waller cut him short. 'I mean that I'm extremely interested in anything that may concern Sir Luke Coniston. For all I know this business may not concern him at all. The fact remains that he appears to be staying at a house where a young woman has committed suicide—if it was suicide—under the threat of blackmail. Unless'—he added tersely—'your bright young brother is inventing it all.'

'No, sir. He seems to have got the facts pretty straight.'

'Very well then. How soon can you get down?'

'I ought to be able to do it in the hour at this time of night.'

'Then tell your brother you'll be down by . . .' Waller glanced at his watch . . . 'by two o'clock. But don't go to the house. Tell him to meet you at his digs, get the outline of the story, and then go up in the morning at crack of dawn.'

'Why not tonight, sir.'

'We don't know the set-up yet. There may be nothing in it at all. Apart from that, I don't want Sir Luke to get the impression that we're too concerned . . . not yet, at any rate. I'll be down at eleven. By then, you'll have been able to get a pretty clear picture of what it's all about. I'll leave the general interview to you.'

Bates beamed all over his face. 'Thank you, sir.' The general interview was an essential part of Waller's technique of investigation. It had been suggested to him by a paragraph in *First Principles of Detection,* the classic work of his old friend, Horatio Green. It was based on the principle that what people do not say in an interview is often more important than what they do. From which Waller had deduced the general interview, an apparently casual affair, almost like a family chat, in which all those who were, or might be, concerned said their little piece. It was remarkable how much they forgot in public which they afterwards remembered in private—remarkable, and highly rewarding.

There were muffled sounds, as of protest, from the telephone.

'That young brother of yours seems to be getting restive', said Waller. 'I'll leave you to deal with him.' He hesitated for a brief second. There were a dozen reminders that he would have liked to give Bates. 'Unless you'd like me to have a word with him?'

'No, thank you, sir,' replied Bates firmly. 'I think I'd best manage that myself.'

Waller took the hint. 'O.K.' he grunted. I'll be seeing you tomorrow. Good night.' He went out, shutting the door softly behind him.

6

At the top of the short flight of steps that leads down to the inner courtyard, Waller paused. He was seized by a sudden feeling of guilt. Instead of going home to bed he ought to have returned to his office and sent for the file on Sir Luke Coniston . . . if Sir Luke were really involved in this case. But why *should* he be involved? Just because a man was staying in a house when a woman committed suicide it didn't mean that he need have had anything to do with it. If it *was* suicide. But again, what reason had he for assuming that it was anything else? There was the question of blackmail, of course . . . and that reminded him that he hadn't even asked Bates what form the blackmail had taken!

Hell . . . he was tired. A man couldn't work twenty-four hours a day.

Ought he to go back and look at that file, or did he know enough already? He entered his car, leaned back, and lit another cigarette. He closed his eyes and evoked the image of Sir Luke Coniston. He must be about forty by now. One of the bright young millionaires of the fifties— a boom bubble boy. Married a rich widow and promptly began to turn the real estate business upside down. His method, as far as he understood it, was to gain a voting majority in the shares of some old-established business, and then—having replaced the directors by his own nominees—to revalue the assets and issue new stock to the shareholders at a heavy premium. All perfectly legitimate business, of course, in the jungle warfare of the city. The only trouble was that during three of his biggest deals in the past two years, one of the directors whom he was seeking to replace had conveniently committed suicide, at precisely the right moment for Sir Luke Coniston. One suicide, or even two, might have been overlooked, but at the third the authorities began to sit up and take notice. In theory there are no connecting links between Scotland Yard and the City; no underground passages run from Whitehall to Cornhill; no detectives, disguised as jobbers, mingle with the noisy crowds on the floor of the great money market. In practice, however, the links are many and various. Because the love of money is the root of all evil, Cornhill is fertile soil for the seeds of crime. Many of the heavier speculators would be surprised to learn with how keen an interest the Yard regards their activities. Sir Luke was one of these speculators. Enough was already known about him to prove that he was sailing so close to the wind that he was heading for the rocks. This time, maybe, he had struck them.

Well, tomorrow would show. In the meantime it was nearly one o'clock, and even Chief Superintendents must get some sleep. He threw away his cigarette and pressed the starter.

MR. WALLER'S BEWILDERMENT

Iт was a perfect October morning when Waller, at a quarter to eleven, stopped his car outside the great gates of Broome Place. He had arranged by telephone to meet Sergeant Bates here at eleven sharp, but he was glad of the extra fifteen minutes in which to stretch his legs and to breathe the golden air—and also to gain a general sense of the lay of the land.

Through a gap in the hedge he could see the main outlines of the estate, stretching far below, down to a valley hazed in autumn mist. The house stood on a narrow plateau of land about half a mile distant. From his present vantage point it was hidden by a high belt of trees, but he had often seen photographs of it, and he remembered the superb sweep of the Jacobean façade and the melodious lines of the terraced gardens that surrounded it. In front of the house the land plunged downwards for nearly a mile in the direction of the great lake, on whose borders in the eighteenth century the Brothers Adam had erected one of their most delicate temples. It was this precipitous slope of land which gave to the gardens their special character; a series of owners, over the centuries, had taken the fullest advantage of the natural terraces to plant them with the finest rhododendrons and azaleas, to say nothing of the eucryphias, the andromedas, the camellias and the rare heathers which rejoiced in the shelter and the rich, peaty soil. To stand on the terrace of the Italian garden in spring was to be dazzled by giant cataracts of foaming colour, to stand there in autumn was to assist at a conflagration that seemed to light up the distant hills. Even from where he stood at the moment, the colour was of a richness that one seldom sees in England.

The crunch of heavy footsteps behind him made him turn round. It was Sergeant Bates. A glance at his beaming face made him realize that the young man was feeling on top of the world.

'Everything O.K., Bates?'

'Very much so, thank you, sir.'

As they walked back to the car Bates began to give him a brief résumé of the routine steps which he had taken. He appeared to have worked with remarkable speed. The photographers had come and gone, the arrangements for the inquest were in hand, and even at this moment his brother Ron was making a final check of objects in the room of the deceased woman that might show marks of fingerprints.

Waller cut him short. 'You've not fingerprinted the guests? Or the servants?'

'No, sir.'

'Good man.' Waller chuckled to himself. 'It's extraordinary how frightened the average man is of having his fingerprints taken. You'd think you were putting the noose round his neck. All the same, I suppose they *are* suspicious? What about Sir Luke Coniston?'

'No more than any of the rest, sir. You see, Mr. Lloyd's told them all about the letter. So they just think it's a plain case of blackmail and suicide.'

'Does Mr. Lloyd think that?'

Bates hesitated for a moment. 'I'm not sure, sir.'

Waller frowned. 'But if they think it's plain blackmail and suicide, how do they account for the Yard . . . for us? I'm asking these questions because I want to know the general atmosphere when I start examining.'

'I understand, sir. Well, Mr. Lloyd's seen to that, too.'

'The devil he has! How has he seen to it?'

'He's been making rather a point about the fire-escape, sir. It connects with the balcony of the deceased woman's bedroom. After they heard the shot they all ran upstairs . . .'

'All?' barked Waller. 'Who do you mean by all?'

Bates glanced at him reproachfully. 'Well, sir, I've got

a full list of names, but I thought you wanted a general outline.'

'Sorry,' grunted Waller. 'Go on.'

'They ran upstairs, but the door was locked. So Mr. Lloyd went outside and got in by the fire escape. A minute or so later, he opened the door, and several of them went in.' He glanced again at Waller. 'I've got the list of them, too, sir, if you want it.'

'No. Go on. I only want to know how this fits in with what you said about disarming suspicion.'

'Well, it's obvious, isn't it? If Mr. Lloyd could get in by the fire escape, so could anybody else. That's the point he's been making. And if you ask me, sir, he's been making it rather more often than is strictly necessary.'

Waller nodded. Bates was talking very good sense. He had done well to let him come down first and do the spade-work.

'Your Mr. Lloyd,' he said, 'seems to have been pretty busy.'

'He's certainly been helpful, sir,' replied Bates. He drew out a bulky sheet of parchment from his pocket and unfolded it. 'Look at this. It's an architect's plan of the house. And you see those numbers in red ink, sir? That's where everybody in the house was at 10.40 last night. There's a list of names, corresponding with the numbers, at the bottom.'

'Lloyd gave you this?'

'Yes, sir. He was just finishing it this morning after breakfast, when I arrived. He said he was drawing up a balance sheet, sir. "A balance sheet of possibilities"—that's what he said. He's a queer cuss, sir. Treats it all as if it were a company meeting.'

Waller stared at the parchment. A curious detail caught his eye. In the top right-hand corner, near the compass sign, Lloyd had doodled a rough sketch of a cherub. It had been drawn in pencil, and partly erased and scribbled over, but it was still clear enough to be recognizable. It might have been a fragment of a heraldic design. Although it was skilfully drawn, it was faintly repulsive. The cherub had the suggestion of a hump, and a distinct squint. Strange, the sort of thing that an intelligent man would do when his nerves were taut.

'Have you checked up on this list?'

'Yes, sir. We had it out at the general interview. Saved a lot of time.'

'Does everybody agree with it?'

'Yes, sir.'

Waller bent closer over the parchment. Then frowned and grunted.

'Anything wrong, sir?'

'Not exactly. But I wouldn't say there was anything particularly right, either. If you look at this plan, you'll see that most of the numbers are isolated. Everybody seems to have been scattered about in all directions.'

'Meaning what, sir?'

'That we've only their own word for where they were.'

'But Mr. Lloyd says . . .' began Bates, and then he stopped. It occurred to him that perhaps he had said enough about Mr. Lloyd, to whose strange, glittering charm he had succumbed. 'You'll understand when you meet him, sir.'

'I'm looking forward to it,' said Waller.

2

Superintendent Waller was to experience a number of shocks during the course of his investigations at Broome Place, and they were not long in developing. They began at the front door.

This was flung open before he had time to ring the bell. Standing on the threshold was the butler. He was younger then the average butler—in his late twenties. He was tall, dark and handsome, and he was grinning all over his face.

'Well, sir,' he said with a cheery assurance, 'this *is* a pleasant surprise.'

Waller stared at him. Where had he seen that face before? Then he remembered.

'Palmer!' he exclaimed.

'That's right, sir.'

'Francis Palmer, if I remember rightly. Two years, wasn't it? For forging share certificates?'

'Eighteen months, sir, if we *are* being accurate. *And* there was an element of doubt.'

'Not in my mind,' retorted Waller coldly. He gave the man his hat. 'What are you doing here?'

Before replying the butler held up the hat, sniffed, and flicked a speck of dust off the rim. Then he set it down, with much reverence, on an old Tudor chest. 'Mr. Lloyd, sir, he replied, 'is a very generous gentleman. He is also a gentleman of imagination.'

'So it would seem.'

'When I had that little trouble in his office, sir, he didn't take it badly. After all, what's a few thousand to him? So when I come out, he offers me this job. "Palmer," he says, "there's a lot of funny people come down to Broome Place" . . . or words to that effect . . . "and you might be just the man I want, to see that nobody pinches the silver." ' He gave the superintendent a sidelong glance. 'How's that for a story?'

Waller did not reply. He was trying to remember more about Palmer. There had been a curious feature about the case—something that had struck him, at the time, as inexplicable. No doubt he would recall it in time.

Palmer turned his head, evading those searching eyes. When he spoke again, his voice was cold and formal. He was once more the perfect butler.

'I expect you'd like to go straight up to Miss Larue's room, sir,' he said .Without waiting for a reply he led the way slowly down the long gallery. He walked slowly, proudly, like a young nobleman surveying his domain.

Waller turned to Bates, who had been a silent witness to this conversation. 'Let's get going,' he said.

3

Twenty minutes later, Waller came out of the room of death, with Bates behind him.

He had a vague feeling of disappointment. In the heart of every police officer, however experienced, however disillusioned, there lurks a secret hope that one day fate may cast him in a role where he can play the star—that one day he may find the clue to end all clues and make the deduction to end all deductions.

But here there was nothing. The situation was in every respect as it had been reported to him by Bates and his young brother, by the doctor, and by all the other testimony that was available. Even the fire escape, which might have afforded some sort of clue, had nothing to tell him. There was some disturbance in the creepers that trailed round it, but this could be explained by the fact that Andrew Lloyd had used it. Whether anybody else had done so would never be known; the heavy rain of the night before had eliminated any trace of footprints.

There was only one thing that puzzled him. The key of the bathroom door which led directly on to the outside corridor, was lying on the thick rug by the side of the bath. Why? Of course, keys sometimes fell out of doors if they were slammed. That might be the explanation. On the other hand, it might not.

He turned to Bates. 'That key hasn't been touched?'

'No, sir. My young brother noted it. D'you make anything of it, sir?'

'Not for the moment. But we'll bear it in mind.'

Palmer was waiting for them as they came out. 'Everything satisfactory, sir?'

Waller looked at the young man sharply. He seemed to detect a note of anxiety in his voice. 'If you can call it satisfactory. Any reason for that question?'

'No, sir. It's just that . . .' he hesitated for a moment . . . 'there's something I feel I ought to tell you.'

'Go ahead.'

'It's about a key, sir.'

'The key that's lying on the floor of the bathroom?'

'Oh no, sir. Not that one. The key to the door of Miss Kane's room.' He pointed to the door of the room on the right.

'What about it?'

'It's missing, sir.'

Waller raised his eyebrows. 'Is Miss Kane in her room at the moment?'

'No, sir. She's on the terrace with Lord Richard.'

'Perhaps you'd show me.'

'Certainly, sir.'

Palmer opened the door, and Waller stepped inside. As he glanced around him the thought flashed through his mind that it would be wonderful to give his own wife a room like this. It was pale grey and rose, with an exquisite Aubusson carpet stretching the whole length of the room. The walls were hung with Fantin Latours. The bed was a masterpiece of the Empire period, surmounted by a gilded swan.

'This is the door, sir,' said Palmer.

Waller concentrated his attention. 'It leads directly to Miss Larue's bathroom?'

'Yes, sir. In the old days this used to be a sort of suite, sir.'

'I see. And the key was kept on this side of the door?'

'That's right, sir.'

'When did you see it last?'

'Last night, sir. Just before dinner.'

Waller nodded. 'That was very observant of you, wasn't it?'

Palmer shrugged his shoulders. 'Not particularly, sir. I happened to be passing the room when Ella called out to me. Ella's the second housemaid.' A grin crept over his face. 'And if you ask me, sir, she's . . .'

'I don't ask you,' interrupted Waller. 'Go on.'

'Sorry, sir. Well, Ella called to me to help her to fix the

window, which had got stuck. Anything to oblige Ella, so I went in and fixed it. When I'd done it I noticed something smelling very nice. It was Ella. I asked her what she'd got on. She just laughed and pointed to this door. "Pinched a bit of Miss Larue's special," she said. And she said it must cost about a guinea a drop. And I said . . .'

'Never mind what you said. That's when you noticed the key?'

'That's right, sir.'

'Have you mentioned this to anybody else?'

'No, sir.'

'Then don't.' Waller stared at the door intently, as though he were trying to compel it to speak. Maybe it would, later on.

'Thank you,' he said abruptly. 'That may be useful. And now I think I'll see Mr. Lloyd.'

4

As Waller followed the young man along the winding corridors, down the great staircase and through the long gallery, it occurred to him that Broome Place would be an ideal location for a game of hide and seek. It must have contained at least seventy rooms. If all these rooms were as rich in treasures as the great drawing room into which Palmer now conducted him, one would need a lifetime in which to study them. The drawing-room was long and lofty, with big bays giving on to the terrace. The wall nearest the door was covered with a Gobelins tapestry that had once hung in the Palace of Potsdam. Against this tapestry stood a pair of Queen Anne tables in silver gesso. The curtains were of faded crimson Genoese velvet, and as the sunlight shone past them it sparkled on a chandelier of Waterford glass, as delicate as a flower. He suspected— rightly—that the chairs, the cabinets and the tables, which were arranged about the room with such careless grace, were museum pieces. And though he was unfamiliar with the artists whose names he could read on the labels of the pictures, he had an instinctive taste that made him respond to their quality.

However, this was no time to go mooning around after pictures. He had scarcely taken his bearings when a quick step behind him announced the arrival of his host.

'Superintendent Waller? My name is Lloyd. Please sit down. I think you will be quite comfortable in this chair.' He spoke in crisp, clipped accents. 'A cigarette? No? You have your notebook? Then let us begin.'

Mr. Lloyd, evidently, was not a man who wasted time in coming to the point. Having spoken, he walked briskly over to the fireplace, folded his arms and waited, tapping his foot impatiently.

Waller looked up, and for five seconds he submitted the figure of the financier to an intense scrutiny. In the space of five seconds a trained observer can see a great deal; it is a sort of mental time exposure. What Waller saw struck him, in some way which he could not explain, as incongruous. In spite of Lloyd's baldness his face was still a schoolboy's, unwrinkled, rosy, almost cherubic. He had a boy's figure, too. If he had been wearing a hat he might still have posed for the photograph of the Cambridge undergraduate that Waller had noticed hanging in the cloakroom.

But there were other incongruities. If Lloyd was a schoolboy, he was a very mondain and sophisticated one. In deference to the dead woman he had changed into a black suit; he looked glossy and elegant; he might have been setting out to some board meeting in the city. And yet, staring down at him from the wall above was a Madonna of the seventeenth century, a work of the greatest austerity and restraint; on the huge chimney-piece stood a primitive wood carving of Saint Anthony, and on the table by his side lay an ivory crucifix, grimly realistic, the work of an unknown master in Siena. Well, other millionaires, whatever their spiritual convictions, had collected religious master-pieces; indeed, Waller had once been shocked by hearing an art dealer describe a really first-class Madonna as "a hedge against inflation". Perhaps it was for such reasons that Lloyd had purchased these works. And yet, they were not the sort of works that one would have expected him to collect; there was nothing flamboyant or pretty-pretty about them; they all bore the stamp of melancholy, of austerity, of the denial of the flesh. Why? What did it mean? Or did it mean anything at all . . . except that Lloyd was a man of exceptional taste?

But his five seconds were up. He blinked, as though he were closing the shutter of his brain on a negative that would be developed at some later date.

He opened his notebook.

'I hope you understand that this is only a preliminary cross-examination, sir,' he began.

'Quite,' interrupted Lloyd. 'Which is why, of course, you are not cautioning me.' He spoke as though he were impatient with the lumbering methods of the law. Very well, thought Waller; two can play at that game.

He took his tempo from Lloyd. 'Exactly,' he retorted. 'I should therefore be glad of every relevant detail concerning the deceased lady. Her age. Her circumstances. Her financial position, if you are aware of it. And her connexion with . . .' here there was a momentary pause . . . 'with your household.' He had been about to say "yourself."

'The most relevant detail, I should imagine, is that she was my mistress.'

The answer came casually, without a second's hesitation, as though he were uttering a commonplace.

Waller was unprepared for it. This was a tempo to which he was unaccustomed. He felt something akin to a social embarrassment. 'I see,' he murmured.

Lloyd smiled—a schoolboy smile. 'Do you? I doubt it.' The smile faded as quickly as it had come. 'I'm sorry, superintendent. That was in very bad taste.'

Waller did not contradict him. There was a moment's silence. Lloyd stepped forward and reached for a chair, which he drew up beside him. Even in this moment of embarrassment Waller noted the swift agility of Lloyd's movements; it was a heavy chair, but he moved it effortlessly with his left hand; at the same time he tossed a cushion from it on to the settee and, as he did so, seated himself on it, with his back to the light. Only an actor, thought Waller, and a very accomplished actor, can move with such dexterity.

But was he acting? Waller flattered himself that he was a good judge of the tones of a man's voice. And as Lloyd spoke, he seemed to hear the ring of truth.

The financier leant forward and looked him straight in the eye.

'It wasn't a pleasant thing to have to tell you,' he said. 'I wanted to get it over quickly. So I tried to do it flippantly. Does that make sense?'

The superintendent nodded. 'Perhaps we'd better define our terms,' he said. 'In my class of people, that word "mistress" . . . it sounds sort of . . . continental.'

Lloyd gave the shadow of a smile. 'That's a very shrewd remark. And I suppose my relationship with Margot was . . . sort of continental. That is to say, it was a business relationship. It is true that the business concerned the body, but it was business none the less. Does that shock you?'

'No, sir. But it puzzles me.'

'Why? I should have thought it was obvious. Try to look at it in terms of a balance sheet. I am a very busy man; I work at the highest pressure; time has, for me, a very special value. I simply cannot afford . . .' He paused and flicked his fingers, as though searching for the right phrase . . . 'physical distractions. If I could have my way I should destroy my body. I don't want it. It bores me. And when I am bored, I work badly; I make errors in judgement. Hence Margot. Her function was quite simple. She was retained—I use the word deliberately—in order to satisfy certain elementary physical demands. I can assure you that she was not overworked. I am not a particularly—physical —person. Does that sound very cold-blooded?'

'Frankly, sir, yes.'

'Perhaps it is. However, that does not make it the less intelligent. In any sensibly conducted country a man in my position should be allowed to put a person like Margot on his expense account. However, we have had enough theories. Let us have some facts.' He rose abruptly, and thrust his hand into his inner pocket. He drew out a sheet of paper, closely typed. 'When this situation developed, last night, I realized that certain facts would be disclosed, sooner or later. I thought it as well to set them down on paper. You may care to glance at them now, and study them later at your leisure.'

He handed the paper to the superintendent, and without waiting for an answer walked over to the window, where he stood staring out on to the terrace.

Waller put on his spectacles and studied the dossier before him. It was neatly typed, on office writing paper; it might have been a stockbroker's memorandum on the merits of an industrial share.

5

MARGOT LARUE. Spinster. Deceased.
Statement by Andrew Lloyd, Esq., Broome Place.
October, 14th, 1956.

Miss Larue, who died by her own hand on the night of October 13th at or about 10.45 p.m., was approximately 27 years old, and was, as far as is known, unmarried.

Her antecedents were obscure, and the name Larue was presumably assumed. According to her own account —(to which reputable witnesses will testify, if required)— her girlhood was spent in Dublin, and she first came to London in the year 1946, at the age of 17. She claims that she was then accompanied by an "uncle", who is presumably fictitious, though there is no reason to doubt that she was under the protection of some man.

My first meeting with Miss Larue occurred in June

1950, at a small night-club called L'Etoile, situated in the basement of 99A Minton Street, Mayfair. She was at that time earning a precarious living as a photographer's model, with occasional small parts on the stage. An intimate association developed between us. Our meetings took place in Miss Larue's flat, which was situated on the third floor of the Minton Street premises. The meetings were not frequent, and were sometimes separated by a lapse of several months.

This situation, which was satisfactory to both of us, continued for over five years. In this period, Miss Larue acquired a certain poise and a superficial appearance of good breeding. She urgently desired me to remove her from the environment of Minton Street, and since I was grateful to her—(she had never been unduly exacting)—and amused by her—(she had a shrewd native wit)—I purchased for her the lease of a small house in Elvira Place, Hampstead. The details of this transaction can of course be verified.

Her first visit to Broome Place was in March of this year. My invitation coincided with a period of intense business activity. I trust there is no need to explain the connexion. She was described to the other guests as the sister of an old school friend.

There seems no doubt that Miss Larue did, in fact, commit suicide. At the same time, I feel it my duty to state that I can conceive no reason why she should have done so. She had no financial anxieties; at the time of her death I was preparing to arrange a settlement which would have made her independent for life. She was in excellent health. She had, as far as I am aware, no emotional entanglements. There may have been other men in her life—it would not have troubled me if that were the case —but I strongly doubt if they were important to her. She was a young woman who was ruled more by the head than by the heart . . . which was one of the reasons why I was drawn to her. She had one weakness; she drank too much. But that is a fault shared by many ladies of more delicate fibre; she could in no way be descibed as an alcoholic.

These observations, for what they are worth, are given in order to assist the enquiries of those who may be called upon to investigate the circumstances of her death.

Without prejudice,
Andrew Lloyd.

Waller folded the paper and transferred it to his wallet. He cleared his throat to attract Lloyd's attention.

'That statement will be very useful, sir,' he said. 'My job would be easier if I always had collaboration like that.'

Lloyd nodded casually. 'No doubt,' he said. 'I have a tidy mind, as you may have gathered. So, presumably, have you. I don't like loose ends. Nor do you. And it seems to me that there are quite a number of loose ends in this business. That is why I prepared that other little plan, which I handed to your assistant. It marks the approximate position of all the people in this house at the time the shot was fired last night. Have you studied it?'

'I have glanced at it, sir.' Waller took the plan from his wallet and unfolded it. 'A very concise document, if I may say so.'

'Thank you. You may care to check it with the persons concerned.'

'I shall certainly do so, sir.' He laid the paper face downwards on the table before him. 'But there is one last question I should like to ask you, sir.'

'Yes?'

For a moment Waller hesitated. Then he came out with it. 'Did Mrs. Lloyd know of your relationship with Miss Larue?'

'But of course.' Lloyd seemed genuinely surprised by the question. 'She entirely approved of it. Why not?'

The superintendent scratched his head. He felt out of his depth in Lloyd's strange amoral world.

Lloyd sat down on the stool beside him. 'Look at it like this, inspector. My wife has a very keen sense of values.

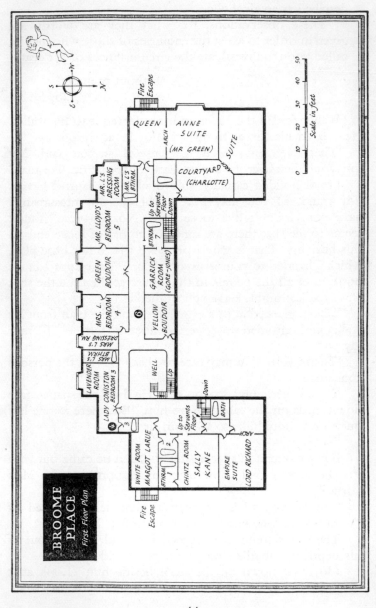

BROOME PLACE
First Floor Plan.

Fire Escape

N W S E

Scale in feet
0 10 20 30 40 50

WHITE ROOM
MARGOT LARUE

BTHRM 1
2

CHINTZ ROOM
SALLY KANE

Up to Servants' Floor

Down

BATH

EMPIRE SUITE
LORD RICHARD

ARCH

LADY CONISTON
BEDROOM 3

LAVENDER ROOM

MRS. L'S BTHRM
MRS. L'S DRESSING RM

MRS. L
BEDROOM 4

GREEN BOUDOIR

MR. LLOYDS
BEDROOM 5

MR. L'S DRESSING ROOM

MR. L'S BTHRM.

WELL

Up

YELLOW BOUDOIR

GARRICK ROOM
(GORE-JONES)

BTHRM 7

Up to Servants' Floor
Down

Fire Escape

ARCH

QUEEN ANNE SUITE
(MR GREEN)

SUITE

COURTYARD
(CHARLOTTE)

44

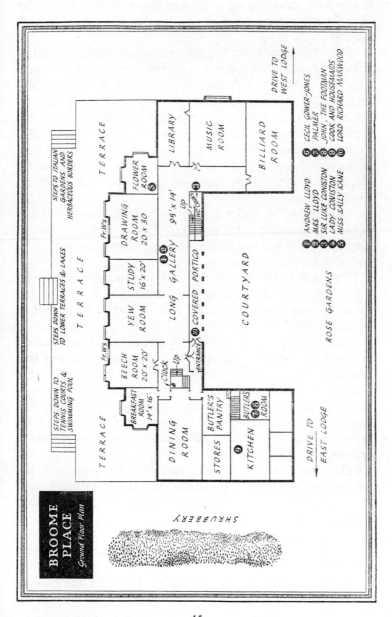

BROOME PLACE
Ground Floor Plan

① Andrew Lloyd
② Mrs. Lloyd
③ Sir Luke Coniston
④ Lady Coniston
⑤ Miss Sally Kane
⑥ Cecil Gower-Jones
⑦ Palmer
⑧ John, the Footman
⑨ Cook and Housemaids
⑩ Lord Richard Marwood

45

If she were drawing up a balance sheet of the things she thought most important in this world, she would put at the top . . .'

For the first time in the interview Lloyd's facility failed. He came to a sudden stop, like a runner who meets a hidden obstacle. The pause was so abrupt, so unexpected, that Waller glanced up sharply. He saw that Lloyd was staring with a look of extraordinary intensity at the picture of the Madonna over the fireplace. Waller tried to interpret that expression . . . there was pain in it, a sort of agonized entreaty. But Lloyd was back on his guard. He looked away from the picture. In a harsh voice he continued:

'Firstly, in her balance sheet of values, she would put her companionship with myself. It has never been strongly physical; today it is not at all so. But it is important to her . . . and vital to me.'

'Secondly, she would put her personal fortune, and mine. Neither of us is in the least ashamed of the fact that we enjoy being rich, extremely rich. We are. We intend to be still richer.'

'And thirdly . . . though perhaps this should be regarded as a sub-section of paragraph two . . . she would put this house, and its contents, and in particular, its pictures.' He glanced round the room. This time, his eyes deliberately avoided the Madonna over the fireplace. 'There are not many private collections that can compare with it, at least in Europe. When you have finished your inquiries, I should be happy to show it to you.'

He rose to his feet. 'Will that be all?' Although the words were phrased in the shape of a question, they were obviously intended as a statement of fact. As far as he was concerned, the interview was over.

Waller saw no reason to prolong it.

'Thank you, sir. If Mrs. Lloyd is available, I should like to see her.'

Lloyd nodded. 'I will send her in.' He went out, closing the door behind him.

6

Waller took up the plan from the table, and scrutinized it closely. This is what he saw.*

It was an admirable document, though there were several points on which he would need further elucidation, either from Lloyd or from the other members of the house-party. It might be a good idea to confront them with it, one by one. On the other hand, it might not. He would make up his mind as the occasion arose. Meanwhile he folded it into his wallet.

There was the sound of voices outside, and the door opened abruptly. Waller looked up. Standing in the doorway was a short, fair-haired woman with her hands thrust deep into a loose-fitting scarlet coat.

'May I come in?' Her voice was high and harsh. 'I'm Lady Coniston.'

Waller hesitated. 'I was expecting Mrs. Lloyd.'

'I know. But she's somewhere in the garden with the dogs. Andrew . . . Mr. Lloyd's gone to look for her. I thought that as I had to see you in any case I might as well get it over. Will it take long?'

'Only a few minutes, my lady.'

'Thank heavens.' She walked forward and flung herself into the depths of a Knole settee. Waller gave her a swift scrutiny; there was something strained and unnatural about her appearance which, for the moment, he could not interpret. Then he realized what it was. Her face had been "lifted". It had the mask-like quality of all such faces, the faintly Chinese tilt to the eyes. But it was her hands that betrayed her most. As she lit a cigarette he saw that they were the hands of a woman nearing fifty. They contrasted oddly with the doll-like prettiness of her face.

'It's too ghastly,' she exclaimed, 'all this happening, when one hasn't a thing to wear.'

* The plan on pages 44–45 is in all essential respects identical with the original at Scotland Yard, but it has been redrawn for the sake of clarity.

Waller was unprepared for such a reaction to the situation. However, no reply was necessary, for she continued ... 'I can't *tell* you how embarrassed I feel, trailing round in this scarlet coat, but I'm chilled to the *bone*—(they never start the central heating in this house till one's practically *rigid*)—and I can't borrow anything of Nancy's—Mrs. Lloyd's, I mean—because she's ten times my size. It's all very well for her in her own house, with a hundred dresses on the hook, but how was one to *know*? I said to Luke ... that's my husband ... that we ought to send my maid up to London to get something black ... in case there were any photographers ... will there be?'

'Not as far as you are concerned.'

'That's *one* thing to be thankful for, anyway, but he said it wasn't important, which is really the most *extraordinary* attitude to adopt, when you think of that poor wretched woman lying upstairs ...'

Waller took the opportunity to interrupt. 'It was of her that I wished to speak to you.'

'Of course. I'm terribly sorry to rattle on. But I just wanted you to understand that this is *not* the sort of costume I should normally wear on an occasion like this, but as I said before, how was one to *know*? If one had been warned ... but how *could* one have been warned?' Her Chinese eyes narrowed as she stared up at him. 'Or could one? D'you think there's something peculiar about it all?'

'That is for us to find out. If you will answer a few questions ...'

'But I'm *longing* to answer questions. What are we waiting for? Do go on. I think I shall lie back and close my eyes and concentrate.'

Waller sighed with relief. He took out his notebook. As he did so she opened her eyes widely. '*Do* put that horrid thing away,' she said. 'It dries me up. They always do.' As though the matter were already settled, she closed her eyes again.

Waller put away his notebook. Lady Coniston, he was beginning to realize, was not an easy customer. He noticed something else. She had not closed her eyes completely. She was still studying him, through those narrow Chinese apertures.

'The main point on which I should like confirmation concerns the time of the shot last night. You heard it, of course?'

Was it his fancy, or was there a sudden stiffening in the muscles round her mouth? One could never be sure about expressions, with these women who have been "lifted".

'Of course. It happened about five minutes after I got to my room. So that would make it a quarter to eleven.'

'You are sure of that?'

'Quite. I know it was twenty to eleven when I went to bed because I stopped on my way up the stairs to look at Andrew's new Queen Anne clock and I felt quite sick with envy. My husband was after it too, but Andrew snapped it up. *Quite* the prettiest clock in the world. The *most* exquisite seaweed marquetry on faded walnut. I suppose you'll say that a Queen Anne clock wouldn't be efficient. If so, you don't know Andrew. (I can't go on calling him Mr. Lloyd.) Everything about Andrew is hideously efficient. It *was* twenty to eleven. And whatever anybody says, that's the story I shall tell the judge. Do go on.'

Waller felt the corners of his lips twitching. Lady Coniston might be a headache, but she was not a bore.

'What did you do when you reached your room?'

She raised her eyebrows ever so slightly. 'If you must know, I went into the bathroom and creamed my face. Does it matter?'

'Only to the extent of deciding the precise direction of the shot.'

'Well, that was obvious, wasn't it? There's only quite a thin wall between my bathroom and Margot's bedroom. The shot came from just the other side of the wall.'

'You are sure of that? I ask you because you are our most important witness on this point. You seem to have been very much closer to the event than anybody else.'

Again he thought he detected that strange tension

round the muscles of her mouth. But there was nothing tense about her reply. 'I suppose I was,' she retorted. 'And you make it all sound most sinister. However, I can't help that. It happens to be true.'

He nodded. 'Thank you.' He reached for his notebook, but thought better of it. 'There's just one other thing, my lady.'

'Oh dear! I thought you'd finished.' She had already risen from the settee. She sat down again on the edge of a chair. 'What is it now?'

'I'm trying to find some sort of reason for this tragedy. So far with no effect. It seems to have come out of the blue.'

'I wouldn't say that. After all, when a girl's constantly threatening to commit suicide . . .'

Waller looked up sharply. 'Are you sure of that?'

'I wish you wouldn't keep on asking me if I'm sure of things.' Her voice had the shrill petulance of a spoilt child. 'It fusses me.'

'I'm sorry, my lady, but this is important. You said Miss Larue was constantly threatening to commit suicide . . .'

'Did I? Well, perhaps not constantly, but she *did* threaten it.'

'Recently?'

'Yesterday afternoon.'

'To you personally?'

'To me and Mrs. Lloyd, when we were walking in the garden.'

'Do you remember what she said?'

'I suppose it was something about being tired of life and making an end of it all and that sort of thing.'

'You *suppose*? But if you heard her . . .'

'Of course I heard her. What makes you think I didn't hear her? D'you think I'm inventing it?' She spoke with a greater intensity than she had yet shown. Waller noticed that her fists were clenched.

'Not at all, my lady. But I had hoped that as it was such an unusual conversation you might have a clearer recollection of it.'

'Well, I haven't. I hate people who talk about suicide. They bore me. I just let them ramble on and think of something else.' She had control of herself again. 'If you think it's so terribly important why don't you ask Mrs. Lloyd about it? She was there too, and she never forgets a thing.'

'I shall certainly do so, at the earliest . . .'

He did not finish the sentence, for Lady Coniston had suddenly risen to her feet. 'Nancy darling . . . thank heavens!'

Waller turned. Framed in the doorway stood a tall, slim woman in a black dress.

Lady Coniston hurried towards her with outstretched arms. 'Darling, you've saved my life. I've been on the rack, my dear.' She turned briefly towards the superintendent. 'Not that this gentleman hasn't been the soul of courtesy' . . . she flashed him a conventional smile. 'But he *does* make one feel exactly like Crippen, and if he doesn't want me any longer . . .' She put her head on one side, in an inquiring gesture. She did not wait for an answer. She blew a kiss to her hostess and hurried out.

7

For a few seconds the woman in black stood in the doorway, looking after Lady Coniston with a quiet, reflective smile. Then she closed the door.

'I am sorry to have kept you waiting,' she said.

She moved towards him with the slow, almost languid grace that is more often associated with the professional model than with the English countrywoman.

As Waller took her extended hand, he made good use of his customary five seconds "mental time exposure". Her dark hair was worn flat and parted in the middle; it had a single streak of white which stood out so sharply that for a moment he mistook it for a silver ribbon. He guessed her age at about thirty. She had a clear, untroubled beauty; her eyes were wide-set, grey and candid; she wore little make-up, but the delicate shadow of her eyebrows had been plucked out and redrawn in a thin artificial curve which suggested the formal beauty of a madonna. Indeed, although there was nothing studied nor affected about her appearance, and although her simple dress bore the stamp of Paris, the immediate effect she created was not so much that of a contemporary woman as of a figure who might have stepped from the landscape of one of the early masterpieces which hung on the walls around her.

Immediately she put him at his ease.

'Before I say anything else, may I offer you a drink?'

'It's very kind of you, madam. But not on duty.'

'As you wish. I suggested it because I thought you might be beginning to feel the strain. You must think this a very peculiar household.'

She walked over to a chair and sat on the edge of it. Again Waller was reminded of a model taking a pose.

'I believe my husband has told you of his relationship with Miss Larue?'

'That is so, madam.'

'Do you understand it?'

Waller shrugged his shoulders.

'Perhaps I should have asked if you understood my reaction to it.'

'It is certainly unusual, madam.'

She raised her eyebrows. 'Is that all you can say about it? I should have said it was unique.'

Waller made no comment.

'And yet,' she continued, 'it is entirely natural. And as far as I am concerned, entirely moral.' She waited for him to speak. Then she smiled. 'Don't you ever contradict a lady?'

'Would you like me to do that?'

'Frankly, yes, in this case. I want to explain my point of view.'

'Is it important, madam?'

Waller's question was shrewd. He was extremely

interested in Mrs. Lloyd's point of view, but he did not wish her to know it.

'I think it is important,' she retorted, with some sharpness. 'You see, I believe that your presence in this house is unnecessary. I'm sorry if that sounds impolite, but it is better to be frank.'

'Much better, madam.'

'Thank you. You are obviously here because you are not satisfied with the cause of poor Margot's death. In other words, you think that she was murdered. Which means, that she was murdered by one of us. Is that correct?'

Waller nodded.

'I happen to think that is nonsense. For one thing, Margot was a suicidal type.'

'There seems some doubt about that, madam.'

'Really? From whom, I wonder.' Her eyes narrowed. 'Didn't Lady Coniston mention it?'

'Lady Coniston, yes.'

'I can confirm her statement. I know of at least three occasions when she threatened to do away with herself.'

'Did she give any reason?'

'No. Do these people ever give any reasons? However, we are losing the point—at least, my point. As I was saying, I believe your presence in this house is unnecessary. I may add that it is also inconvenient. In short . . .' she paused, and looked up with a disarming smile . . . 'I want to get rid of you as soon as possible. Is that clear?'

'Quite clear.'

'Very well. In order to do that, I must co-operate. And the best way I can co-operate is by trying to explain this curious triangle between my husband, Miss Larue and myself. When you have understood it, you will no longer see anything sinister in it. At least, I hope not. And you will be able to look elsewhere for your culprits . . . not that I expect you to find any.'

'I'm all attention, madam.'

She reached for a cigarette box by her side. It was an exquisite little object by Fabergé, in crystal, with a design of vine-leaves in emeralds. Then she shook her head. As though to herself she murmured 'I am smoking too much.' She pushed the box away.

'There is only one thing you need realize about Andrew Lloyd,' she continued. 'Andrew Lloyd is a genius.' (It was curious, thought Waller, that she should use both her husband's names. It was almost as though she were speaking of a stranger.)

'He is not merely a financial genius . . . though if you knew the methods by which he made his money, you might see the working of an entirely exceptional brain. I will give you one example. Some months ago, he began to take an interest in some of the new gold mines on the borders of the Orange Free State.'

'Do you remember the precise date, madam?'

She looked surprised at the interruption. 'As it happens, I do. Does it matter?'

'I am assuming that everything in your story is important.

'You flatter me.' She shifted in her chair. For the first time, her movement seemed uneasy, without her usual grace. 'It was in January. I remember because the story got into the papers. There were big headlines, with Andrew's picture on the front page. May I go on?'

'Please.'

'As a result of this interest, I found myself entertaining a number of mining experts at this house. Not merely financiers—engineers, surveyors and the like. One night, after dinner, one of these men said to me: "Your husband has the most fantastic memory of any man I ever met. He knows those mines backwards—every seam of them. And yet—surely he can only have spent a comparatively short time in them? When was he last in South Africa?" And then I told him. Andrew Lloyd had never been in South Africa at all. All his knowledge was gained from maps and diagrams and reports. They would not believe me.' She gave him a sudden smile. 'Do you?'

'Yes, madam. But where does it get us?'

'I deserved that question. It gets us precisely to this

point.' She put the tips of her fingers together, as though she were summing up. 'Andrew Lloyd' . . . (the use of the double name seemed even stranger by repetition) . . . 'is a genius. The brain of a genius needs exceptional treatment, particularly from those who love him. I happen to love Andrew Lloyd's brain. That is the whole point. What he does with his body does not even interest me. It bores me. It is of less concern to me than where he gets his hair cut. He knows that. Margot Larue knew it. Now, you know it too. And because you know it, I hope that I may have saved you some trouble. I should hate to see you following a false scent.'

She rose abruptly to her feet. 'This must be the most extraordinary conversation between a suspect and a police-man that has ever been recorded. Or do you hate being called a policeman?'

'It is my profession, madam.'

'And am I a suspect?' She laughed—easily, naturally. 'I'm sorry. I shouldn't have asked that question. But it gave me a sort of morbid thrill, for the moment. To pretend you're in danger when you aren't . . . to assume that something terrible is happening to you when it isn't . . . that's a feminine privilege. However, I have talked more than enough, and you will be wanting to ask me some questions.'

8

Waller had a sense of anti-climax. As she had suggested, this was indeed one of the strangest conversations in which he had ever taken part. He felt, too, that it had a significance deeper than he yet realized. A woman of Mrs. Lloyd's intelligence and sensitivity did not indulge in such intimate revelations without a very good reason. Of course, it was just possible that this reason might be as she had stated; she might merely be anxious to be rid of him. On the other hand, she might be shielding somebody. But if so . . . whom?

The rest of the cross-examination, he suspected, would be flat by comparison with what had gone before.

He began with the inevitable question:

'Is there any member of your party who, in your opinion, might have had a grievance against Miss Larue?'

She permitted herself a faint smile. 'In any party where there are several women there is bound to be a sense of grievance if one of them is prettier than the others.'

'My question was quite serious, madam.'

Her smile faded. 'I beg your pardon. I did not mean to be facetious. It was only that . . .' She paused and shrugged her shoulders. 'The whole affair was so ridiculous.'

'Which affair?'

'The quarrel between Miss Larue and Miss Kane.'

'When was that?'

'On Friday afternoon. The day before this horrible thing happened.'

'What was the cause of the quarrel?'

'Of all things—a jar of cold cream.'

Waller raised his eyebrows.

'I don't wonder that you look astonished. It must be difficult for any man to believe that women can be so idiotic. But really, for a moment I thought there was going to be murder.'

'Would you tell me the circumstances of the quarrel?'

'If you think it worth while. We were walking by the lake, the three of us . . . Miss Larue, Miss Kane and myself. There was a cold wind and Miss Larue said something about its effect on one's complexion. And then—I'm quite certain she was deliberately provoking Miss Kane—she said that nothing like that ever worried her, because of this extraordinary cream she used.'

Waller stared at her. 'In what respect was it extraordinary?'

She laughed. 'Personally, I don't believe that it existed at all. I think that Miss Larue was inventing it. It used to amuse her to provoke Miss Kane, and this was a good way of doing it. Miss Kane has a very poor skin, although she has spent a fortune on beauty treatment. She is vain and spoilt, and absurdly superstitious. She pours out money on fortune-tellers. So Margot invented this magical cream. She said that she had discovered it in the East. (I very much doubt if she ever travelled further east than Margate.) It was all too silly and bogus, but Miss Kane swallowed it. And that was when the quarrel began. Miss Kane implored her to give her some of the cream and Margot refused. Miss Kane offered fantastic sums, and Margot merely laughed. And there they were, by the edge of the lake, facing each other in the cold wind . . . two silly women, who had begun talking about their complexions and had ended by saying the bitterest things and wishing that the other was dead.'

She looked up at Waller with an expression of genuine bewilderment. 'I wonder—am I making a great deal out of nothing?'

Waller tapped his notebook. It was a difficult question to answer. The whole situation seemed strange and remote, like a passage in a surrealist novel, lit by a lunatic glare. Death—and a lake blown by the wind—and two women, screaming about their complexions.

'That remains to be seen, madam.'

'You sound very sinister. Perhaps I was wrong to mention it at all. And yet . . .' She paused; she seemed to be thinking aloud. 'Some women will go to almost any lengths to gain beauty. Look at poor Lady Coniston! She risked her life for the sake of a few wrinkles.'

'Her life?'

'Certainly. Surely I don't have to tell you that her face has been lifted?'

'But why should that have endangered her life?'

'Because she has a weak heart. None of the London surgeons would operate. They told her that she wouldn't stand up to it. So she had to bribe an unscrupulous doctor in Paris—and nearly died under the anaesthetic. Are you beginning to see what I mean?'

'The general trend, yes.'

'I am afraid it is nothing more than a general trend. But

I am trying to help you, Superintendent. And it seemed to me that by being completely personal and—if I may say so—almost aggressively feminine, I might be of more assistance than if I merely tried to remember dates and hours and positions and all that sort of thing.'

Waller smiled. 'It is quite possible that you are right, madam. At the same time, I should like your personal check on people's movements at the time the shot was fired.'

'By all means.'

With Lloyd's chart before him, he took her through the few crucial minutes of the tragedy. Nothing new emerged, with one exception. As the guests had hurried along the corridor, Mrs. Lloyd had knocked on Lady Coniston's door and opened it.

'Why did you do that?'

'Why not? For all I knew, it might have been her.'

'I see.'

She spoke rather sharply. 'You sound as though you thought it were an odd thing to do. Why? How was I to know what had happened, or to whom?'

'I was not questioning your statement, madam. I was only trying to ascertain the facts.'

'Well, those are the facts.'

'Did you say anything to Lady Coniston?'

'Naturally. I asked her if she'd heard the shot. Or words to that effect.'

'And that was all?'

'There was no point in saying much else, was there? As soon as I saw that she was all right, I hurried next door . . . and that was that.'

Waller closed his notebook. She rose to her feet. She suddenly became the polite hostess.

'I must go and make arrangements for your luncheon.'

'There is no need, madam.'

'But I insist.' She hesitated for a moment. 'I would have suggested that you had it with us, but perhaps, in the circumstances, that might be embarrassing?'

'Thank you, madam. It would.'

'Some other time, I hope.' She glanced out of the window. 'I see Miss Kane is walking across the terrace with Lord Richard. Shall I send them in?'

'I should prefer to interview them separately.' He paused. Sometimes two heads, under cross-examination, were more rewarding than one. 'On second thoughts, I will see them together.'

She gave him a charming smile, and went out.

Waller absent-mindedly tapped the cover of his note-book. He was beginning to feel that this was the strangest case in which he had ever been engaged. It was a case in which trivialities—feminine moods and shadows of emotion —seemed to be assuming an unwarranted importance. Two women, standing by the side of a lake, with the wind cutting across the water, screaming at one another about a pot of cold cream. It was just plain silly. But it was more than that. There was something obscurely disturbing about it, even if it meant nothing. Which, in all probability, it did.

He was getting nowhere, very fast.

He heard a knock on the door. There entered Sally Kane and Lord Richard Marwood.

9

He saw a young lady with a sallow complexion, green eyes and a retroussé nose. She had a good figure and pretty legs, but she was very short, and in order to counter this disability she wore shoes with absurdly high heels, her hair was piled high, and she held herself unnaturally erect, so that she seemed to be straining for something. Her simple black dress spoke with a French accent, she herself with the accent of Philadelphia.

'Come along, Richard.' The voice was high and petulant. 'We might as well get it over and done with.'

Lord Richard stepped forward. He was an open-faced young man of about twenty-four, powerfully built. He looked as though he would be happiest in rugger clothes.

He had fair hair and very blue eyes, with lines of laughter round them.

'I don't think I shall have to keep you young people very long,' said Waller.

'That's a comfort at any rate. I don't see why you should keep Lord Richard at all. He wasn't even here.'

'In that case I will begin with him.'

But Miss Kane had not finished. 'He *ought* to have been here for dinner, but his wretched car broke down and . . .'

'Sally, darling!' The young man raised his hand. 'Do let the inspector get on with it.'

She scowled at him and looked away.

'Thank you, sir.' Waller turned to Lord Richard. 'As Miss Kane was saying, you arrived at the house only a few minutes after the tragedy?'

'I wouldn't say a few minutes. I'd say a few seconds. In fact, I was practically in on it.'

Waller nodded with approval. He liked this young man. There was something disarming about him. And obviously he had no intention of evading any responsibility.

'But you were not in time to hear any shot?'

'No. I didn't hear anything.'

'Nor see anything? Nor anybody?'

Lord Richard looked puzzled. 'No. Ought I to have done?'

Waller smiled. 'Not at all. I was merely asking. You see—in the event of this affair being something other than suicide—it might have been possible for some person to obtain entrance to Miss Larue's room by the fire escape.'

'But that's round the other side of the house.'

'Quite. All the same, it is just possible that you might have seen somebody after they had come down it. Or that you might have walked round to that side of the house yourself.'

'Why should I do a thing like that?'

'Frankly, I don't know. I'm only trying to eliminate certain factors. So you went straight to the door and rang the bell?'

'I rang the bell, yes. But I didn't wait. I never do, in this house. The door was ajar and I walked in. I saw a housemaid scurrying down the gallery, looking sort of scared. And there was a lot of nattering upstairs. So I went up.'

'Did you go inside the room?'

'Well, yes and no. I stepped inside. But Sally was in there, looking ghastly . . .'

Miss Kane sat up sharply. 'I was *not* in there. At least, only in the doorway. As for looking ghastly, how would you expect a girl to look, after seeing a sight like that?'

'So you did go in the room?' Waller's voice was gentle but firm.

'Not *in* the room . . . at least, not really. I suppose I may have stepped inside for a few seconds.' She threw out her hands. 'How can one be certain?'

'You see, it was all a bit of a mix-up,' observed Lord Richard apologetically. 'And naturally, I wanted to get Sally—Miss Kane out of it.'

'Quite.' Waller made a pretence of writing something in his notebook. 'You've nothing you care to add to that statement?'

'I wish I could think of something, but honestly I can't.'

Waller turned to Miss Kane. 'And now, miss, I'd just like to check up on one or two things.' He pointed to the chart on the desk. 'I take it that you've seen this?'

'We've all seen it.'

'Would you say it was accurate?'

'As far as I'm concerned it is. I can't vouch for the others.'

'Does that mean you think that some of the other positions may not be accurate?'

'No, it doesn't mean anything of the sort. Really!' She tossed her head. 'There's no need to put words into my mouth.'

Waller bent over the chart. 'When you heard the shot did you come straight out of the flower-room?'

'I suppose I did.'

'Suppose?'

'Well, I must have done.'

'I see. And you ran straight upstairs?'

'Yes.'

'Did you see anybody on the way?'

'Not till I'd got to the bedroom door.'

Waller glanced at the chart again. 'Not Sir Luke
Coniston, for example? He is marked here as having been
near the staircase which you ran up.'

'So what? He must have gone on ahead.'

'Nor Mr. Gower-Jones? He seems to have been walking
down the upper gallery.'

'I can't help what he was doing. I didn't see him.'

Waller had a sudden instinct that she was lying. 'Would
he have been in a position to see you?'

'How do I know? You'd better ask him when he comes
back.'

'From where?'

'He went up to London at crack of dawn. At least, so
my maid tells me. He's coming back tonight.'

Waller frowned. He had no reason to suppose that Mr.
Gower-Jones was an important witness, but his absence
made the pattern incomplete.

He closed his notebook. He had not quite finished, but
he wanted to give Miss Kane the impression that he had
done so.

'I don't think I need detain you any longer, miss.'

'Thank goodness.' She held out her hand to Lord
Richard. 'Coming?'

The couple began to walk towards the door. Waller
stepped forward. 'Perhaps there is just one other thing,
miss.'

'Oh dear! What is it now?'

'Can you think of any reason why anybody should have
wished any serious harm to come to Miss Larue?'

She dropped Lord Richard's hand. 'No, I can't.'

'As far as you know, she was on good terms with all
the rest of the party?'

'Very good terms.' She shot a glance at her fiance. 'Particularly with the men.'

'No quarrels, or anything like that?'

She threw back her head and stared at him. 'None that I ever heard of.'

'Thank you. That will be all.'

With a final toss of the head she led Lord Richard from the room. It was she who opened the door—and slammed it, very loudly.

Waller lit a cigarette. He sighed, but it was not a sigh of despair. At least he had discovered one thing. Miss Kane had been lying.

He heard footsteps outside, echoing on the polished floor. They came up to the door and then stopped. Waller stared at the door. It was his experience that people who walked up to doors and then stopped had a very good reason for doing so. He went on staring. Somebody was taking a long time to make up his mind.

Then at last the handle turned. There was a moment's pause. And then, into the room walked his last witness— Sir Luke Coniston.

10

Sleek, dark, suave. Good-looking, in a Sicilian sort of way. Courteous and apparently straightforward.

Not quite a gentleman. Why did Waller, in those first few seconds of intense scrutiny, make this decision? Who was he, to presume to classify men socially? He could not have told you himself. Mr. Lloyd now, he was a gentleman. He wore the same uniform—the uniform of the City; he had the same aura of wealth. But he did not speak the same language, and, so Waller suspected, he did not think the same thoughts.

Waller wasted no time on preliminaries.

'Have you any theories as to why Miss Larue should have committed suicide, Sir Luke?'

'None. It was a profound shock.'

'Had she ever threatened to do so?'

'Certainly not in my hearing.'

'I see. How well did you know the lady, sir?'

'Really superintendent, that might be rather an embarrassing question to answer . . . in this house.'

'At the same time, I must ask you to answer it.'

'Of course. I did not say it *was* embarrassing. I merely suggested that it might have been. As it happens . . .' he shrugged his shoulders . . .' my acquaintance with her was very slight.'

'I see.' Waller was sure that he was lying. 'You never saw her, except on her visits to Broome Place?'

'Oh, come! I wouldn't go so far as that. One ran across her from time to time in London. Usually in public places.'

'Did she ever go to your house?'

'No.'

'Did you ever go to hers?'

Sir Luke shifted impatiently. 'These are questions that would be more suitably addressed to Mr. Lloyd.'

'Perhaps. But I am addressing you. Did you ever go to her house?'

'No, Superintendent, I did not. I didn't even know that she had a house.'

Again Waller was sure that he was lying. But he made no comment.

'Now let us come to last night. Did you notice any unusual incidents, apart from the major tragedy?'

Sir Luke appeared to consider the question. 'Well—I had a rather heated argument with Mr. Lloyd—though that wasn't perhaps so very unusual.'

'What was the argument about?'

Sir Luke told the story of the picture. 'It was all very childish. I'm afraid I lost my temper. I always do, when Andrew buys something that I'd have liked to buy myself.'

'I believe that you have often found yourself in opposition to Mr. Lloyd?'

'In what respect?'

'In the City.'

Sir Luke laughed lightly, showing a row of perfect teeth. The thought flashed through Waller's mind that those teeth were too good to be true. 'We have had our little battles.'

'Would I be right in assuming that one of those battles is in progress at the moment?'

The smile remained fixed. 'You must have been reading the *Financial Times.*'

'The story has spread to more popular papers.'

'Really? Very well. Yes, there is a battle, if the word appeals to you.'

'It was your word, sir.'

'So it was.'

'Would it be in order to ask who is winning?'

The smile was as broad as ever, but there was little mirth in it. 'No, superintendent, it would not. I do not give financial tips out of office hours.'

Waller ignored the insolence of the retort; indeed he welcomed it. Sir Luke, he suspected, was getting rattled. Swiftly he asked the next question:

'Where did you go, after this quarrel?'

'What do you mean . . . where did I go?'

'Precisely what I say, sir.'

The smile was beginning to fade. 'I see. I went to wash my hands, to use a conventional expression.'

Waller glanced at the chart before him. 'You must have seen this plan.'

'Yes. I helped to make it.'

'Your position is marked as being in the washroom at the bottom of the stairs.'

'Quite.'

'For nearly seven minutes. That is rather a long time, isn't it?'

Sir Luke shrugged his shoulders. 'Nature is unaccountable, superintendent.'

Waller frowned. 'Were you in the washroom all that time?'

C

'As it happens, no. I came out and walked a few steps up the staircase. There was a picture I wanted to see. I was looking at it when I heard the shot.'

'What picture was that?'

'It was . . .' He hesitated for a moment. 'It was the portrait of a lady. By a Dutch artist.'

'You don't remember the name of the artist?'

'Not for the moment. Has it any sort of significance?'

Waller did not answer the question. He continued to stare straight at Sir Luke. 'If I could give you a word of advice, sir, I shouldn't hold anything back.'

'Why do you suggest I am doing that?'

'I don't suggest it, sir. I merely advise against it.'

'You seem to be making some sort of insinuation.'

'Not at all, sir. But you will remember that there have been other occasions—three I think—in which you have been involved in a case of suicide.'

'So that's it!' The financier sprang to his feet and took a step forward. Waller thought he was about to spring at him. He looked a very ugly customer.

'So that's it!' he cried again. 'I might have known! Suicide . . . suicide . . . suicide!' With an obvious effort he controlled himself. 'You've been reading the Sunday papers, superintendent! "Trail of Blood Follows Ruthless Financier." That was one of the headlines, wasn't it?'

'It stated the facts, sir, none the less.'

'So what? Am I to blame if a silly old woman speculates in one of my companies and jumps off the edge of a cliff? Is it my fault if one of my own directors starts a bear account behind my back and ends up with his head in a gas oven? Am I to take the responsibility if a young idiot in the Life Guards tries to pick my brains, and fails, and blows his own brains out?'

He suddenly realized that he was shouting. He straightened himself and stretched out his hand for a cigarette. 'I beg your pardon, superintendent. But I am rather tired of these insinuations.'

Waller made no reply.

Sir Luke lit a match. His fingers were trembling. 'Is there anything else you wish to ask me?'

'Not for the moment, sir. You will be available, of course?'

'I do not intend to disappear, if that is what you mean.'

The eyes of the two men met, and for a moment they seemed to be measuring each other. Sir Luke was the first to turn away. As Waller watched him go, in silence, he wondered how much he had gained from this stormy scene. Of only one thing could he be certain. He had made an enemy.

4

ENTER MR. GREEN

At about the time when Superintendent Waller was conducting his interviews in the drawing room of Broome Place, a very ancient baby Austin motor-car was panting its way up the hill that led to the great house. It was driven by a pretty young lady with dark hair, very wide eyes and a slightly turned-up nose. By her side sat a person of some consequence to our story—a small, tubby gentleman, with features that inevitably recalled Leech's conception of Mr. Pickwick. This person was none other than the author of *First Principles in Detection*, Mr. Horatio Green, once famous as a private investigator of exceptional ability, but now—so he wished it to be understood—finally retired, and firmly uninterested in anything that could possibly be connected with crime.

It might be imagined that Mr. Green's arrival in the neighbourhood, so soon after the events that have been described, was in some way connected with the death of Miss Larue. On the contrary, his presence was a matter of coincidence. Mr. Green was a passionate lover of gardening; Broome Place offered one of the finest gardens in the country; and this was the last Sunday in the year on which it was open to the public. Hence his appearance. He had not even heard of the tragedy, and even if he had done so, he would not have concerned himself with it. His mind was on pleasanter things.

'I think, my dear Charlotte,' he said to the young lady by his side, 'that we should begin with the *polymorphums*.'

'Yes, darling,' replied his neice. 'That would be lovely.' She spoke somewhat absent-mindedly, for whenever she was driving the baby Austin she was convinced that it

68

should long ago have been put to bed. It had no business, at its advanced age, to be climbing up this long steep hill, on a fine Sunday morning, with all these vulgar Jaguars and Fords and Bentleys sweeping contemptuously past it.

However, it was no use speaking to her uncle about it. Although he had a brand new Sunbeam coupé, in a beautiful shade of sage green, which would have been a charming foil to the copper-coloured dress she was wearing, he had insisted on using the Austin. It might rain, he had said, and the Sunbeam's beautiful new chromium would be spoiled. Now that was a point of view which she could have understood; and if Mr. Green had been really worried about the Sunbeam's complexion she would have been the last to object. But she was quite sure that he did not care in the least about spoiling the Sunbeam. He was thinking only of the baby Austin. Not about its complexion, but about its feelings. Mr. Green had a habit—endearing in some ways but maddening in others—of endowing inanimate objects with human emotions. His home was cluttered up with junk that had long ceased to serve any useful purpose. There were typewriters in the attic that would never type another word; he kept them merely because, on some occasion in the dim past, they had typed letters which had been important in his life. He was grateful to them, so he cherished them, and protected them against the indignities of the sales room or the flea market. It was the same with the baby Austin. Long ago, in the case of Lady Bessingham's diamonds—the case which had made him an international celebrity—the little car had served him faithfully on many hazardous journeys. He could not turn it out into a cold, competitive world as though it were a mere machine. And since, this morning, he had a fancy that it looked lonely and neglected in the tool-shed to which it had been banished, out it had to come. So here they were, trundling up this long hill at an unsteady fifteen miles an hour, to the scornful hoots of the aforesaid Jaguars, Fords and Bentleys.

Charlotte changed gear, with an effort, from bottom to

second. The speedometer trembled from fifteen to nearly twenty.

'It still goes wonderfully, considering its age, does it not?' observed Mr. Green. He gave an affectionate pat to the dashboard, as though he were stroking a dog. 'We are nearly at the top already. After that it is only five minutes to the entrance of the drive. I seem to remember that the finest of the *polymorphums* are grouped round the lake, which is some little distance from the house. After that touch of frost last night they should be magnificent.'

It was nearly forty years since Mr. Green had stayed at Broome Place, as a shy young Oxford undergraduate, the least important member of a very grand house-party from which he had been delighted to escape. But he still remembered, with remarkable clarity, the superb sweep of the Jacobean façade, and the melodious lines of the terraced gardens that surrounded it. And he recalled, very vividly, the fine eighteenth-century gates at the entrance to the drive. They were of considerable elaboration, flanked by two massive columns surmounted by griffons in carved stone.

The gates were open, and the Austin, having passed through the lodge gates, proceeded to free-wheel down the twisting half-mile of the drive, which gave many enchanting glimpses of woodland colour. At last it glided gently into the great courtyard. There were no other cars standing there, except for a single black Wolseley outside the front door.

'This is very strange,' murmured Mr. Green, staring out of the window. 'One would have thought that on a fine day like this the place would have been crowded with visitors.'

'Are you sure the gardens *are* still open to the public?'

'Of course.'

'Then why isn't there anybody to sell us tickets?'

'I imagine that one buys them at the front door. Ah . . . here is somebody.'

2

Mr. Green alighted, and turned towards a tall, burly man who was crunching across the gravel towards them. And then he gave an exclamation of astonishment.

'Waller!'

'Mr. Waller!' echoed Charlotte.

The tall man approached at a leisurely pace. Sketching a salute he clicked his heels and bowed curtly to Charlotte. Then he folded his arms and shook his head and glared at Mr. Green, as though he were greatly disgruntled by his sudden appearance.

'Well, well,' he growled, 'I might have known that you'd be along.'

'I assure you that I had not the faintest idea . . .'

'Don't try and pull that stuff on me!' The superintendent took a step nearer, so that he towered over the minute figure of his friend. 'I was expecting you!'

Mr. Green was quite pink in the face. 'This is preposterous,' he retorted. 'Charlotte, my dear, will you kindly explain to Mr. Waller . . .'

'There is no need to explain anything to him,' she interrupted gently. 'Mr. Waller is merely having one of his little jokes.'

The superintendent glanced at her with a twinkle. 'I'm always bad news as far as you're concerned, Miss Charlotte, aren't I?'

She hesitated for a moment. Then she said, 'Frankly, yes.' She did not like saying it, for she had a fondness for this great bear of a man. 'As soon as you come along, uncle starts getting mixed up in things.'

A scornful snort came from Mr. Green. 'There is not the smallest danger of *that* happening again, I can assure you.'

Charlotte took his arm affectionately. 'There, Mr. Waller! I hope you heard that. Whatever you may be doing down here, my uncle is not to be mixed up in it.'

'I heard all right.'

'Then please remember it. He is far, far too fatigued for any extra effort.'

This was too much for Mr. Green. 'I am not in the least fatigued,' he protested vigorously. 'I have never felt more energetic in my life. It is simply that I am no longer interested in . . . but I have explained all that before.'

Waller grinned. 'Don't you even want to know what brings me down here?'

'Not at all.' However, even as he spoke, Waller noticed that the little man resisted, ever so slightly, the tug of Charlotte's arm. 'No doubt it is something unpleasant.'

'Very unpleasant,' agreed Waller. 'Suicide.'

Mr. Green shook his head. 'Dear me!'

'The suicide of a beautiful young woman. If . . . of course . . . it *was* suicide.'

Charlotte gave an extra tug to Mr. Green's arm. This time his resistance was more marked. 'Have you any reason to suspect otherwise?'

Waller assumed a very innocent expression. 'None that I could really put into words.' He gave a sidelong glance at Mr. Green. He felt as though he had a very wary little fish at the end of a line; he must be careful how he played him. 'It is really a question of . . . atmosphere.'

He could not have chosen—for his purpose—a more effective bait. The word "atmosphere", to Mr. Green, was like a red rag to a bull. It always reminded him of an inferior detective story. When the author was at a loss for a concise plot, when he could no longer marshal his events, conduct his characters and contrive his clues, he fell back on "atmosphere", and filled his pages with vague hints and empty sighs and meaningless shadows.

Mr. Green detached himself from Charlotte's restraining arm. 'My dear Mr. Waller,' he said, 'how often have I been obliged to remind you that in your profession there is no such thing as "atmosphere"?'

'What do you mean?' inquired the superintendent, who knew very well what he meant.

'I mean precisely what I say. There are degrees of temperature, there are variants of light, there are specific densities of texture . . . just as there are tones of voice and changes of expression. But these are *facts*, that can be measured and interpreted. To describe them as atmosphere . . .'

Charlotte felt it was time to interfere. 'Uncle darling,' she said in a warning voice, 'he is only saying it to draw you on . . .'

'Not at all,' interrupted Waller.

Mr. Green drew himself up to his full height of five feet two inches. 'I trust he knows better than that,' he retorted.

He stood there, shaking his head at the superintendent, in the manner of a very small schoolmaster reproving a very large schoolboy. Charlotte, feeling that this was a crucial moment, prepared to bid Waller a crisp good morning.

And then there was the sound of steps on the gravel behind them. Mr. Green turned and saw the slim figure of a man in a dark suit. The man was walking towards Waller, but his eyes were on Mr. Green. He stopped abruptly.

Then he walked forward with outstretched hands. 'I think I recognize you, sir' he said. 'Mr. Green, is it not?'

'That is my name, yes.'

'I am Andrew Lloyd.' He took Mr. Green's hand and held it. 'I am glad to see you. I am very glad indeed.'

And Mr. Green, who was not unpractised in his judgement of men, was convinced that he was speaking the truth.

3

Looking back on this strange case in after days, Mr. Green admitted that it was his conviction of Andrew Lloyd's sincerity, in this first moment of their meeting, that persuaded him to become involved. Had he guessed, at that time, the tangled motives that caused Lloyd to invoke his aid, things might have been different.

c*

Or might they? Could any man have resisted such a combination of flattery and expert pleading? Before he quite realized what was happening, he found himself being conducted through a gate on to a wide terrace, from which there were dazzling views of the valley below. The financier held him gently but firmly by the arm, guiding his footsteps over the wide stone flags, in whose crevices—he noticed them with a thrill of delight—were growing many magnificent clusters of autumn's brightest blossom—the *sternbergea lutea*.

'But of course you must stay with us,' Lloyd was saying. 'And your charming young friend.'

'I am afraid . . .' began Mr. Green.

'Your arrival is quite providential. It alters the entire situation.'

'Not at all.' Mr. Green's voice sounded very feeble. The situation to which you refer . . . whatever it may be . . .'

'I will give you a résumé of it as soon as we have decided upon your rooms.' He turned and pointed upwards towards the right wing. 'There is a pleasant room up there, where I believe you would be comfortable. The bay window has a very good view of the plantation of polymorphums.'

'Ah—the polymorphums!' Mr. Green clutched at the word as though it might afford him some means of escape. At this moment he felt that there was nothing he would welcome more eagerly than a large polymorphum, under which he could retreat and hide himself in its crimson shade.

'It was solely in order to see the polymorphums . . .'

Lloyd interrupted him again. 'You shall see them. And a great deal else. It will be a privilege to show you the gardens.'

'But my arrangements . . . my programme . . . ' The words lacked conviction, for Mr. Green, apart from a desire to steep himself in the colours of autumn, had no arrangements and no programme.

'I am absurdly rich, Mr. Green. If it were a question of compensating you for any inconvenience . . .' He broke off. 'This is one of the things one can't say without sounding boorish.'

There was a brief silence.

Then the financier dropped Mr. Green's arm, and turned swiftly towards him. He seemed for a moment to lose his sophistication . . . and in some curious way to shed his years. He was like an unhappy, bewildered young man.

'Mr. Green, I am in great trouble.' His voice had softened and grown deeper. 'Something has happened in this house which greatly affects my life. How greatly . . .'

He stopped dead. It was like a gramophone being switched off. Mr. Green felt the old familiar tingle of excitement which always came to him when he found himself in the presence of something which he could not explain, something which did not fit into the pattern. Why had Lloyd stopped so abruptly? Was he hiding anything? And if so, why was he apparently anxious for his help?

Mr. Green heaved a long sigh. For a fleeting moment his eyes met those of the financier. He saw a desperate pleading in them. He looked away across the valley. He saw the crimson glow of the polymorphums.

'Very well,' he said gently.

And so it came to pass that Mr. Green was installed at Broome Place without further ado. No—perhaps that would be an exaggeration. There was a considerable amount of ado, from a protesting Charlotte, on whose slender shoulders later in the day, fell the burden of arranging the numerous domestic upheavals involved in transporting their luggage from the little Regency house which Mr. Green had rented in Brighton. There was also a certain amount of ado on the part of the servants. Andrew Lloyd maintained a large staff but . . . there were limits.

There were even signs of ado from the guests at luncheon. Mr. Green was placed next to a lady with a mask-like face, who was introduced to him as Lady Coniston. She treated him with a mixture of condescension and contempt which suggested that she was under the illusion that he had come to tune the pianos. This behaviour greatly encouraged Mr. Green. He hoped that all the other guests would adopt the same attitude. To be treated with condescension and contempt was just how he would desire to be treated. It made his task so much the easier . . . whatever that task might prove to be.

He allowed himself nearly half a glass of Chateau Yquem with the trout. It went straight, or nearly straight, to his head. He sat back and said nothing, and gazed benignly around him.

He saw a long panelled room, lined with glowing pictures by Peter Brueghel. There was a great deal of red in them—the vivid scarlet which that master splashed over his canvases. He saw Charlotte's disapproving face. He noticed how pretty she looked, and how elegant, with that new touch of vermilion lipstick. He looked out of the window. Over the top of the balustrade he saw the glowing crimson of the polymorphums. Red . . . everywhere there was this colour . . . red. Involuntarily his eyes strayed to the ceiling. For a moment it seemed almost as though there were red shadows in the dark, clustering beams.

He checked his fancies with a frown. This was morbid folly. It was fortunate, he reflected with a grim smile, that Superintendent Waller was not here to read his thoughts. He would have had something to say about "atmosphere". There was no such thing as "atmosphere". It was solely because of the draught from the open window—so Mr. Green told himself—that he felt a tendency, ever so slight, to shiver.

5

NOTHING OF IMPORTANCE?

'WELL, that's the story', said Waller, pushing back his chair and relaxing. 'What do you make of it?'

Mr. Green raised his eyebrows in mild protest. 'My dear Waller! That is hardly a fair question, at this stage of the proceedings.'

Waller grinned. 'But surely the great Horatio Green decides his plan of campaign in the first few hours?'

'When you are facetious, my dear Waller, you are not at your best.'

The grin broadened. 'Can't you let me in on what you're thinking? Can't you give me a hint or two? Isn't there some book or other I ought to read?'

Mr. Green appeared to ponder the question seriously. 'Yes,' he said at length. 'I think I can recommend a book that you should read.'

'What is it?'

'Any good book on Flemish mediaeval art.'

Waller's grin faded. 'Is that one of your wisecracks?'

'It was not intended as such.'

'Why should I read a book on Flemish whatever it is?'

'Because there are several masterpieces of the period in this house, of great importance.'

'Importance in this case?'

'Really, Waller . . . a work of art is a work of art in its own right.'

'And so you suggest I should go round looking at the pictures?'

Mr. Green beamed upon him. 'I am always delighted to assist in your education.'

With which Waller had to be content.

It was two hours later, and they were sitting in Mr. Green's room in the west wing. Andrew Lloyd had not exaggerated when he had described it as "quite pleasant". The room was enchanting, and unlike most of the rooms at Broome, very English. There was a fine George Morland over the chimney-piece, and some delicate water-colours by Richard Wilson. The carpet was of Queen Anne needle-work.

The two men had not wasted time, and Waller, as usual, had been struck by the uncanny swiftness with which Mr. Green had mastered the essentials of the situation. After only the briefest inspection of Andrew Lloyd's plan, it seemed to be photographed on his memory, so that he was able to re-enact the movements of the various suspects—for so they must be called—as though he had been on the spot at the time of the tragedy. And re-enact them he did . . . opening and shutting doors, hurrying up staircases, striding down corridors and retracing his steps, to the considerable astonishment of John, the footman, who reported in the servants' hall that the new guest must be "a bit queer in the head".

As usual, Waller was mystified by some of the apparently irrelevant objects by which Mr. Green's attention was suddenly engaged. Why, for example, when they were in the music room, did he display so keen an interest in the record lying on the turntable of the gramophone? He took it up, sniffed at it, and read aloud the inscription on the label.

' "Mad at the Moon. Played by Blue Joseph and the Ebony Ensemble". '

Waller stared at him. 'So what?'

'It is the title of the record,' explained Mr. Green, giving another sniff. 'Blue Joseph is a coloured gentleman who plays an ulta-modern form of syncopated music . . . if one can call it music.'

'I still say . . . so what?'

Mr. Green shrugged his shoulders. 'It seems a curious object to find in this house, that is all.' He bent over the turntable and adjusted his glasses. 'I see that the record immediately underneath is Bach's "Jesu, Joy of Man's Desiring", played by Dame Myra Hess. There is a certain difference.'

Even more marked was his interest in the painting of the Madonna over the chimney-piece in the drawing-room. It was the same picture at which Andrew Lloyd had stared with so strange an expression while Waller had been cross-examining him. As soon as Mr. Green entered the room the picture caught his eye. He walked straight up to it and studied it with intense concentration.

He turned to Waller. 'You see what I said about the masterpieces of the Flemish school?'

Waller regarded the picture coolly, indeed with some distaste. He could see its power, but it did not appeal to him. The features of Our Lady were gaunt and drawn with suffering; there was none of the radiance of divine maternity. As for the Infant . . . well, as a staunch Methodist, Waller would call it positively blasphemous. True, he never had much fancy for holy babies as portrayed by old masters, they usually struck him as obese and complacent. But this infant, well really, it was pitiful. A poor stunted little brat, with shrivelled limbs and a face with such a vacant expression that you'd think it was half-witted.

'I'm afraid it's not my cup of tea,' he grunted.

Mr. Green gripped his arm. 'But can't you see?' he demanded. 'Can't you see?'

'See what? Ought I to think it's beautiful?'

Mr. Green merely sighed.

'Well, I'm sorry, I don't think it's beautiful. I think it's damned ugly. I suppose it's worth a lot of money?'

'It is unique,' observed Mr. Green, shortly.

Such conduct was apt to try a man's patience.

And then there were the sniffings. Waller was used to the sniffings; they were part of the technique for which Mr Green was famous; indeed, they had been greatly exaggerated by the caricaturists. It would be unjust to regard Mr. Green as a sort of human bloodhound; he merely happened to have an exceptionally developed olfactory sense which had proved of service on certain occasions. But today he was sniffing all the time . . . upstairs, downstairs, in my lady's chamber. Especially in my lady's chamber. Indeed, when they had been passing the bathroom that adjoined the room in which Margot Larue had met her death, he began to sniff so violently that Waller asked him, with some sarcasm, if he had a cold.

However, the two men were such old friends that when they eventually returned to Mr. Green's study they settled down quite amicably to discuss procedure.

'There's one bit of luck for us,' said Waller. 'Usually, after a business like this, all the people concerned scatter as soon as they can; they run off abroad or something like that. But in this case they've got to stay put, here in this house.'

'But surely you cannot compel them?'

'It's nothing to do with me. They're putting on a play next Saturday. A sort of revue.'

'Where? In this house?'

'No. At the local theatre in West Greenstead. And they're all in it.'

'Do you mean to say that Sir Luke Coniston is acting in a revue?'

'No, but his wife is. So he's staying on. It's the same with Lord Richard. He isn't in it, but Miss Kane is. So he's staying on too, to give her moral support. Gower-Jones is helping with the music. That accounts for all of them.'

Mr. Green nodded reflectively. 'So for at least a week we shall be able to study them, as it were, on the spot.'

'*You* will' retorted Waller. 'I'm only a poor policeman, pigging it at the local pub.'

'On the contrary, you are the arm of the law. And as such you will be able to open a great many doors which are closed to me.'

'You know quite well that any information I may collect is at your disposal.'

Mr. Green accepted this remark with some reservation.

There had been times when Waller had been none too co-operative.

'You are very kind,' he said.

'I wish I could say the same about you,' grunted the superintendent.

'My dear Waller, if I had any information I should share it. But I have none.'

'All the same, you've got a hunch, haven't you?'

'I have never cared for the word "hunch",' observed Mr. Green loftily. 'It should be reserved for the race-course.'

'Well—an instinct then.'

'Hunches—instincts! One would really think that this was the first time we had worked together! I am not a fortune-teller, my dear Waller, as I have told you a hundred times. I merely examine the puzzle before me in order to see if there are any pieces which do not fall naturally into place. If there are, I ask myself why. There is nothing more to it than that.'

2

Nothing of great importance, or so it seemed, transpired during the rest of the day. The final witness, Mr. Cecil Gower-Jones, returned shortly after tea, and was duly interviewed by Waller in the library, after which Waller made his departure. Mr. Green took the opportunity of intercepting him as he was about to step into his car.

'Was there anything significant in Mr. Gower-Jones's evidence?' he asked.

It was Waller's turn to sniff. 'Don't you think you'd better have a go at him yourself?'

Mr. Green drew himself up haughtily. 'If that is your idea of co-operation . . .'

Waller grinned and patted his hand. 'Keep your hair on. I was only joking. No. There was nothing significant.'

'You were satisfied with the account he gave of his movements?'

'He seemed to be telling the truth.'

'As far as I recall from the plan, he was walking towards the staircase from the direction of the east wing, a few seconds after the shot was fired. Does he keep to that story?'

Waller regarded Mr. Green with some respect. 'For an old gentleman of your advanced years, you have a remarkable memory. Yes, he sticks to it. He says he went upstairs to powder his nose, and took the wrong turning. It wouldn't be difficult in a house of this size.'

'No,' agreed Mr. Green. 'It would not be difficult. Indeed, there are times when it might be almost imperative.'

'Meaning?'

'Nothing. I was speaking at random.'

'If I choose to believe Gower-Jones,' said Waller, 'it's not because I've taken a fancy to him. He's not my type.'

'May I ask why?'

'I don't like young gentlemen who go round pinching housemaids' bottoms.'

Mr. Green blinked.

'One of the maids has been complaining about it only this morning.' His eyes twinkled. 'I suppose one might find some significance in *that*?'

'One might indeed,' observed Mr. Green, with complete gravity.

'So might the housemaid, when you come to think of it.'

This marked the end of their exchanges, and Waller departed, after telling Mr. Green that he would be driving to London in the morning with Andrew Lloyd, in order to visit the house of the dead woman and examine her effects. He did not ask Mr. Green to accompany him, nor did Mr. Green suggest it.

Mr. Green walked slowly back to the library. There was still some time before dinner and he wished to follow the advice that he had given to Waller—to find a book on Flemish art of the seventeenth century.

He closed the library door after him, crossed the room and was about to consult the card index system. Then he paused, staring intently at a door which connected with the music room. He heard a curious noise, like somebody tapping on a piece of wood. And yet—was it wood? He listened intently. There were three more sharp taps, and then the sound of something breaking and falling. Finally a rustle of paper, and silence.

Walking very softly he went towards the door and pushed it ajar. As he did so, a door at the further end was swiftly closed, but not before he had seen the gleam of a woman's dress.

He stood there staring about him. After a few seconds he stepped across to the gramophone. There was a record on the turntable. Mr. Green read the title and blinked. His eyes strayed towards the waste-paper basket. He walked to it and lifted up the crumpled newspaper on top. Some fragments of black wax fell out. The title was printed on one of them. He picked it up and read it. "Mad at the Moon" played by Blue Joseph. Mr. Green blinked again, more rapidly.

Then he sighed and ran his hands through his scanty hair. It was all very confusing. Of a sudden he felt fatigued. A little music would be refreshing.

He went back to the gramophone. The record lying on it was the one which he had previously mentioned to Waller —Bach's "Jesu, Joy of Man's Desiring", played by Dame Myra Hess. He turned it on, sank back in a chair, and closed his eyes. As he listened to the gentle cadences he could not help reflecting that if everybody began his day by listening to music such as this, the world would be saved from a great many disagreeable occurrences.

6

A HOUSE OF SECRETS

MR. GREEN slept very soundly that night, and it was not till nearly ten o'clock on the following morning that Palmer, the young Adonis of a butler, knocked on the door and entered with the breakfast tray.

In his wake came Charlotte.

'Thank you, Palmer,' said Charlotte, for Mr. Green was still rubbing his eyes. 'That looks very nice.'

'I brought tomato juice as well as orange juice, miss, as I wasn't sure which the gentleman preferred.'

'I think the orange juice will be enough in future.'

'If the gentleman would like a nectarine, miss, or some grapes?'

'I don't think so, thank you, not just now.'

He seemed disappointed that Mr. Green was so un-enterprising. He poured out a glass of iced Vichy water and set it by the coffee. 'This is what Mr. Lloyd always likes, miss, to start the day. but if the gentleman would prefer Evian . . . or Vittel?'

By this time the gentleman was awake. 'You are very kind. The Vichy will do very well.'

With a sigh Palmer bowed and went out, closing the door softly behind him.

'That young man is really quite impossibly good-looking,' observed Charlotte.

Mr. Green smiled, sipping his orange juice. 'I should warn you that he is a criminal.'

'Really?' Charlotte showed no great interest. She was used to this sort of thing.

'Though I should not regard him as a criminal type. He merely happens to have been in gaol.'

She nodded absently. 'There's a note for you from Mr. Lloyd. Shall I read it?'

'If you please.'

Dear Mr. Green, she read . . . *I regret that there has so far been little opportunity to talk to you in private. As you will understand, I have been somewhat preoccupied. By the time you read this, I shall be on my way to London with Superintendent Waller. We are going to Miss Larue's house, in the hope of finding some evidence which may assist our enquiries. After this I shall be occupied with various affairs until the late afternoon. So, I understand, will Mr. Waller. I trust, however, that I shall be able, this evening, to present you with some new facts which you may feel worthy of consideration.*

I hope you will ask for anything that you may need. I should like you to regard Broome, if not as a home, at least as a fairly comfortable hotel.

She put down the letter. 'I must say he couldn't be more considerate. And Mrs. Lloyd's a darling.'

'Have you been seeing her?'

'We both had breakfast early, and went a walk afterwards. When I came back I felt quite dizzy. It's the most fabulous place.'

'In what way?'

'Well, darling, you knew houses like this before the war. I didn't. And I really don't think there can be many of them left—not in England at any rate. I mean . . . fourteen gardeners!'

'When I stayed here, as a young man,' observed Mr. Green with a sigh, 'there were twenty. Times have changed.'

'You're being tiresome, darling, and spoiling my story. There are half a dozen woodmen as well. There are acres and acres of kitchen garden, and miles and miles of glass, and an orchid house and a carnation house and a camellia house and a house for tropical ferns, and heaven knows what else. There's a quite fantastic swimming pool and four tennis courts and three lakes, and the most enchanting temples and statues in the woods, and I haven't seen a quarter of it yet. What it must cost to keep it up!'

'Surely Mrs. Lloyd did not omit to tell you?'

She looked at him curiously. 'As a matter of fact, she did tell me. How did you guess?'

'She struck me as that sort of woman.'

'But she couldn't be less . . . less vulgar.'

'I am not suggesting that she is vulgar. I am merely remembering that she is Andrew Lloyd's wife, and as such, money has a special importance for her. I might almost say, a special morality.'

'I'm not quite sure what you mean by that.'

Mr. Green twinkled at her. 'I am not quite sure what I mean by it myself.'

2

Had Mr. Green been eavesdropping on Andrew Lloyd an hour before this conversation took place, he could not have made a more apposite remark than his observation about money, and it's "special morality". For as Lloyd ushered the superintendent into the car—a Rolls Royce which seemed to sparkle with a special richness of its own— he turned to him and said, in the most casual of tones: 'If we are to understand one another, there is only one thing that need concern you about myself.'

'And what is that, sir?'

'My god is money.'

Waller had no immediate retort to this statement. Even if he had been able to think of one, it would have been trite.

Lloyd glanced at him. 'Your silences are devastating.'

'So are some of your remarks, if I may say so, sir.'

'Don't you believe me?'

If Waller had been truthful he would have said no. A man whose god is money did not choose the sort of pictures that Lloyd had chosen, nor respond to them as he responded. Waller had been in millionaires' houses before; Broome Place was like none of these There was great richness, but always that feeling of restraint, of reserve.

Nor did a man whose god was money show the same almost passionate solicitude for green, growing things. Waller had watched Lloyd as he walked round the terraces of the garden after the storm. His fingers would touch a broken branch or a bruised tendril as gently as a father tending the limbs of a hurt child.

'Don't you believe me?' repeated Lloyd.

'Of course I believe you, sir.' If this were the mask that Lloyd chose to wear—the mask of the inhuman, ruthless materialist—let him wear it. Men who wore masks had a sense of false security, which sometimes led them to betray themselves.

Lloyd smiled and nodded. He had made his point.

'And now,' he said. 'will you forgive me if I study the *Financial Times*?'

Without waiting for a reply, he opened the paper. At the same time he flicked a gold pencil from his pocket and made a note on a pad in front of him. By the time the journey was over, a dozen pages of the pad were covered with figures and symbols. Waller had a momentary feeling of bitterness. All that money—just for ringing up on the telephone and buying a lot of slips of paper! Then he reproached himself. After all, it wasn't as simple as that. You had to buy the right slips of paper, and maybe that wasn't so easy.

The car was speeding up Fitzjohn's Avenue. Lloyd tore off the sheets of paper on which he had written, folded them neatly and pushed them into the inner pocket of his jacket.

'That's that,' he said, with a sigh of relief.

'Satisfactory I hope, sir?'

Lloyd shrugged his shoulders. 'One has one's ups and downs.'

He felt that it would be embarrassing to inform the

superintendent that his operations in the last ten days showed a loss of slightly over thirty thousand pounds.

3

Number One Elvira Close might have been specially designed to accommodate the mistress of a discreet millionaire. It lay at the end of a cul-de-sac off a quiet road that led to Hampstead Heath. On one side of it rose a tall Queen Anne building, shabby and neglected, its windows largely obscured by ancient plane trees. To the other side lay half an acre of land on which there were no buildings at all—an undeveloped bomb-site. Number One itself was a small box-shaped house of red brick, in the Georgian tradition.

Sergeant Bates was waiting for them outside. He sketched a salute as the superintendent stepped from the car. 'Any developments, sir?'

'Nothing to write home about,' grunted Waller.

The young man sighed, very audibly. If *he* had been running this case . . .

Lloyd paused at the entrance. 'By the way,' he said, 'if you want to have a word with the housekeeper alone, I need hardly say that I have no objection. She might feel embarrassed in my presence.'

'Thank you, sir. Mrs. Cartwright, I think you said her name was?'

'Yes. She's only been here for about four months, and she's not very intelligent; I don't suppose you'll get much out of her. While you're interviewing her, I'll show our young friend the run of the house.'

As he spoke, he pressed the bell with one hand and inserted his latchkey with the other, and before the door was fully open he was calling 'Mrs. Cartwright!' in an impatient voice. Lloyd, reflected Waller, knew the full value of each second in the unforgiving minute.

Waller's interview with Mrs. Cartwright took place in a small study on the left of the hall. The housekeeper was a stout, flaccid woman, dressed in deep black. As she spoke she constantly sniffed and dabbed her eyes with a handkerchief; in spite of these manifestations of grief Waller suspected that she was enjoying the situation.

'Such a terrible thing to happen, sir,' she proclaimed in tremulous tones. 'I'd never have credited it. Always so bright and happy, she was. Of course . . .' with a glance towards the door . . . 'I know she wasn't what you'd call straight-laced, but that was her affair. And as for Mr. Lloyd, he was always the perfect gentleman.'

Waller took her through the usual routine, and once again received the usual collection of negatives. Any signs of depression? On the contrary. Ever seen a revolver about the house? Good heavens, no! Money troubles? What—with Mr. Lloyd being so generous?

And then, at last, he got something.

'Any suspicious visitors?'

Mrs. Cartwright stopped dabbing her eyes and frowned in concentration.

'Well, I wouldn't say exactly *visitors*, sir, because, you see, he never came inside.'

'Who?'

'He just sneaked around like, usually at the end of the road.'

'Yes, but *who*?'

'Why, the man in black, sir.'

Waller looked at her sharply. The man in black? She spoke with such relish that she made it sound absurdly melodramatic. He wondered if she was trying to pull his leg.

'Can you describe this man?'

'He was about six foot, sir. Very dark. Fortyish, I should say. A fine figure of a man.'

'What did he do?'

'Just hung around, sir, at all times of the day and the night. As likely as not he'd be there at breakfast time.'

'Did you ever speak to him?'

'No, sir. I went out, once or twice, but he always gave me the slip. Just faded away, as it were.'

'Did Miss Larue ever speak to him?'

'Yes, sir. She ran out once and caught him, and I think she must have given him a piece of her mind.'

'Did she tell you who he was?'

'No, sir. But I think she knew. Because when I said she ought to send for the police she got very angry, and told me not to be a fool. It was the only time I've ever known her to speak like that.'

'Have you seen this man since her death?'

'No, sir. Not a sign of him.'

Waller stood there for a moment, thinking. The past of the late Miss Larue was singularly slow in yielding up its secrets. A man in black, standing in the shadows—it was not much to go on, but maybe it was better than nothing at all.

4

The interview with Mrs. Cartwright had taken longer than he expected. When he went out into the hall, he saw that Lloyd and Bates had already gone upstairs.

He walked into the drawing room, immediately opposite. It was a room that proclaimed the taste of the man who had decorated it—Andrew Lloyd. It was exquisite, but relentlessly austere—panelled walls of faded pine, Queen Anne tables with Ming horses. The brightest touch of colour, if silver can be called a colour, came from the sconces round the walls. He wondered if Miss Larue had appreciated it. He suspected that there must have been days when she longed to modify the chastity of the Adam settees with a few brilliant cushions.

There was a step behind him. It was Lloyd. 'I've left your young man in the bedroom,' he said. 'He seemed to be enjoying himself. For me it is a room with rather painful associations. Did you have any luck with Mrs. Cartwright?'

'I wouldn't go so far as to say that, sir. But she told me one thing on which I'd like your comment. About a man that's been hanging round the house.'

He was looking straight into Lloyd's eyes as he spoke, and he was certain that he read fear in them. It was only for a brief second—a fleeting shadow, a twitch of the lids—but it was unmistakable.

'What sort of man?' Lloyd had full control of himself again.

'Fortyish. Dark. Well set up. Always wore black'.

'He sounds rather cloak-and-dagger.'

'That's what I thought, sir. But she seemed to be telling the truth. Apparently this man was to be seen at all times of the day and night. Even before breakfast.'

Lloyd gave a careless laugh. 'Perhaps he was crossed in love. Or he may have been a peeping Tom. I'm afraid I can't help you, superintendent. It can hardly be very vital, can it?'

Waller appeared to ponder the question.

'Can it?'

Before Waller could reply there was the sound of a knock on the door.

'Come in,' cried Lloyd impatiently.

The door opened, revealing Bates. He held a letter in his hand.

'Excuse me, sir, but I thought I'd better come down and show you this. It might be important.'

He handed the letter to Waller, who glanced at it and frowned.

'Where did you find it?'

'In the wall-safe, sir.'

Lloyd stepped forward. 'The wall-safe?' he repeated. 'Where?'

'In the bathroom, sir.'

'You mean to tell me that there is a wall-safe in the bathroom?'

'That's right, sir. Behind the towel-rail.' There was a note of some satisfaction in Bates' voice. 'If you didn't know it was there, you wouldn't be likely to notice it. Very neat little job. But not too difficult to open if you know how.'

Lloyd seemed too astonished to make any comment. Meanwhile Waller was studying the letter, which was typewritten on notepaper bearing the address of Garside, Payne and Garside, 30A Throgmorton Street, E.C.2. It was dated October 11th, 1956 . . . the previous Thursday.

As he studied it, he frowned. Then he handed it to Lloyd. 'You'd better have a look at this, sir.'

Lloyd took it. As soon as he saw the heading on the paper he paused and lifted his head, and for a moment he stared up to the ceiling; it was as though he had heard a movement on the floor above, from the dead woman's room. Then he lowered his head and read . . .

Dear Miss Larue,

This is to confirm that I am prepared, through my nominees, to purchase from you your holding of 250,000 ordinary shares in Wild Range Oil Development, Ltd. The price paid will be the current quotation at the opening of the Stock Exchange on Monday morning next. At the close of the market today they stood at 3/1d. buyers.

This is also to confirm that in consideration of your selling these shares I will personally transfer to your account the sum of £25,000, which is the equivalent of a bonus of 2/- per share above the ruling price.

In order that this transaction shall be binding on both of us, my legal advisor is preparing a document to which your signature will be required. Normally I would send this through the post, but there are some technical details which I should like to explain to you. I will therefore bring it with me tomorrow to Broome Place, where I understand we are both to be guests for the week-end, and when I trust we shall have an opportunity for some private conversation. I am sure I need not reiterate the desirability of keeping this matter strictly confidential.

Yours sincerely,
Luke Coniston.

Waller watched him closely. Lloyd was keeping a good grip on himself; his hand did not tremble; but the muscles round the chin showed that his teeth were tightly clenched. He was obviously very angry indeed.

Waller spoke. 'Do you make anything out of it, sir?'

Lloyd's lips parted in the parody of a smile. 'No, superintendent. I don't make anything out of it.'

'Are you sure, sir?'

'Quite sure. I am answering your question literally. I make nothing out of it. On the contrary, I may lose a fortune.'

Suddenly he stepped forward and took up the telephone on the desk. He began to dial a number; then he glanced at his watch and put down the receiver. 'What's the use?' he muttered. 'He'll have put the deal through by now.' He threw the letter on to the table and walked over to the window. For a moment he stared out, tapping his foot on the parquet floor.

Then he turned. 'Well, Superintendent,' he said, 'you have just witnessed a classic example of what I believe is known as the double cross.'

'I'm afraid you'll have to put me wise, sir. I'm not much of an expert on financial matters. These shares . . . do you know anything about them?'

Lloyd gave a short laugh. 'Wild Range Oil? Quite a lot! I financed the original exploration in Canada. I chose the technicians, and paid them. I floated the company . . . if you can call it a company. To all intents and purposes, the company was myself.'

'Did you know that Miss Larue had such a large holding in them?'

'Of course. I gave them to her. I wanted a fifty-one per cent control of the company, and there were technical reasons why I preferred not to have it all vested—to outward appearances—in my own hands.'

'And now you have lost that contol?'

'So it would seem.' He looked up to the ceiling. 'That she should sell my secrets to Luke Coniston, of all people!' There was a world of bitterness in his voice. 'I think I deserved a little better from her than that!'

He turned again towards the window. He seemed unwilling to face Waller's calm scrutiny.

'I'm sorry to have introduced so intimate a note,' he said at length. 'After all, this is a matter of business, and should be treated as such.' His voice was cold and hard again. 'A matter of business,' he repeated. 'That is why, as far as I am personally concerned, my relations with Sir Luke will remain outwardly unchanged. I imagine that you would also prefer it like that.'

'Very much so, sir. In fact, I should have suggested it myself. The less Sir Luke is aware that his movements are being watched, the better. As a technical matter, sir, is there any reason why you are bound to know that he is the purchaser of these shares?'

'None. As he says in the letter, he purchases through nominees. Needless to say, he'll know that I suspect him, but he'll also know that I can't prove it.'

'From a stock exchange point of view, is there anything irregular about such an arrangement as this?'

'None that I can think of. If it comes to that, I can see nothing illegal about it either.'

'To tell you the truth, sir, nor can I.' He heaved a deep sigh. 'As for this cheque for £25,000, I think we can assume that no more will be heard of that!'

Lloyd gave a short laugh. 'I don't think Sir Luke is likely to waste much energy in handing it over to Miss Larue's heir . . . if she has any.'

'So everything's worked out very nicely for him—for the time being.'

'For the time being,' echoed Lloyd. 'I wonder how long that time will be.'

He threw a last fleeting glance towards the ceiling. Then he walked swiftly to the door.

7

LORD RICHARD DRIVES FAST

WHILE these things were happening, the morning was passing uneventfully for Mr. Green. A stroll in the garden, a wander down the long gallery, another stroll—this time to the stables, where he had an interesting conversation with one of the gardeners about the age of the chiming clock in the tower—and a saunter round the west wing, where he was especially attracted by one of the late-flowering magnolias . . . that was all.

He asked no questions, and was told no lies. But wherever he went, in his quiet way, he made friends. Even Lady Coniston, who had been inclined to resent his presence with some bitterness, observed to Mrs. Lloyd that 'one would hardly know he was a detective.'

Mrs. Lloyd smiled gently. 'I don't think he would care to be described as such.'

'But isn't that what he's here for?'

'I hardly know. He came quite by chance. And Andrew thought it would be a good idea if he stayed on.'

'Do *you* think it's a good idea?'

'I suppose so.' She hesitated. 'Though I can't really see that it's necessary.'

'Neither can I. When one starts raking things up, one never knows where it's going to end.'

'If there *is* anything to rake up.'

Lady Coniston gave her hostess a malicious glance. 'Well darling . . . you should know.'

Not for the first time, Mrs. Lloyd felt that she would be extremely glad when Lady Coniston, and all the rest of the party, had taken their leave.

It was round about noon that Mr. Green decided to

walk down to the lakes, in order to indulge in a little meditation. He was partly persuaded to do so by the excessive attentions of Palmer, who seemed to have developed a dog-like devotion to him, and was constantly appearing, in the most unexpected places, with suggestions of sherry and biscuits, grapes, coffee, Vichy water, and even hot milk.

'We must keep up our strength, sir' he said, regarding Mr. Green with adoring eyes.

Mr. Green agreed that this was most desirable, but added that as far as he was concerned, his strength was not dependent upon quite so large an intake of fluids. Having said this he instantly regretted it. He feared that he might have wounded the young man, who had departed looking greatly disappointed. Mr. Green sighed. Life would be very much easier if one had no consideration for the feelings of others.

So to the lakes he decided to take himself. But he never reached them. For as he opened the front door, a thunderous sound, only a few yards away, made him start back with a shock.

2

Mr. Green turned, and saw that the sound came from a large, eccentrically designed automobile that was standing near the porch.

The thunderous sound ceased as quickly as it had begun. 'Scared you?'

A young man in greasy overalls lifted his head from under the bonnet. For a moment Mr. Green did not recognize him. Then he remembered.

'Lord Richard!' he exclaimed.

'That's me.' He wiped his hands on his knees, and looked up with a grin. 'Or should it be "That's I"? I never know.'

Mr. Green appeared to ponder the question. ' "That

is me," ' he murmured, cocking his head to the left. ' "That is
I," ' cocking his head to the right. 'I am no grammarian. But
speaking as a human being . . .'

'And as a detective?'

Mr. Green looked up sharply. He was inclined to like
this young man, with his tousled hair and turned-up nose
and his casual smile. But he had old-fashioned notions that
the young should not interrupt.

'Speaking as a human being . . .' he repeated, in somewhat lofty tones.

The young man interrupted again. 'Sorry sir,' he said.
'I always seem to speak out of turn.'

Mr. Green's heart melted within him. The "sir" had
been charmingly stressed, and the admission of error had
been nicely timed.

He beamed upon Lord Richard. 'This is a fruitless
discussion,' he observed. 'But speaking as a human being,
I should be inclined to prefer the man who said "That is
me" to the man who said "That is I." '

Lord Richard nodded. 'Me too,' he said

The eyes of the two men met in a mutual twinkle.

'And now,' said Mr. Green, 'perhaps you would care
to tell me something about this singular conveyance?'

Lord Richard's car was indeed a singular conveyance.
It had begun its life some ten years ago as an open touring
Bentley, but it had been so supercharged and streamlined
and invigorated—so painted and repainted and generally
gadgetted—that it now looked like a large and ferocious
mongrel.

But if the conveyance itself was singular, even more so
was Mr. Green's request to examine it. His mind was so
unmechanical that even the setting of an alarm clock called
for considerable deliberation. As for motor-cars, and
especially the insides of motor-cars, they were a closed
book. If ever the bonnet of a motor-car was raised in his
presence, he looked the other way, particularly if it was one
of his own motor-cars, for which he had a fondness. It
would have been as distasteful to look into the inside of a

motor-car as to peer through an X-ray into the stomach of an intimate friend.

And yet here he was, accompanying Lord Richard to this outlandish contraption and displaying every sign of interest in its functions.

'A powerful piece of mechanism' he observed.

'There's not many buses on the road that'll pass her.'

'How fast would you estimate it . . . that is to say, she . . . will go?'

'Well, I've done a hundred and twenty on the Portsmouth Road.'

Mr. Green, with an effort, repressed a shudder. The thought of doing even fifty on the Portsmouth road appalled him. However, this was no time to air his predilections.

'That must have been most exhilarating.'

His lordship grunted. 'Of course, she wasn't going all out. Not really. You can't. Not in this darned country.'

'Does it . . . she . . . does she give much trouble?'

'Good Lord, no! Never had a day's illness in her life.'

'But I understood that last Saturday . . .'

'Oh . . . that!' He gave a short laugh. 'That wasn't much. Just a spot of bother with the distributor.'

He took a screwdriver from his pocket and bent low over the engine. Mr. Green came a little nearer. He pointed at the carburettor.

'The distributor, I take it, being this object?'

'No. That's the carburettor. The distributor's this chap.' Lord Richard's voice sounded gruff. 'D'you mind if I concentrate for a minute? This is a rather tricky adjustment.'

'Not at all. Please do not let me disturb you.'

Mr. Green stepped back and regarded the motor-car with a pensive eye. Although his bent was not mechanical, he had quite an affection for motor-cars, simply because he transformed them, in his mind, into animals. He usually thought of them as cats, because of their purr, though certain very smart sports-cars were dogs, like prize setters.

This car was a sort of panther, he felt—a lean and rather battered panther that had escaped from the zoo—and he had a fancy that it might be dangerous.

However, it looked comfortable enough. Perhaps Lord Richard would not mind if he sat in the front seat for a moment? He opened the door, and as he did so a thin slip of paper fluttered out on to the dashboard. Mr. Green was the tidiest of persons, and he swiftly picked it up and transferred it to his pocket. Then he placed himself in the seat next to the driver's. Yes, it was very comfortable indeed, though his short legs did not reach the floor.

What a formidable collection, he thought, as his eyes roved over the dashboard. So many clocks and gauges and dials! He was reminded of the instrument panel of an aeroplane. There was only one of them, apart from the speedometer, that he recognized—the petrol gauge. He switched it on for a moment. He saw that it was nearly touching Empty.

'Care to go for a run?'

Mr. Green started. He had not noticed Lord Richard come up behind him.

'Thank you indeed. But I think not, this morning.'

'I'm only going down to the station and back again. Do you good.'

Mr. Green blinked. 'To the station?' A sudden thought struck him. He glanced at his watch. 'If you are going immediately' he said, 'I might catch the twelve thirty.'

'To London?'

'I have just recollected some business.'

'We'll have you there in five minutes.' He wiped his hands on a rag, vaulted into his seat and pressed the starter.

Mr. Green gave a sickly smile. He leant forward and raised his voice over the roar of the engine. 'There is no great urgency,' he shouted. 'It is not a matter of life and death.'

Even as he spoke his smile faded. Not a matter of life and death? He wondered.

3

In spite of Lord Richard's solicitude in moderating his
speed to suit the nerves of his passenger—a mere eighty
through the narrow winding lanes—it was not till the train
was half way to London that Mr. Green had recovered his
self-possession. Never again, he thought, would he entrust
his person to so diabolical a contraption as that young man's
car. He had flattered it by calling it a panther. It was a how-
ling, roaring tiger, gone berserk . . . a wild beast crashing
through the jungle, trying to shake its riders from its back.
So breathless and battered had he been on his arrival at the
station that he had forgotten to warn his hostess that he
would be out to luncheon. She would think him very ill-
mannered. He must bring her some flowers from London.
No. That would be carrying coals to Newcastle, with a
vengeance. Perhaps a bottle of scent? Coals to Newcastle
again. He had noticed a glittering array of Dior and Chanel
and Molyneux on her dressing table. However, he had also
noticed that on this table there were none of the odours of
Floris—the exquisite little establishment in Jermyn Street
to which his sensitive nose had so often conducted him.
No woman, surely, could savour the delicacy of Floris's
rose geranium without being the better for it. He would
buy her a bottle of rose geranium, and if she did not like
it he would annex some of it for himself.

Yes, thought Mr. Green, he would have been glad of
some fragrance on his handkerchief at this moment, for
he seemed to have landed himself into a most unsavoury
situation. If only he had not picked up that slip of paper
from Lord Richard's car! But then—he had to pick it up;
he always picked up slips of paper. The trouble was that
he also read them. And the message he had read on this
particular slip of paper was a message that it was his duty
to decipher.

He felt in his pocket and read it once again. To the
casual observer it would have seemed innocuous enough.

It was merely a printed receipt from the Ma-Phare Garage—
Mr. Green shuddered as he read the name—for fifteen
gallons of petrol. It was dated 13.10.56. But Mr. Green's
face was grim and unhappy as he studied it. He had
developed quite a liking for young Lord Richard.

4

The Ma-Phare Garage—apart from its appalling name—
was an agreeable enough institution, situated in a quiet mews
behind South Audley Street. Across one of the windows
was the sign "Garage to Let", and underneath this window
stood an elegant Rolls Royce, which was being hosed by a
young man with ginger hair and a plentiful crop of freckles.

Mr. Green walked over to him. 'Excuse me,' he murmured, 'might I speak to you for a moment?'

The young man looked up. 'Yes, sir?' He saw that Mr.
Green was regarding the hose, which was streaming very
near to his feet, with some apprehension. 'Just a minute,
sir. I'll turn it off.'

'It was about the garage to let,' said Mr. Green when he
returned. 'Is it still available?'

'That's right, sir. Thirty-five bob a week. Was you
thinking of it?'

'Yes. Which one would it be?'

'Over 'ere, sir. I'll show you. It's in a bit of a mess
now, but we'll soon get rid of that.'

They walked over to an open door, and Mr. Green
looked in. He felt that some comment was expected of him,
but it was difficult to find any very original adjectives for
a cement floor littered with packing cases.

'Very nice,' he murmured.

'That's what I always say,' agreed the young man. 'Very
nice little garage. Very central too. When was you thinkin'
of movin' in?'

'I could let you know tomorrow. You have a telephone?'

'Just a minute, sir. I'll give you one of our cards.' He

fumbled in his waistcoat and produced a grimy trade card which he handed to Mr. Green. 'Sorry it's a bit mucky, sir.'

'Not at all.' Mr. Green put the card in his pocket. For a moment he seemed as though he was going to turn away. Then he paused and said: 'I believe that you also oblige a young friend of mine—Lord Richard Marwood?'

The man's face lit up. 'You know 'im, sir? There's a wild 'un for you! Ever seen his car, sir?'

'I have not only seen it. I have driven in it.'

'Phew! That'd take some nerve.' He regarded Mr. Green with increased respect.

'It is not an experience I would care to repeat.' Mr. Green smiled ruefully. 'A very expensive car to run, I should imagine?'

'That's right, sir. Eats it up. Just eats it up. When 'is lordship come in 'ere last . .. '

'Let me see' interrupted Mr. Green. 'That was on Saturday morning, was it not?'

'No, sir. Saturday afternoon, round four o'clock. Should've been my week-end off, but one of the blokes got sick.' He noticed that Mr. Green was blinking painfully. 'Got something in your eye, sir?'

'Nothing. Just a speck.'

'Very painful, anything in the eye, sir, that's what I always say. Worst place to 'ave anything, in the eye, and no mistake.'

'It is certainly an inconvenience. You were saying?'

'Oh yes, sir. About 'is lordship. Well, when 'e come in 'ere Saturday, we 'ad a bit of an argument like. I give 'im 'is usual fifteen gallons . . .'

'Dear me. As much as that?'

'That's right, sir. Fifteen of the best, every time. And I says to 'im: "This lot won't get you very far, m'lord." Joking like. And 'e says: "It'll get me over 250 miles." And I says: "Over fifteen to the gallon in this outfit? Not on your life." Or words to that effect. Quite short 'e was with me, 'is lordship was, not believin' 'im. Not like 'is lordship.'

'Perhaps he was annoyed at the car breaking down?'

'Did it break down, sir?'

'I seem to have heard so. I may have been mistaken.'

'Must've been, sir. I'd 'ave known about it. I'm the only one in this outfit as 'e ever allows to touch 'is car.'

'Perhaps—if I should rent the garage—you will be able to look after mine.'

'It'd be a pleasure, sir.'

'I am much obliged to you.' Mr. Green extended his hand and slid half a crown into the young man's palm with the apologetic smile which was one of the signs of his perfect manners. People who were tipped by Mr. Green were always given the impression that it was they who were conferring the favour.

5

Mr. Green went straight from the Ma-Phare Garage, in a taxi, to the ancient house of Floris, and purchased not one bottle of rose geranium but two. One at thirty shillings, for Mrs. Lloyd, and one at eighteen shillings for himself. He quite startled the young lady who attended him by the urgency with which he seized the packets, and the almost ferocious tones in which he assured her that there was no need to wrap them up. He might have been a drug addict, craving relief from some intolerable stress.

Then he hurried down the street to an Espresso coffee bar, ordered a large black coffee—which he would almost certainly have cause to regret—undid the stopper of the smaller bottle and sniffed. For a few moments the lines on his face were softened, and the corners of his mouth lifted with a smile. as he savoured the familiar odour of lemons and roses and dew, mingled in a moonlit night of June.

Then one of the young Espresso ladies—(he found himself wondering, inconsequently, if they were called Espressettes)—arrived with her deadly concoction, and demanded a shilling and sixpence. And he came back to the sordid realities of life.

BULLS AND BEARS

WHEN Mr. Green returned to Broome Place shortly before six o'clock, he found that Waller had preceded him, and was waiting in the library.

'What have you been up to?' growled the superintendent staring at him suspiciously.

Mr. Green had expected this question. Indeed, all the way down in the train he had been speculating on the answer he should give to it. Should he tell Waller what he had discovered? Or should he keep his secret?

It was by no means the first time that he had been faced with this dilemma, and it always disturbed him. His sense of fair play prompted him to confide in Waller. After all, Waller had laid all his cards on the table; he had withheld no information; he had been scrupulously co-operative.

And yet Mr. Green hesitated. He had always had a strange almost psychic sense, that as soon as an idea was put into words, it lost the power of growth. As long as the idea—call it a clue if you must—remained in your mind, as long as it was not clipped and limited by verbal definition, it could expand, it could stray into unexpected places, it could go on sending out tentacles of inquiry. But as soon as you expressed it, gave it a subject, a verb and an object, it remained static.

He had proved this in his early contacts with Waller. On more than one occasion, in the early stages of a case, an idea had occurred to him—a tenuous, shadowy idea that needed the most delicate treatment, like a moth that had fluttered out of the darkness and was still hovering in the outer circle of the light. He had felt it his duty to speak to Waller about it. And what had happened? Waller had pounced on it, with his great policeman's hands, and captured it, and pinned it down, and that was the end of it. The moth was no longer a live thing, with gold-dust in its wings, it could no longer flutter into strange places. It was a dead, dumb exhibit in a file in Scotland Yard, that could tell no secrets, even if it had any.

Mr. Green looked Waller straight in the eye. Like all essentially truthful men he was an admirable liar, when it came to the point.

'What have I been up to?' he repeated. 'If it is of any interest, I have been buying some scent.'

'Don't tell me you went up to London just to buy scent.'

'No. I had some private business.'

Waller snorted. 'If you expect me to believe that . . .' Then he gave a reluctant grin. 'O.K. Keep it up your sleeve. I don't suppose I'd understand it, even if you told me.'

Mr. Green made no comment.

Waller heaved a deep sigh. 'And now, I expect you want to pick *my* brains?'

'If you care to tell me what transpired in London this morning, I should be interested.'

'I suppose I'd better. I shan't have any peace until I do.'

Waller plunged into the story of his discoveries at Elvira Place. He was a good reporter and he omitted no detail. He was anxious to see what effect these revelations would have on Mr. Green. The old gentleman could be irritating, but his comments were very much to the point.

So it was on this occasion. He finished his story, lit a cigarette, and waited for Mr. Green to speak.

Mr. Green was frowning in concentration. 'How very curious!' he murmured. He seemed to be speaking to himself. 'How extremely improbable!'

'What's improbable?'

'The mysterious man in black.'

D*

Waller stared at him. 'I don't follow. I should have thought that the man in black was the least important part of the story. Why, there are millions at stake. There's double-crossing on a gigantic scale, the dead woman's directly involved, and . . .'

'All of which was to be expected' interrupted Mr. Green. 'For men who live in the world of Andrew Lloyd and Luke Coniston there are always millions at stake; there is always double-crossing on a gigantic scale. It is part of the inevitable pattern of their lives. Even if you had not discovered evidence of these things, I should have assumed them. I should also assume that a woman of the type of Margot Larue would have been involved in them. The one thing I should not have assumed would have been a man in black.'

'But who the devil *was* the man in black?'

'I think we can safely say that he was not employed by Scotland Yard.'

Waller sat up with a jerk. 'You mean . . .'

'I mean that he answers perfectly to the description of a private detective. And that is the only description that suits him . . . unless we are to conclude that he is a stray lunatic. If you recall the description of him given to you by the housekeeper you will find that it fits at every turn.'

'But who would want to have her shadowed? And why?'

'The second question might be easier to answer than the first. Why should she be shadowed? Well, I think we can forget about finance for the moment. One does not employ a detective to watch a house all night in order to keep track on a stock exchange speculation. So we are left with only the romantic alternative . . . if one can use the word romantic in such a connexion.'

'You mean, some man wanted to make sure that she wasn't putting a fast one on him?'

Mr. Green pursed his lips and nodded.

'But who? It couldn't be a jealous lover. He wouldn't behave like that. He'd come and batter down the door.

Besides, he'd have no illusions about her, in any case. It couldn't be a husband, because she wasn't married . . .'

'I wonder.'

'Have you any reason to think she might have been?'

'No. I was merely reflecting how little we know about her.'

'I'm beginning to think we know damn all.' Waller threw his cigarette into the fire with an impatient gesture. 'Still, let's keep to the facts we do know. There are only two men left who might have employed this man . . . Sir Luke and Andrew Lloyd. I'm inclined to eliminate Sir Luke, for the reasons you mentioned. This isn't a financial affair. But if it was Lloyd . . .' He looked up at Mr. Green with an expression of bewilderment. 'It just doesn't make sense.'

Mr. Green smiled. 'That was my original contention. Everything we know about Andrew Lloyd suggests that he would be the last person to go to these extremes—for any sentimental reason. His relationship with Margot Larue was as cold-blooded as any of his business transactions. At least, that was how he has described it to me.'

'To me, too. And I believed him.'

'Quite. I think we *must* believe him. Otherwise the attitude of Mrs. Lloyd becomes totally inexplicable.'

'It's pretty hard to swallow whichever way you look at it.'

'Not if we accept the fact that neither of them is quite normal. They have their own peculiar scale of values. In any normal household, the presence of a woman like Margot Larue would have been unthinkable. The wife would have sent her packing. But at Broome Place she became an item on a balance sheet. I have no doubt whatever that this was how Mrs. Lloyd regarded her.'

'Then why did he have her shadowed? If it wasn't a question of love or of money?'

Mr. Green shook his head. 'Your guess,' he said, 'is as good as mine.'

And then there was a knock on the door.

If Andrew Lloyd was still suffering from the strain of the morning's revelations, he showed no sign of it. He was as suave and as immaculate as ever. As he entered the room Waller was struck, once again, by the astonishing swiftness of his movements. He was smiling, and holding a scarlet carnation. He advanced, slipped the carnation into Mr. Green's buttonhole, drew up a chair, threw a log on to the fire, and lit a cigarette, and the effect was of one swift co-ordinated gesture.

'I am glad to have found you both together,' he said. He turned to Waller. 'You have told Mr. Green what happened this morning?'

'Yes, sir.'

'Good. I shall be interested to learn his comments. But first perhaps you would allow me to sum up the situation as I see it, to date.'

He looked at Mr. Green. 'I should like to begin with a question that may seem irrelevant. Have you ever heard of the Oxford Group?'

Mr. Green blinked. Before he could reply, Lloyd continued: 'Of course you have heard of it. What I should have said was are you aware of its four cardinal principles? They are . . . absolute honesty, absolute purity, absolute unselfishness and absolute love.'

'Indeed,' said Mr. Green.

'The application of these principles may be explosive, on individuals or on communities.'

'I can well believe that.'

'I propose to apply them, or rather the first of them, to the present situation. Absolute honesty. I will be absolutely honest with you, Mr. Green, if you will be absolutely honest with me. Is that a bargain?'

'By all means.'

There was a sense of tension in the room. Waller leant forward in his chair.

'Very well. Then let me say this. I believe that Margot Larue died by her own hand. I believe that this is a case of suicide, and that any other line of inquiry will prove unprofitable.'

Mr. Green put the tips of his fingers together and stared into the fire.

'And now, Mr. Green, let me ask you a question. *Do you believe that I am speaking the truth?*'

Slowly Mr. Green raised his eyes. 'Yes,' he said gently. 'I believe that you are speaking the truth.'

It was Waller's turn to speak. 'Does this mean that you share Mr. Lloyd's opinion?'

Mr. Green smiled. 'Absolute honesty is fatiguing,' he parried. 'I think we will leave it as it is. I believe that Mr. Lloyd is speaking the truth when he tells us that, in his opinion, this is a case of suicide.'

Waller glanced at Lloyd. 'That may be so, sir. But where does it get us?'

Lloyd laughed shortly. 'I don't know where it gets you, Superintendent. But it would certainly seem to eliminate me from your list of suspects, if you persist in your theory of murder.'

Waller made no comment.

'Why *do* you persist in it, Superintendent? Surely your first interest in this case was entirely due to the fact that it *was* a suicide . . . the fourth suicide with which Sir Luke has been associated. That seemed to you, as it seemed to me, a very strange coincidence. It seemed a more than adequate reason for calling in the Yard, and also for enlisting the co-operation of Mr. Green. Has anything happened to change your opinion?'

'We are only at the beginning of our investigations, sir.'

Lloyd made a gesture of impatience. 'But if you are on the wrong track . . .' He paused abruptly. 'Forgive me. I oughtn't to have said that. What I am trying to suggest is this. Might there not be cases of suicide which were, in fact, tantamount to murder? Might not there be cases where a woman was so harried and driven that she would have no alternative but to take her own life? That was what happened in at least two of the previous affairs in which Sir Luke was involved . . .'

'But in the case of Miss Larue? Is there any evidence that she was being harried and driven?'

'We know that he had involved her in financial transactions behind my back.'

'They seem to have been pretty profitable, if I may say so, sir.'

'Yes . . . but if I had found out!' Lloyd clenched his fist. Then he let his hand relax. 'Apart from that, there was the blackmailing letter found in her room.'

'Are you suggesting that Sir Luke wrote that himself, sir?'

'Hell, man! How do I know?' He drew his hand over his eyes in a sudden gesture of fatigue. 'All I know is that I want you to get that man.'

At that moment the telephone rang. He sat up abruptly and reached for the receiver. 'Hullo? Andrew Lloyd speaking.' For a moment he listened. 'I see. What was the closing price?' He listened intently and nodded. 'What's that you say? Sell?' His voice was very cold. 'Either I misunderstand you, or one of us is out of his senses.'

Suddenly he seemed to realize that he was not alone. 'Just a moment—hang on; I'll take this in my study.' He held out the receiver to Waller. 'Perhaps you'll be good enough to replace this for me?'

Waller took the receiver. It was damp with sweat.

At the door Lloyd paused. His lips twitched to a smile. 'If you care to listen,' he said, 'you might make a fortune. Or lose one.'

He went out. Mr. Green noticed that he had left the evening paper by the side of the chair in which he had been sitting. There was a headline on the front page:

CITY SPECIAL
FLARE UP IN OIL
Duel of Financial Giants

He scanned the opening paragraphs:

"In frenzied dealings late this afternoon the shares of Wild Range Oil Development Ltd. were hoisted a further four shillings to the record price of 28/6.

"Behind these sensational developments a grim battle is being waged between two of the City's most daring speculators, Sir Luke Coniston and Mr. Andrew Lloyd.

"Only a few weeks ago Wild Range shares stood at the nominal price of 11½d. The company was regarded as the exclusive perquisite of Mr. Andrew Lloyd, and its affairs were a closely guarded secret.

"Rumour has it that there has been a leakage in information, and that because of this large blocks of shares have passed out of Mr. Lloyd's hands. He is now fighting to regain control.

"A certain piquancy is added to this drama by the fact that in private life Sir Luke and Mr. Lloyd are close friends. Indeed, Sir Luke is at present staying in Mr. Lloyd's palatial residence, Broome Place."

Mr. Green handed the paper to Waller, who read it in silence. Then he threw it back on to the sofa.

'It's enough to turn a man into a Commie,' he snorted. 'All the same, I wish I'd got some of those shares myself. That's a good one about them being close friends.'

'They will no doubt continue to behave as such.'

'Dinner tonight ought to be interesting for you,' said Waller. 'All those smiles and small talk, with murder in the air. Now that Lloyd's not in the room, I suppose we *can* use that word? Or do you rule it out too?'

'My mind is quite open.'

'But you believed him when he said that in his opinion it was suicide.'

'I did.'

'Well, that's got us a little way along the road. Or has it?'

Mr. Green frowned. 'I wonder,' he said. And indeed, he wondered very much.

He glanced at his watch. 'It is time for me to go and change. We meet tomorrow?'

'I'll be up in the morning.' At the door he turned, with a grin. 'And let's hope that by the time I get here you'll have done a little hard thinking.'

Mr. Green nodded absent-mindedly. 'A little hard thinking,' he said, 'is precisely what the situation seems to demand.'

9

THE OLD SCHOOL TIE

Mr. Green had every intention, on regaining his room, of indulging in the hard thinking which Waller had recommended.

However, the opportunity was denied him. For when he opened the door of his bedroom he found that Palmer had preceded him. The young butler had fallen under Mr. Green's spell to such an extent that he had volunteered to valet him, instead of John the footman. John, in Palmer's opinion, was too heavy-handed to serve a person of Mr. Green's distinction. He did not understand the finer touches.

One of these finer touches was engaging Palmer's attention at this moment. He was squeezing paste on to Mr. Green's toothbrush, and laying the brush, with loving care, on top of a goblet of luke-warm water into which he had sprinkled a few drops of rose-geranium. If Mr. Green had been frank, he would have requested Palmer to discontinue this practice. It fidgeted him. He liked to squeeze out his own tooth-paste. To have it squeezed for him made him feel faintly decadent; apart from that, the tooth-paste did not taste so fresh.

However, he realized that this ceremony of the tooth-brush was one in which Palmer took a special pride, and since he had no desire to hurt the young man's feelings, Mr. Green beamed upon him, as though specially prepared toothbrushes were among the principal delights of his existence.

'You spoil me, Palmer,' he observed blandly.

'It's a pleasure, sir.' He opened a drawer, extracted a handkerchief, arranged it in the shape of a fan, and tucked

it neatly into the breast pocket of Mr. Green's smoking
jacket, which was hanging over a chair. This action also
fidgeted Mr. Green. He did not like fan-shaped handker-
chiefs protruding from the pocket of his smoking jacket.

'Yes, sir. It's a pleasure to work for a man if he isn't
temperamental. That's what I always say.'

'I'm sure you are right, Palmer . . .'

The young man gave the handkerchief a final pat. He
frowned, as though in deep thought. Then he said:

'You wouldn't call Mr. Lloyd a temperamental man,
would you, sir . . . not to look at him?'

Mr. Green, before answering, blinked several times in
rapid succession. He found himself faced with a dilemma
that was all too familiar—whether to behave as a gentleman
or as a detective. Gentlemen did not discuss their hosts
with servants. Detectives did. He blinked again. His eye
caught the toothbrush, laid out on the glass of perfumed
water. It seemed to reproach him. He decided to behave as
a detective.

'No, Palmer,' he replied. 'I should have formed a very
different opinion.'

'Well, sir, you'd be surprised. Now take that business,
last spring, over all his old school things.'

'I am afraid I do not quite follow you.'

'Sorry, sir. I should have explained. You know Mr.
Lloyd went to Marlbourne College?'

'So I had heard. I believe he had a very distinguished
record there.'

'That's putting it mildly, sir. He was top of everything.
Senior prefect, captain of rugger, captain of cricket, the
whole works. Same as when he went to Cambridge. Seems
to me Mr. Lloyd just can't help being head boy, if he puts
his mind to it.'

Mr. Green perceived that Palmer, though he might
criticize his master, was not devoid of a streak of hero-
worship.

'Well, sir, he didn't usually talk much about that sort
of thing. In fact, he was . . . well . . . sort of contemptuous

about it. He used to say that the bright boys who
got all the prizes at school were the ones who always
came to a bad end. But last spring, everything suddenly
changed.'

'Last spring?'

'Yes, sir. End of March it must have been, because the
daffodils was just coming out.'

It occurred to Mr. Green that Palmer was an unusually
observant young man.

'As I was saying, sir, everything suddenly changed.
It was Marlbourne College all the time. Not so much in
front of other people, but whenever he got a chance to
talk to me. You'd be surprised, sir, how much a gentleman
will talk to his valet, if he gets the opportunity. Well sir,
he talked to me all night. What's more, he got me to go up
in the box-rooms and go through all his old trunks—there's
acres of 'em up there, sir, that's got to be seen to be believed
—and bring down all the old things he hadn't worn for
twenty-five years or more. College blazers, school ties,
sweaters, that sort of thing. And books of school songs.
And then there was the prizes, too. Whole shelves of books,
bound in leather, and stamped with a gold crest and a
motto underneath.

'*Virtute studio ludo,*' murmured Mr. Green.

'That's it, sir. I asked Mr. Lloyd what it meant.'

'Do you recollect his reply?'

'No, sir. He just laughed and said it was a lot of hooey.
But I do remember what he said when I asked him what all
this was in aid of—meaning, why was he getting all these
things out.'

'And what was that?'

'He looked at me, sir, and said . . . "Well, Palmer, you
know very well that I never do anything unless there's
money in it. So there must be money in this, mustn't
there?"'

'And did you believe him?'

'I didn't know what to think, sir. At first I wondered
if there might be something valuable in all this junk. You

never know with books, like. But I gave up that idea, on the night it happened.'

'What precisely . . . happened?'

For the first time in his narrative the young man hesitated. 'I don't know as I should be telling you this, sir.'

By now, the detective in Mr. Green had completely ousted the gentleman. He spoke in the gentlest of voices. 'I assure you it will go no further.'

'Thank you, sir. I'd be obliged. Well—it must have been about six weeks later. Sometime during May. And one night Mr. Lloyd came home looking as though he'd seen a whole graveyard of ghosts. I met him in the long gallery— Mrs. Lloyd was up in London—and asked him what time he'd be wanting to dine. He said "Don't talk to me about dining, Palmer, we've got some business to do first".'

'Then he led the way upstairs, into his suite. I don't know if you've seen Mr. Lloyd's dressing room, sir? It has built-in cupboards on three sides. One of the cupboards was full of the things I've been telling you about. He threw it open and said "I want you to pack all these in a couple of suitcases". I asked him when? He said "Now, this minute". He was acting so strange that I didn't argue. He went into his study and I heard him pouring himself three quick drinks, one after the other. When he came back I'd just about finished. The suitcases were pretty heavy, but I'd got everything in. "Now we're going out to burn all this stuff," he said. I beg your pardon, sir, I said. I didn't think I'd heard aright. "Burn it," he said again. Pretty well shouting he was. And he was white in the face, clenching his fists, and standing there looking like murder. Then he must have realized that he was carrying on pretty peculiar, because he pulled himself together, and tried to relax, and muttered something about the things in the cupboard having the moth in them. Now sir, that wasn't true. Those things hadn't got the moth in them. They were so stinking of moth balls that any moth which had come within a mile of 'em would have turned up its toes. So I began to say I didn't think they had the moth. But he cut me short. He didn't shout any more, but he looked at me as if he could kill me. And he said, very quietly, that I was to pick up the suitcases and follow him. He led the way down the long gallery and out through the front door. We went up through the azalea walk, to the edge of the beech wood. And there we dumped all the stuff out of the suitcases. All the books, in their lovely bindings. And the sweaters with the crests on 'em. And the football boots. And the school songs. And the caps with the tassels. Mr. Lloyd told me to start a bonfire with them. So I did. And there we stood, throwing things on, acting like a couple of lunatics.'

He stopped abruptly. 'I've never spoken about this to anybody before, sir. I wonder why I should be telling you?'

'Perhaps it has been preying on your mind.'

'That's it, sir. It *has* been preying on my mind.' He looked at Mr. Green curiously. 'What do you make of it, sir?'

Mr. Green sighed. What could anyone make of it?'

'One can only assume . . .' he began. And then he blinked, and blinked again. Palmer regarded him sympathetically. A regular nervous twitch the old gentleman had, on some occasions.

Mr. Green spoke again, in a flat voice. 'One can only assume that Mr. Lloyd has what is sometimes described as the artistic temperament.'

'Yes, sir,' agreed Palmer. But he looked disappointed. He had hoped for a more illuminating comment.

Mr. Green stopped blinking. 'I have had rather a difficult day,' he said. 'I think that perhaps I will lie down for half an hour before dinner.'

'Of course, sir.' The young man was all contrition. 'I shouldn't have kept nattering like this.'

Mr. Green beamed upon him. 'I hope you will continue to . . . to natter,' he said mildly. 'It may prove of the greatest assistance.'

After Palmer had left him, he lay back in his chair and closed his eyes. Yes, he had certainly had a difficult day—

one of the most difficult he could ever remember. He had been presented with a series of fragments of a jigsaw puzzle, none of which seemed to bear the least relation to the other, either in colour or design. And yet dimly, in the background, he felt that a shape was emerging—a shape so grotesque, and so ugly, that he scarcely dared to contemplate it.

10

MR. NOBODY

NEXT day was Waller's day, and once again it was Palmer who advanced the action.

The young butler, like his master, had his own touch of what Mr. Green had described as the artistic temperament. He took instant likes and dislikes, and these decided his conduct. For Mr. Green, as we have observed, he had conceived a feeling verging on adoration; for Mr. Waller, on the other hand, he had no use at all.

This was partly due to Waller's profession. Palmer detested all policemen; one might, indeed, say that he had a policeman complex. This hatred arose from an episode in his youth. As a boy of seventeen, new to London, with very little money in his pocket, he acquired the habit of wandering at night under the bright lights of Piccadilly and Leicester Square, marvelling at all he saw. His startling good looks, his shabby clothes, and his general appearance of vagabondage, encouraged certain elderly gentlemen to assume that he might be seeking their company. The assumption was incorrect, but it was shared by a bright young policeman who had learned the first lesson of the force—that by far the quickest, easiest, and most popular way to promotion was through the detention of homosexuals, or those who might conceivably be construed as such. As a result, Palmer was arrested for importuning.

So Palmer disliked policemen. Nor was his dislike diminished by his later contact with them, in the matter of the forged share certificates, when he had been employed in Andrew Lloyd's office.

None the less, Palmer, though he hated policemen, was not a fool about them. He realized their power. They could be very unpleasant, if one did not co-operate. They could be very nasty indeed, if one kept secrets from them, at a time like this. It would be better to come out with it.

He came out with it, at ten o'clock on the following morning, in the long gallery, just after Waller had arrived to see Mr. Green.

'Excuse me, sir. May I have a word with you?'

Waller turned. The young man looked worried, and was flicking his fingers in a nervous gesture.

'What is it?'

'It's something I want to tell you, sir. About a letter. I suppose I ought to have mentioned it before, but what with one thing and another . . .'

'Fire away.'

The young man hesitated. 'Could we be a bit more private, sir?' He glanced towards a door on the left. 'There's nobody likely to come into the flower-room.'

'Very well.'

Palmer opened the door and stood aside for the superintendent to enter. It was an exquisite little room, panelled in faded yellow satin. Waller looked round for somewhere to sit down. Most of the furniture seemed too fragile for his heavy bulk. He chose the window ledge.

'I'm waiting,' he said shortly. He had no more liking for Palmer, than Palmer for him; he had no desire to put him at his ease.

Palmer closed the door softly.

'This letter, sir . . . it was one that Miss Larue gave me on the day she died. Addressed to a man staying at the Red Dragon.'

'Why did she give it to you?'

'Wanted me to deliver it by hand, sir. Said it was very important.'

'Well?'

'I didn't deliver it, sir.'

'Why not?'

'I suppose you might say because I was fed up, sir.'

Waller raised his eyebrows.

'Always wanting me to fetch and carry for her, sir, Miss Larue was. You'd think I had nothing better to do. Always making excuses to put more work on my shoulders. The way she'd send for me sometimes, about nothing at all, you might almost wonder whether . . .' He shrugged his shoulders.

'Whether what?'

The young man flushed. He'd be a menace to the teen-agers if he ever went on the movies, thought Waller.

'Well, sir,' he said. 'I've seen that look in women's eyes before.'

'I've no doubt you have,' grunted Waller. 'So what happened to the letter?'

'I just put a stamp on it and dropped it in the box at the end of the drive.'

'Although she'd told you that it was so important?'

The young man scowled. 'She'd queer ideas of what was important. There were times when she thought it was important that I should hook up her dress.'

For a moment there was silence. Waller's brain did not work at lightning speed, but it was methodical and not insensitive. He liked to docket his impressions as he went along. His impression, at the moment, was that Palmer was telling the truth.

'What time did you post the letter?' he asked.

'Just before six, sir. The last collection's at six-thirty.'

'Then it would be delivered by the first post on Monday —yesterday morning?'

'That's right, sir.'

'You say it was addressed to a man staying at the Red Dragon. Do you remember the name of this man?'

'Grey, sir.'

'Any initials?'

'One of them was S. I don't recollect the other.'

'Was there anything unusual about the envelope? Was it bulky? Did it look as though it might contain any-thing but a sheet of notepaper? Anything like a wad of notes?'

'Oh no, sir. Just an ordinary letter. By the feel of it there was only the one sheet in it.'

'Broome Place notepaper?'

'That's right, sir. Same as they all use, with the crest on the back.'

Waller nodded. 'I'll follow this up straight away. I hope you realize that it's a serious offence to withhold evidence in a case of this nature?'

Palmer made no reply.

'There's nothing else you're keeping up your sleeve? No? Very well. I'll be seeing you.'

At the door he paused. 'If anybody asks for me, I've gone out. You don't know where or why. Is that clearly understood?'

'Yes, sir.'

Waller strode out.

2

The exterior of the Red Dragon was not of a nature to allure the weary traveller. It was shabby and down-at-heel, its thatched roof was unkempt, and its small garden was full of weeds.

It stood by itself in a quiet lane leading towards one of the new building estates that were springing up on the outskirts of South Greenstead. Sooner or later, no doubt, it would be bought by some enterprising speculator, and refurbished with the inevitable façade of bogus Tudor beams. In the meantime it mouldered in solitude—a convenient refuge for any man who did not wish to draw too much attention to himself.

The door was opened to Waller by a middle-aged woman with bare arms and a dirty apron. Her eyes had the glassy film of the all-day drinker.

'Don't you know the hours?' she snapped, preparing to shut the door again.

Waller stepped forward. 'Mrs. Barker?'

'That's the name. What about it?'

'I am a police officer.'

The woman's mouth fell open as if it had been drawn apart by elastic.

'There's nothing to worry about,' said Waller quietly. 'This is merely a routine enquiry.'

'If it's about last Monday night . . .' stammered the woman.

'It has nothing to do with that.'

'Or Thursday morning . . .' she began.

'Nor that either.'

The woman heaved a sigh of relief. It occurred to Waller that the record of the Red Dragon's proprietors might repay local investigation.

'Then if it's not Monday or Thursday, what is it?'

'It concerns a letter. To a Mr. Grey, who I believe has been staying here.'

'Oh, *'im*.' She folded her arms and sniffed.. "E's gone. Good riddance too, if you ask me.'

'When did he leave?'

'Sunday morning. Crack of dawn. *And* forgot to pay for two double gins.'

'Do you remember a letter coming for him?'

'Sure I remember it. It come on Monday morning and it 'ad a crest on the back. Not the sort of letter you'd expect a man like that to get.'

'And you still have it?'

'Oh no. I sent it on to an address 'e give me. A London address.'

Waller sighed. He had a sudden vision of his job as an eternal paper-chase, in which the scraps of paper were always blowing over the hills and far away. Even as he asked the next question he knew the answer to it.

'Did you keep this address?'

The answer came, as he had expected. 'No. As a matter of fact I didn't. When I'd forwarded the letter I threw the bit of paper into the sink.'

'And you don't remember what was written on it?'

'No. Why should I?'

'No chance of finding the paper again?'

''Eavens no! It must 'ave gone into one of the dustbins, and they was emptied yesterday.'

It was always like that, thought Waller.

He obtained a description of the man which was even more anonymous than usual. He was tall, but not too tall, in fact she supposed some people would call him short, if you compared him with her husband. She wouldn't say he was dark, but she wouldn't say he was fair. He was sort of brown. Age? She never was good at judging a man's age . . . now if it had been a woman that would have been a different matter. But Mr. Grey . . . well, he wasn't old and he wasn't young, and really, why she should be expected to know such things she did not understand. Any peculiarities? Not unless you'd call going away without paying for two double gins a peculiarity. He kept himself to himself.

The longer he questioned her the more dim and shadowy became the portrait of Mr. Grey. He was Everyman and no man—a composite of negatives.

'You're quite sure you can't remember the address on that piece of paper?'

'I've told you, 'aven't I?'

'Not even the London district number? It might be very important.'

'Wait a minute. Now I come to think of it . . .' She held up a finger in concentration. 'S.W.3. That's what it was. Chelsea, S.W.3. And the reason I remember it is because it made me think of three buns.'

'And that's all?'

'Well, I could 'ardly be expected to remember any more, could I?'

No, thought Waller as he met the glazed eyes. It was indeed remarkable that she had remembered so much.

He bade her a brief good-day. To her rather agitated query as to whether he would be calling again he replied that it was very probable. It would do no harm to the proprietors of the Red Dragon to be reminded that the law had a very long arm.

He got into the car and headed for Broome Place. An old slogan of the war days recurred to him. "Is your journey really necessary?" He wondered whether this particular journey had been necessary.

What had it told him? It had told him that somewhere in Chelsea S.W.3 lived a Mr. Everyman, to whom a woman had sent an urgent message a few hours before her death. This Mr. Everyman was neither old nor young, tall nor short, dark nor fair; and Chelsea was an extensive district. To search for such a person, on such slender evidence, would seem the height of folly.

And yet, Mr. Waller had a curious hunch that sooner or later he would meet Mr. Everyman face to face.

II

CONVERSATION WITH A CRITIC

'POSITIVE thinking,' said Mr. Green briskly. 'That is what we must remember. Never negative thinking.'

'I don't know what you mean by positive thinking.'

'It is the basis of Christian Science.'

'How will Christian Science help us to find Mr. Grey, when all we know about him is that he lives in Chelsea?'

'I have no idea. But if we say to ourselves that we *shall* find him, that is a step in the right direction. I refuse to harbour thoughts that we shall not find Mr. Grey. Such thoughts are Error, and a proof of the fallibility of Mortal Mind.'

Waller glanced at his companion suspiciously. He had a feeling that Mr. Green might be pulling his leg.

It was on the following morning, and the two men were strolling down the main azalea walk which led to the great lake. It was a sensational prospect that stretched before them; bank upon bank of azaleas flamed gold and vermillion as the sun caught their frosted leaves; behind them were groups of liquid ambers, flecked with purple and lemon yellow; and in the background were sheets of crimson from the polymorphums.

He allowed his thoughts to wander for a moment.

'Has it ever struck you,' he said to Waller, 'that there is something about this garden which makes it quite different from any other garden you have seen?'

'Yes.'

'And what is that?'

'Money,' he grunted.

Mr. Green beamed upon Waller. 'That is precisely what I hoped you would say. Money. An extraordinary

sense of richness.' He stopped walking and took Waller
by the arm. 'You see those Scots pines in the distance?
And the silver birches to the left? Does anything appear
unusual about them?'

'They're pretty good specimens.'

'Quite. But what makes them exceptional? I will tell
you. They have all had beauty treatment. Every dead twig
has been removed from the firs. And the trunks of the
silver birches have actually been scrubbed with soft soap.
Our host told me so himself.'

Waller emitted a snort of disapproval. 'Unnatural, I
call it. Do *you* like it?'

'I cannot make up my mind. It is unnatural, but I do
not know if that is a reason for condemning it. It is certainly
beautiful. One has a feeling that one is walking through
some finely stitched tapestry.'

'None of which,' retorted Waller, 'gets us much nearer
to Mr. Grey. Or to making any sense out of the whole of
this business.'

Mr. Green returned to the point.

'I think you are unduly pessimistic,' he said. 'The mere
fact that Mr. Grey exists is an advance, even if we cannot
for the moment lay our hands on him.'

'How is it an advance?'

'Surely it had occurred to you that Mr. Grey might be
the author of the original anonymous letter?'

'It had. But where does it get us?'

'Not very far, but a little way. It enables us at least to
place Mr. Grey as a person who is in need of financial
assistance. If we were to meet him walking towards us at
this moment I should expect him to present a seedy appearance. And I should not be surprised if the heels of his shoes
were in need of repair.'

Even as he spoke, they turned the corner, and were
greeted by the figure of a young man walking swiftly
towards them. But Mr. Cecil Gower-Jones did not present
at all a seedy appearance, and his shoes gave no sign of
needing repair. They were of pale grey suede, and he

pointed them delicately and precisely, for the grass was damp.

'This is where I get off,' grunted Waller. 'That young gentleman gets my goat.' He turned swiftly and strode away towards the house.

2

'Have I frightened that horrid man away?' demanded Mr. Gower-Jones, falling into step with Mr. Green.

'I fancy he had an appointment.'

'I can't bear him. He looks at one as if one had stolen the silver. Which, heaven knows, one would adore to do, if one could get one's hands on it. Really . . . with all this money staring one in the face, it's enough to make one scream. Did you ever see anything like this garden?'

'I had been remarking upon it.'

'Did you know about the pines and the silver birches? Yes. I remember hearing Andrew tell you about them. But did he tell you about the chloroform?'

Mr. Green looked up sharply. 'The chloroform?'

'That really was something. Dear Andrew read in some ridiculous American paper that if you wanted to transplant big trees . . . really enormous trees, I mean . . . you could do it quite safely if you chloroformed the roots. The idea was that it deadened the shock, just as it does with human beings.'

'Dear me!' remarked Mr. Green.

'You may well say "dear me", and I adore you for making it sound so sinister. Well, dear Andrew is always wanting to transplant enormous trees. He's got some idiotic idea that he's not going to live very long; he says he can't afford to wait to watch things grow; he wants things to happen here and now. Do you know his favourite motto? It really is quite profound. I'll tell you. "The only thing that money cannot buy is . . . Time".'

'That observation . . .' Mr. Green's voice was dry and

precise . . . 'is usually attributed to the late Thomas Edison. Personally, I regard it as superficial.'

'You really are *divine* when you act in character!' Mr. Gower-Jones made a gesture as though he would link his arm through Mr. Green's. But at that moment a convenient branch of liquidambar crossed their path, and Mr. Green stepped aside.

'And the chloroform?' he enquired.

Mr. Gower-Jones, who was not insensitive, gave a petulant sniff. 'I've already told you,' he said. 'He ordered gallons and gallons of it. How he got it I really do *not* know . . . if anybody like oneself tried to get so much as a sniff one would probably be clapped straight into gaol. Anyway, he got it. With all that money, one can get anything.'

'And then?'

'The whole of Broome was drenched with it. One used to be walking along, and then one would almost plunge into a vast pit that had been dug for some gigantic tree. And before one knew where one was, along would come a lorry with a tree on it and about a dozen enormous men— and there they were, sticking the tree in and propping it up and pouring *oceans* of chloroform on the roots and we were practically *swooning* . . . even the birds and the rabbits.'

'I fancy that you exaggerate,' commented Mr. Green in a voice as dry as a rusk.

'Of course, I exaggerate like mad. It is part of my charm. But he really did move several trees like that. Needless to say, they all promptly died. As for the animals, I really did see a squirrel reeling about once, in the most peculiar way.' He stopped abruptly, and this time he succeeded in catching Mr. Green's arm. 'You know, when one comes to think of it, this is rather a point for you!'

'In what respect?'

'Well . . . surely . . . chloroform, digging pits and all that. If one is suddenly compelled to live in the atmosphere of a whodunnit—and apparently one is, at the moment—

E

one might at least get some fun out of it. Or doesn't the suggestion appeal to you?'

Mr. Green gently detached himself. 'Not conspicuously,' he observed.

'Oh dear! And I was only trying to help.'

'It is very kind of you. But I think I must be making my way back to the house.'

'So must I. I've got a rehearsal.'

They turned together. For a few moments they walked in silence. Then, as though the thought had suddenly occurred to him—'You know, Mr. Green, what you should do if you really want to find out what is going on in this house?'

'What is that?'

'You should take much more interest in this play we're doing. After all, that's what we're all here for. Personally I think the whole thing ought to have been put off in view of what's happened. But that ghastly Lady Coniston would have screamed the place down if anybody had suggested such a thing; so would Sally Kane; they're *besotted* about the idea of appearing in public.'

'How do you imagine that a study of the play might assist me?'

'People let their hair down at rehearsals in the most fantastic way. Last night there was a hideous row in which they stopped the show altogether and began accusing each other of the most appalling things.'

'In connection with this case?'

'Of course.'

Mr. Green appeared to ponder this information, but he made no comment.

'I know I'm right,' persisted Mr. Gower-Jones. ' "The play's the thing, wherein I'll catch the conscience of the king". Do please think about it. At least it might start things moving. As it is, you seem to have come to a full stop. Don't you?'

Mr. Green seemed to detect a tremor of anxiety in the young man's voice, but he still made no reply.

'Don't you?' he repeated. And this time there was no doubt about the tremor.

Mr. Green turned and smiled . . . a deceptively gentle smile. 'When I am investigating a problem,' he said, 'I do not recognize full-stops. However, I am occasionally compelled to acknowledge the existence of a semi-colon.'

The little man seemed pleased with his mild epigram. And that was all, for the moment, that he had to say.

12

FIRST NIGHT

WHETHER Mr. Green had indeed come to a full-stop, or whether he was merely confronted, as he had suggested, with a semi-colon, it was certainly true that for the rest of the week there were, to all outward appearances, no sensational developments in the case of the late Margot Larue.

There was a feeling of pause, of stalemate. Even the inquest on the dead woman seemed an anti-climax. Apart from a few ponderous remarks from the coroner on the snares of life in high society, the verdict had been as expected; Miss Larue had taken her life while the balance of her mind had been disturbed, and that was that. And since the Press had no reason to connect her with Sir Luke Coniston—since, indeed, they knew nothing at all about her that seemed to suggest a "story"—there had been very little comment in the newspapers.

Pause, stalemate; and yet, in the background a feeling of tension. Everybody felt it—in particular, Charlotte, Mr. Green's pretty neice.

'Darling,' she said to Mr. Green, 'what is happening?'

They were breakfasting in Mr. Green's room. As usual, this normally unpretentious meal had its aura of richness. There were late raspberries, there was Devonshire cream, and there was a particularly exotic bottle of water that was neither Vichy, nor Vittel nor Evian nor any such plebeian beverage. It hailed from Yugoslavia and—as Palmer had assured them with reverence—had been imported at enormous expense.

'What is happening?' echoed Mr. Green. He sniffed the

Yugoslavian elixir, suppressed a shudder, and impaled a raspberry on a very heavy fork of Georgian silver. It fell off. He did not attempt to retrieve it.

'Yes. Where *are* we?'

In the most level of tones Mr. Green replied: 'We are at Broome Place, in the county of Sussex, at an elevation of slightly over six hundred feet.'

'I won't be put off. You know quite well what I mean. Where *are* we . . . in this case? And how long are we going to stay?'

He did not answer her question. Instead he asked: 'Are you unhappy here?'

'Not in the least. In fact, I'm rather loving it . . . the incredible luxury of it. I mean, it *is* rather exciting, in this day and age, to be presented with caviar in buckets, every night of the week. I'm sure I've put on pounds. Apart from that, I'm improving my mind. I've learned more about pictures in the last week than if I'd spent months in museums. Nancy Lloyd loves taking me round and talking about them.'

'You like her?'

'I adore her. Don't you?'

'She seems charming and intelligent.'

'I wish I could say the same about the others. They really are rather an impossible collection. Lady Coniston gives me the creeps with that lifted face of hers, and so does Sir Luke. Cecil's quite amusing, but his hands are damp and he's always making dreadful little dabs at one. Sally Kane is vapid and vain and so rude that sometimes I could slap her.'

'And Lord Richard?' prompted Mr. Green.

A faint flush came to her cheeks. 'I like him.'

'Very much?'

'Don't be silly, darling.' But the flush deepened. 'I suppose I'm sorry for him really. It must be ghastly to be compelled to marry a girl like that.'

'Is he compelled to do so, I wonder?' Mr. Green asked the question as if he really wanted to know.

'You surely don't suggest that he would marry her if it weren't a question of money?'

Mr. Green sighed deeply. 'It is a pity,' he said. 'A great pity. For I agree with you that he is a very agreeable young man.'

He rose to his feet abruptly. He seemed to have recollected something. 'I must pack,' he said.

Charlotte stared at him in astonishment. 'Pack? Why?'

'Only a hand-bag.'

'But darling, where are you going? And what about the play tomorrow?'

'I shall be back in good time for it. I am not going far.'

She knew better than to ask him his destination. 'It . . . it isn't anything dangerous?'

'Not in the least,' he assured her. 'On the contrary, I anticipate that it will be very agreeable, with some most interesting conversation.'

True to his word, Mr. Green returned on the following morning, and whatever his mission may have been, it had obviously impaired neither his health nor his spirits. He was in excellent form at luncheon, and Charlotte was happy to observe that he seemed to have acquired a surprising interest in the play, and to be eager to learn all he could about the impending performance. There could be surely nothing dangerous about that?

Indeed, had it not been for a sudden and exceptionally violent onslaught of blinking—always a bad sign—she might have felt justified in assuming that he had detached himself from the recent drama, and was gently preparing to retire from it.

However, the blinking was occasioned by such a trivial incident that perhaps she was wrong in attaching any importance to it. They were having coffee, and Mr. Green had turned to Lady Coniston to make some comment on the magnificent tryptych by Peter Breughel that hung over the chimney-piece. She did not hear Lady Coniston's reply, which seemed to have been brief and casual, but its effect on her uncle was galvanic—a positive fusillade of blinks.

After luncheon she had made an excuse to examine the picture, to see if she could detect any sinister signs in it, such as suicide, or murder, or even a resemblance to one of the guests. She found nothing. It was a bravura performance, by a great master, that had captured on canvas a moment of lusty life. Why should it have made her uncle blink? And yet, he did not blink without good reason.

She sighed. Mr. Green, she feared, was not detaching himself, after all, and had no intention of retiring from the scene. Well, at least there was no prospect of any immediate excitement. They were going to the play that night, and she would have him under her eye. He would not be able to get up to any mischief.

Or would he?

2

The cast of *Back Your Fancy* was so glittering—from a social if not a dramatic point of view—that its success was a foregone conclusion. With an earl as stage manager, a marchioness, a countess and two viscounts in the chorus, half a dozen honorables in the sketches, the widow of a baronet at the piano, and several wives of knights—including Lady Coniston—playing minor roles, it was not surprising that every seat in the old eighteenth-century theatre at West Greenstead was occupied nearly half an hour before the curtain went up, with the exception of a dozen places in the front row reserved for very important persons.

Behind the scenes reigned the chaos which is customary on these occasions. Just before the final dress rehearsal the stage manager—(affectionately known to his intimates as "Kippers Castlemere")—had realized that things were getting beyond his control. He had therefore sent an S.O.S. to his friend Martin Strange, the well-known producer, who had a weakness for the nobility. Mr. Strange's arrival had merely confounded the confusion, and had plunged the performers into alternate fits of rage and gloom, from which they could only be roused by the premature broaching of one of the cases of champagne which "Kippers" had thoughtfully provided for consumption after the performance. Indeed, if it had not been for the presence of a large number of photographers, and the hope of achieving immortality in the glossy magazines, several members of the chorus might well have walked off in a huff and spent the rest of the evening at the Queen's Head.

Mr. Green arrived with Charlotte at about ten minutes before the curtain was due to rise. On the drive down there had been an argument as to the advisability of his coming at all.

'I think it is very foolish of you,' she said, 'with that cold.'

Mr. Green's cold had developed, with remarkable speed, during the course of the afternoon.

'It is nothing,' he replied, stifling a sneeze. 'Besides, one must not always think of oneself. You will have an opportunity to show off that very pretty frock.'

She threw him a suspicious glance. 'I don't believe you've even noticed it.'

'I am not so unobservant as you suppose.'

'It all sounds very fishy to me, as though you were up to something. Are you?'

'Really, my dear, if I cannot escort my neice to a harmless entertainment . . .' He finished the sentence with a shrug.

'Somebody else could have escorted me.'

'Who? The Lloyds—not unnaturally—have stayed at home. Lady Coniston and Mr. Gower-Jones are in the revue, and Sir Luke has gone on ahead with them. That leaves only Lord Richard. And he is dancing attendance on Miss Kane, who—I understand—is playing the role of a conjuror's assistant.'

Charlotte sniffed. 'She's bought a new Dior dress just to stand there and hand him a lot of rabbits.'

Mr. Green sat up sharply. 'There are not going to be rabbits?'

'No, dear.' She smiled and patted his hand. 'I was only

joking. Nothing so ambitious. Only some very old card
tricks and something rather silly with a lot of hoops.'

He breathed a sigh of relief. 'For a moment you disturbed
me. I have a great fondness for rabbits. I should not like
to think of them being cramped in some stuffy box behind
the stage. They would certainly be terrified.'

He relapsed into a silence which continued until their
arrival. He looked very absent-minded as they threaded
their way through the crowded hall, and he failed to
respond to the numerous greetings that were thrown to
him. He hardly even blinked when the photographers
exploded their flash-bulbs in his face.

It was only just before the curtain went up that he spoke
again.

He turned to Charlotte and whispered in her ear. 'You
are *quite* sure, my dear, that there will be no rabbits?'

'Quite, darling.' She put her hand in his. 'Only two-
legged ones. And they will all be in the chorus.'

3

It was fortunate that Mr. Green's seat was at the extreme
end of the front row of the stalls, only one pace from the
exit, which was concealed by a heavy plush curtain. For the
revue had scarcely begun when his cold took a sharp turn
for the worse. He was seized by such a violent fit of sneezing
that he was obliged to rise from his seat and go out. As he
did so, he whispered his excuses to Charlotte, and told her
that on no account was she to follow him.

The comparatively fresh air of the vestibule appeared
to restore him; it did more than that, it stimulated him to a
quite remarkable activity. Indeed, had it not been for the
presence of so many stray visitors, sightseers, photographers,
pressmen and the like, drifting in and around the entrance,
his movements might have aroused some curiosity. He
seemed to have acquired a passionate interest in the geography of the theatre; he hurried upstairs and downstairs,

round corners and along corridors, with such an expression
of anxiety that on no less than three occasions he was
accosted by sympathetic commissionaires who inquired if
he was "looking for the gents".

'No,' replied Mr. Green with the greatest courtesy. 'He
was not "looking for the gents", though it was most kind
of them to suggest it.'

He did not say what he was looking for. Nor was there
any indication whether he had found it, for he suddenly
changed his tactics and darted upstairs again with surprising
alacrity, crossed the vestibule, went outside, descended the
steps into the little courtyard, disappeared, and reappeared
again in the space of ten seconds.

It may have been by chance, or it may have been by
design, that as he stepped across the cobbled pavement, a
figure in a dark blue suit emerged from the shadows and
walked towards him. It was Bates junior, who had been
deputed by the local constabulary for special plain-clothes
duty on this social occasion. Judging from the smile on his
face, the young man seemed very pleased to encounter Mr.
Green. Mr. Green seemed equally pleased to encounter
the young man. They had a protracted conversation,
which ended in a handshake. Whereupon Mr. Green walked
briskly back to the theatre, swinging his arms and humming
the immortal theme of the chorale of the Ninth.

At the top of the steps he paused once more, and
looked around him.

A sympathetic commissionaire approached him.

'Looking for the gents, sir?'

Mr. Green came back to life. He remembered that he
had a busy hour in front of him. Perhaps it might be as
well . . .

4

Very few people noticed Mr. Green's return to the
theatre, so softly did he glide through the plush curtain,
so gently did he sink into his seat. And even if he had begun

to sneeze again, the sound would have been lost in the uproar of the jazz band which now filled the stage. Knowing her uncle's detestation of jazz, Charlotte turned to him, expecting to find his features twisted into an expression of pain. To her surprise he was beaming all over his face; he was even tapping his small feet in time to the music. Mr. Green was a most unpredictable person.

The band finished to a roar of applause.

She glanced at the programme. 'Lady Coniston's piece is coming on now.'

'That,' retorted Mr. Green cryptically, 'should be illuminating.'

'I hope she remembers it, this time. I saw Sir Luke standing at the back and he looked terribly worried.'

'Perhaps he has other things to worry about.'

Charlotte had no time to ask what he meant, for at this moment the curtains parted, revealing Lady Coniston in the disguise of a Cockney charwoman, seated at a kitchen table sipping a cup of tea.

The monologue—entitled simply "Mary Anne"—was one of those trifles which, in the hands of Miss Beatrice Lillie, are transformed into soufflées of delight. In the hands of Lady Coniston it was not so easily digestible. However, a British audience always prefer to see an amateur —particularly a titled amateur—make a fool of herself by accident than a professional make a fool of herself by design.

So Lady Coniston's painful impersonation of a Cockney charwoman was received with rapt attention. Needless to say, a large proportion of those who watched her were thinking how much better they could do it themselves; the assumption of a Cockney accent, in certain sections of society, is often a convenient substitute for wit. None the less, the sketch was "getting over".

And now, at this point, Mr. Green sneezed—the sneeze to end all sneezes, of such trumpet-like resonance that it drew an indignant chorus of "ssh!" from the row behind. But Mr. Green did not seem to hear the protests. He was

staring at the stage. It was lucky that Charlotte had buried
her face in her programme, otherwise she might have noted
that once again he was blinking with exceptional rapidity.
Still he stared at the stage. And then, with a final blink and
a little nod as though he had made up his mind about some
point which had been troubling him, he turned to Charlotte
and whispered something in her ear. A moment later they
both glided out, to the considerable relief of the people in
the adjoining rows.

13

839766041

AT the top of the staircase Charlotte began to protest.

'Darling, I told you it was madness to come—that sneeze . . .'

He put his fingers gently on her lips and drew her to one side.

'I want your help.'

'Are you . . . are you up to something?'

'I'm afraid so.'

'Oh dear!' She stared at him unhappily. She saw a little man with a round, pink face and a turn-up nose. A little man with a gentle smile and pale blue eyes—eyes that held a curious blend of innocence and disillusion. A little man whom she greatly loved, and whom she longed to take home and put to bed like a baby.

There was the sudden flash of a photographer's bulb. For a second it lit up Mr. Green's face from another angle, sharpening the features, distorting them ever so slightly, etching them into the impersonal image that she knew so well—the image that had so often flashed across the headlines in the old days, when murder was in the air. And she remembered that Mr. Green was not only a dear old gentleman who should be put to bed; he was also a world-famous detective.

'Very well,' she sighed. 'What do I do?'

'It is very simple. I want you to go and wait for me at the stage door.'

'Just wait?' There was a hint of disappointment in her voice.

'I will join you in a few minutes.'

'And then?'

'You will see.' He took her by the arm and led her through the vestibule to the top of the steps. 'The stage door is just round the corner, on the right.'

She hestitated for a moment. 'You are not running any risks?'

He smiled. 'On the contrary, this is an entirely social occasion.'

She ran down the steps. As she turned the corner, Mr. Green waved her good-bye.

2

Whether Mr. Green had been telling the truth about the social nature of the occasion, he appeared to be in the best of spirits when he rejoined Charlotte a few minutes later. His arrival at the stage-door coincided with the fall of the curtain, and the corridors were bustling with activity.

'Let us go straight up,' he said. He turned to the stage door-keeper. 'I believe that Lady Coniston and Miss Kane are sharing a dressing-room?'

'Yes, sir. Number six. But I'm afraid that visitors . . .'

'I am Sir Luke Coniston', interrupted Mr. Green with some sharpness. 'Come, Charlotte.'

Before the man had time to protest, he had hurried her upstairs and round the corner.

'Uncle, how could you? Supposing Sir Luke were to come?'

'Sir Luke is otherwise engaged,' he retorted calmly. He peered at the number on the door behind him. 'Let me see. This is Number one. Number six is at the other end.' As he spoke there was the sound of a commotion at the end of the corridor. Lady Coniston and Miss Kane appeared, followed by Lord Richard. They were all talking at once and they appeared to be in sharp disagreement about some matter. They passed straight into Number six, slamming the door after them.

'Charlotte, my dear,'—Mr. Green's voice was suddenly

urgent—'I am very anxious to hear what our friends are saying. Would you kindly go straight into that room, and then pretend that you have made a mistake, and come out again, leaving the door ajar?'

'But supposing they shut it again?'

'That is a chance we shall have to take.'

'And supposing they see you?'

'If it is like any other dressing-room I have ever visited, there will be a screen by the door.'

She bit her lip. She realized that she was not being very co-operative. She nodded and hurried down the passage.

A moment later she had done as he asked. 'They haven't noticed,' she whispered. 'And there *is* a screen. They're having the most awful row.'

Mr. Green nodded. 'Stay here,' he said, 'and try to keep anybody else from coming in.' He squeezed himself a little way inside.

It was one of the most curious pieces of eavesdropping that Mr. Green had ever done. There was a comedy element about it. Outside, the corridor was a bustle of activity, with doors opening and shutting, members of the cast running backwards and forwards, and a great deal of chatter and laughter. From time to time somebody would come up to the door of Number six, and Mr Green could hear Charlotte gently sending them away.

But there was nothing comic about the dialogue that echoed from behind the screen.

'It's absolutely and totally monstrous!' Miss Kane's voice was shrill. 'How *dare* you come up to me with a message like that, just before my act!'

'She was trembling all over.' It was Lord Richard speaking.

'I can't help that,' retorted Lady Coniston. 'This message says it's a matter of life or death.'

'Let me read it again.'

There was a moment's silence. 'Did you recognize the man's voice on the telephone?'

'No.'

'What sort of voice was it? I mean, was he what one calls a gentleman?'

'Heavens, how do I know if he was a gentleman or not when it's a matter of life or death?'

'Whose life? And whose death?' demanded Lord Richard.

'That's for her to say.'

'I know nothing whatever about it,' snapped Miss Kane.

'Then why does the message say you do?'

'I don't know and I don't care.'

'Then I suppose I'd better take it to the police.'

'Sybil!' Miss Kane's voice rose to a scream of protest. 'You wouldn't be so *mean*!'

Lord Richard intervened. 'If you take it to the police, you're involved just as much as she is.'

'I'm not in the least involved.'

'Then why did this mysterious man telephone *you*? If Sally's got anything to confess, why should she confess it to you? The obvious implication is that you've got some sort of inside knowledge yourself.'

'You're quite right, Richard. I never knew you could make such sense. And as for you, Sybil, if you go to the police with that thing I shall never speak to you again.'

'That's a risk I shall have to run.'

'And you won't gain anything by being catty, Sybil dear.' A thought seemed to strike her. 'Wait a minute. How do we know the message applies to Margot at all? It only says "tragic event".'

'What else could it apply to?'

It was Lord Richard who had spoken. 'Be your age, Richard,' she retorted.

'But what *else* could it apply to?' he repeated.

'Heavens! Is Margot's death the only tragic event you can think of?'

He shrugged his shoulders. 'Very well. If you think it's none of my business . . .'

'That's just what I do think.' There was a moment's silence. Suddenly she turned on him. 'Or is it?'

'What do you mean?'

'*Is* it your business, Richard?'

'Don't be funny.'

'I'm wondering if it's you who've been trying to be funny. Is this one of your wretched practical jokes?'

'You know perfectly well I've given those up.'

'I know you promised to, after nearly scaring me to death. But have you started again?'

'I swear I haven't.'

'It's just like the sort of thing you used to do.'

'Sally, I swear.'

'Oh, very well . . . but if I find you've been up to any funny business, I'll . . .'

What Miss Kane might or might not have done must remain a secret. For at that moment Mr. Green sneezed.

3

It was a vintage sneeze, clear and resonant, and it produced an immediate silence.

'I beg your pardon,' murmured Mr. Green as he stepped into the room.

They all stared at him. Miss Kane took a step forward. 'Have you been listening at the door?'

Mr. Green raised his eyebrows. 'Surely you heard my knock?'

'Did you knock?'

His eyebrows went higher. 'It is the usual custom, before entering a lady's dressing-room.' He turned to Lady Coniston. 'I am afraid I have kept you waiting. But I only received your message a moment ago.'

'What message?'

'That you wished to see me. I gather that it is urgent.'

'I never sent any message.'

Mr. Green's eyebrows were as high as they would go. 'Indeed?' He looked at Miss Kane. His expression was that of a man who is not greatly amused, but his voice was soft and urbane. 'Am I to understand that this is some sort of practical joke?'

Miss Kane, who appeared to be on the verge of hysterics, turned to Lord Richard. 'Richard, do you swear you haven't been up to something?'

'For the hundredth time I tell you . . .'

'Sally!' Lady Coniston spoke very sharply. 'Have you forgotten that this is a matter of . . .'

'Life and death' she repeated. 'Go on—life and death, life and death. You drive me mad. Over and over again.'

Lord Richard put his hand over her shoulder. 'Don't you think we should tell him?'

'I'm past thinking.'

Lady Coniston sniffed loudly. '*I* have nothing to hide.'

The young man looked at Mr. Green. 'We've had rather a shock, sir,' he said. 'Maybe you could help us.'

'I should be glad to help . . . you.' There was only the fraction of a second between Mr. Green's pronunciation of the verb and its object.

'Just after Lady Coniston's sketch an attendant came round and told her that she was wanted on the telephone.'

'Yes?'

'She went to the telephone . . .' He turned to Lady Coniston. 'Sybil . . . tell him.'

Lady Coniston shrugged her shoulders. 'Very well. I went to the telephone—it's in a box on the staircase—and a man with the most horrible voice gave me this message.'

Miss Kane intervened. 'You never said he had a horrible voice before.'

'Shut up, Sally,' grunted Lord Richard.

'And the meassage?' inquired Mr. Green. 'May I see it?'

'Give it to him, Sybil.'

She handed him a crumpled piece of paper. Mr. Green adjusted his glasses and held it before him. He read it aloud.

This is a matter of life and death. Miss Kane has something to confess to you concerning the recent tragic event. You must

insist that she tells you all before she leaves the theatre tonight.
Ask her the meaning of the numbers 839766041.

Mr. Green turned to Miss Kane. '839766041?'

'There's no need to look at me like that,' she protested.
'*I* don't know what those numbers mean.'

'Do *you*?' demanded Lady Coniston.

Mr. Green took the paper and gave it a delicate sniff.
'Yes,' he said, 'I fancy that I do.'

'Then for heaven's sake tell us.'

'One moment, if you please.' Mr. Green gave the paper
another sniff. He looked puzzled for a moment, then his
eyes wandered to the dressing table and he smiled. He had
noticed a yellow bottle standing by the mirror. 'Of course,'
he murmured. 'Arpège, by Lanvin.'

'It's hers—not mine,' said Lady Coniston sharply.

'So what?' Miss Kane folded her arms. 'What's my
Arpège got to do with it?'

'Nothing at all. You must forgive me. My mind was
wandering. I was only trying to recollect where I had last
smelt it.'

'Are you going to tell us what those numbers mean?'

'At the risk of seeming discourteous, I am not.'

'Well, I really must say . . . I mean . . .' Miss Kane
finished the sentence with a dramatic shrug.

Lord Richard stepped forward. 'Look here, sir, this is
all a bit unnerving for the ladies. Couldn't you give them a
bit of a clue?'

Mr. Green did not appear to hear him. He was reading
the paper once again. *Miss Kane has something to confess to you.*
He was again staring at the dressing table. 'And we are to
take it, of course, that there is no truth in this allegation?'

'Not a grain.'

Mr. Green nodded. 'Not even the smallest grain,' he
repeated, as though in confirmation of her statement. 'And
the same applies, of course, to everybody in this room?'

'Of course it does.' It was Lord Richard speaking again.
His voice had a harsh note, and Mr. Green noticed that he

had dropped his customary "sir". 'Can't you tell us what
we ought to do, instead of dropping a lot of mysterious
hints?'

Mr. Green looked up slowly. His eyes met Lord
Richard's.

'What would you suggest yourself?'

An angry rustle came from Lady Coniston. 'I say we
ought to go to the police.'

'And you?' Mr. Green was still looking at Lord Richard.

The young man suddenly turned away. He said nothing.

Mr. Green sighed. He looked at Lady Coniston. 'I don't
think that this is a matter for the police.'

'Thank God for *that*!' exclaimed Miss Kane.

Lady Coniston looked almost disappointed. 'Well, I
suppose you know best. All the same . . .'

Miss Kane tapped her foot impatiently. 'Sybil, why
can't you stop nattering about the police? Why can't you
leave it to Mr. Green? *He* knows what it's all about. Don't
you, Mr. Green?'

'I would hardly go so far as that.'

'Anyway, you'll find out, sooner or later. You always
do. If Sybil rushes off to the police with this wretched
message, I shall never have a minute's peace. Nor will she.'
She turned to Lady Coniston. 'Nor will Luke if it comes
to that. You ought to be thinking of Luke, Sybil. A nice
thing it would be, if it got into the papers. Think of the
headlines. "Famous financier's wife involved in murder
message." Those wretched oil shares would go down to
the bottom of the sea and Luke would never speak to you
again.'

She had hit the right note. 'Very well,' she said. 'If
that's what you think. And if it's what Mr. Green thinks,
too. As long as we aren't all had up for being accessories
to something or other.'

Mr. Green gave her a reassuring smile. 'I don't think
you need have any fear of that.' He glanced at the piece of
paper in his hand. 'Would you allow me to keep this?
Thank you.' He folded it and placed it in his waistcoat

pocket. 'And shall we perhaps say nothing about this to anybody else?'

He looked round the room, his eyes pausing for a brief moment on Lord Richard.

'Not even to my husband?' demanded Lady Coniston.

'Perhaps least of all to your husband.'

'Very well. I'm sure *I* don't want to make any difficulties.'

'Then I will not detain you any longer. I think I heard the sound of the bell for the second act. If it is as entertaining as the first, I would not wish to miss any of it.' He made a courteous bow to the two ladies and walked to the door. Then he paused, with his fingers on the handle. 'Oh—by the way, Lady Coniston, I owe you an apology.'

'An apology. For what?'

'I was the person in the front row who interrupted your performance with that very vulgar sneeze.'

'Oh, was that you? I thought . . .' Lady Coniston suddenly dropped her handkerchief. She bent down to pick it up before Mr. Green could retrieve it.

'Yes?' enquired Mr. Green.

Lady Coniston fluttered her handkerchief to remove a trace of dust.

'It was not of the least importance,' she said shortly.

'I am delighted to hear it. I assure you that it will not happen again.'

With a final bow Mr. Green went out, closing the door behind him.

14

A MYSTERIOUS YOUNG MAN

ALTHOUGH Mr. Green would have preferred to drive straight back to Broome Place after the performance, he pretended, for Charlotte's sake, that he would be greatly refreshed by a glass of champagne at Lord Castlemere's party. As Mr. Green required at least an hour to drink a glass of champagne—consuming it in small, staccato sips as though he were dealing with a powerful explosive—it was not till after midnight that he found himself standing on the steps of the theatre, waiting for Charlotte to bring the car.

And here a strange thing happened. As his eyes wandered over the animated groups of people who were still chattering in the courtyard, he observed the figure of a young man, in a shabby black mackintosh. There would have been nothing to make him stare with such sudden interest at this young man were it not for a certain peculiarity in his behaviour . . . he was walking backwards. There was no doubt about it. There would be three quick steps backwards, then a pause, and then another three quick steps, with an occasional furtive glance over his shoulder in the direction of Lord Richard, who was standing at the other end of the steps, holding the hand of Miss Sally Kane.

It needed no exceptional powers of deduction to suggest to Mr. Green that young men in shabby black mackintoshes do not walk backwards towards their social superiors without a very good reason, and as he studied this curious behaviour Mr. Green fancied that he detected the reason in the presense of one of the local police, who was standing in the shadow of the wall. In a moment he was sure that his reasoning was correct, for the policeman suddenly turned and walked away. Whereupon the young man, with evident relief, turned round, and finished his approach to Lord Richard in the normal manner.

As he stood there, at the bottom of the steps, waiting for Lord Richard to notice him, Mr. Green studied him attentively. In spite of the shabby mackintosh, the muddy black shoes and the general air of seediness, he appeared to be a gentleman, or perhaps, should one say, a near gentleman. He was about thirty, with a high forehead and receding fair hair. He had blue eyes, set close together, and a loose, rather feminine mouth. He was very thin, and from time to time he coughed. He might have been a motor-salesman down on his luck, or one of those feckless types who ring the door-bells of prosperous suburban houses in the hope of inducing some kindly housewife to buy a washing machine.

At last Lord Richard noticed him. He regarded him with some surprise, but apparently without recognition. The young man indicated that he would like to speak in private. Lord Richard shrugged his shoulders, said a word to Miss Kane, and accompanied him to the bottom of the steps.

At this point Miss Kane walked over to Mr. Green.

'Really!' she exclaimed huffily. 'I think it's a little much. Did you see that ghastly creature?'

'Yes. Is he a friend of Lord Richard's?'

'I can't believe that Richard has sunk quite so low as that. Still, one never knows. He has the most extraordinary circle of acquaintances, though they're usually women.' She threw a hostile glance in the direction of the two men. 'Why, look! Would you believe it? The creature has actually grabbed hold of Richard's arm!'

She turned back to Mr. Green, but to her annoyance she found that he was no longer by her side. He really was the most irritating little man, here one moment and gone the next. People had no right to vanish into thin air like that. She scanned the crowd, but saw no sign of him.

Had Miss Kane turned round she would have found that Mr. Green had not gone very far. He had merely stepped back a few paces into the shadow of the wall, and was in earnest conversation with a tall young man in a dark blue suit. It was lucky that young Bates was so conscientious; his spell of duty finished at midnight and he might well have signed off. As it was, his appearance at this moment was providential. He listened intently to what Mr. Green was saying, nodded, and saluted. Then he hurried down the steps, keeping to the shadow of the wall, and disappeared round the corner. A moment later he was back again, this time with a bicycle. He bent low over the front tyre, as though he had a puncture; but a careful observer would have noticed that his eyes never left the figure of the shabby young man on the steps.

And now Mr. Green was once more by Miss Kane's side.

She turned with a start. 'Oh, there you are! Wherever have you been?'

Mr. Green merely raised his eyebrows, as though he thought the question uncalled for. She did not wait for an answer. 'That monstrous young man's still grabbing hold of Richard. It's past a joke.'

Mr. Green was inclined to agree. There was a most unpleasant expression on the young man's face, and he had indeed seized Lord Richard's arm with a threatening gesture. This was surprising enough; even more remarkable was Lord Richard's reaction. Instead of displaying any sign of anger, he seemed positively intimidated. He shrank back, without attempting to remove the man's hand from his arm.

The young man was evidently insisting on an answer to some question he had put. At last he got it. He appeared satisfied. He gave Lord Richard a curt nod and said one word. Mr. Green was not a lip-reader, but he fancied that the word was "tomorrow".

For a moment Lord Richard stood there staring. So did Mr. Green. He noticed with a sigh of relief that as the young man turned the corner Bates jumped on his bicycle and pedalled slowly after him.

Miss Kane called out. 'Richard, what *is* going on?'

He walked slowly over to them. He forced a smile. 'Sorry, old girl.'

'You look as if you'd seen a ghost. Who was that frightful person?'

'Just a chap.'

'Was he trying to borrow money.'

'Of course not.'

She looked at him suspiciously. 'He wasn't trying to blackmail you?'

'What should he want to blackmail me about?'

'You might have been running about with one of his girl friends.'

Lord Richard continued to smile, though Mr. Green noticed that his fists were clenched. 'So I might.'

She stamped her foot. 'Richard, who *was* he?'

He hesitated. And then . . . 'Just a chap in the car business.'

'I might have known it. And I suppose he's trying to sell you another car?'

'That's roughly the idea.'

'Well, you're mad if you have anything to do with him.' She turned to Mr. Green. 'Would *you* buy a car from a man like that?'

Mr. Green, whose thoughts appeared to have been wandering, blinked at her vaguely. 'I fear that I have not a mechanical mind.'

'You don't have to have a mechanical mind to see when a man's a complete crook. If Richard has anything to do with him, I shall . . .'

But Mr. Green was not to learn what action Miss Kane proposed, for at that moment he saw Charlotte waving to him through the window of his little car. With a courtly bow he excused himself and hurried down the steps.

'Sleepy, darling?' said Charlotte, as she tucked the rug round his knees.

'Very sleepy, my dear.'

Even as he spoke, he closed his eyes and began to nod.

But perhaps Mr. Green was not so sleepy as he thought
—or as he pretended. A light was still shining dimly through
his curtains long after he had retired to his room. And it
was not extinguished till after the bell had rung on the
house-telephone by his bedside. It was the lodge-keeper
speaking, and he seemed puzzled by the message.

It came from a Mr. Bates, and was to the effect that the
package had been followed to its destination and would be
kept under strict observation until further instructions.

The lodge-keeper hoped that Mr. Green would find
this message comprehensible. Yes, Mr. Green assured him,
it was quite comprehensible. Judging from the smile on
his face, as he put down the receiver, it was also eminently
satifactory.

15

MR. JONES MAKES A CALL

ALTHOUGH Mr. Green had retired so late, he woke early. Or rather, he was awoken by that convenient but implacable apparatus, the house telephone.

He struggled to a sitting position and stared at the instrument, with its elegant ivory panel on which were inscribed the various quarters of the great house. For a moment he allowed the bell to ring, while his sleepy mind played with all the possibilities inherent in this invention.

Beech Room	07	Lavender Room	99
Billiards Room	01	Library	03
Breakfast Room	08	Lodgekeeper, East Gate	76
Butler's Pantry	91	Lodgekeeper, West Gate	75
Butler's Sitting Room	92	Mr. Lloyd's Bedroom	82
Chintz Room	97	Chauffeurs' Room	89
Cook's Sitting Room	93	Secretary's Office	88
Courtyard Suite	85	Secretary's Room	87
Dining Room	09	Valet's Room	70
Drawing Room	05	Mrs. Lloyd's Bedroom	82
Empire Suite	96	Chauffeur's Room	72
Entrance Hall	90	Maid's Room	71
Flower Room	04	Maid's' Sitting Room	94
Forester's Cottage	79	Music Room	02
Garages	77	Queen Anne Suite	86
Garrick Room	84	Study	06
Green Boudoir	81	Swimming Pool	73
Head Gardener's Cottage	78	Tennis Court Pavilion	74
Home Farm	60	White Room	98
Kitchen	95	Yellow Boudoir	83

How often, he wondered, had guests telephoned from their bedrooms to the swimming pool? It seemed to his simple mind a refinement of luxury—even though the swimming pool was a quarter of a mile from the house. It was built in the lee of the hill, with a circle of giant beeches towering in the background. He had a fancy to lift the receiver and call the pool at this moment. Then he gave a slight shiver; there was something uncanny in the thought of the bell echoing in the deserted pavilion, ringing out over the cold dark water on which the leaves had started to fall, mocking the joys of the summer that had gone.

He obeyed the summons of the bell. 'Yes . . . who is there?'

It was Superintendent Waller. 'Well,' he barked. 'your instructions have been carried out.'

'My dear Waller, that is hardly fair. I only made a little suggestion.'

'Anyway, it's been followed up. Two of my best men went down to West Greenstead at crack of dawn. They'll be watching the house till further orders. And now, perhaps, you'll tell me who *is* this mysterious gentleman you're suddenly so anxious about?'

'It is a little difficult over the telephone . . .' began Mr. Green.

'Come off it!' interrupted Waller. 'If you expect me to mobilize the entire resources of the Yard on a vague hint, even if it comes from the great Mr. Green, you're very much mistaken.'

Mr. Green sighed, and drew his pyjama jacket more closely round his shoulders. He saw Waller's point. 'Very well.' In a few crisp and concise phrases he described the advent of the mysterious young man of the night before, and Lord Richard's strange reaction to him. He omitted no relevant detail.

Waller gave a low whistle. 'It sounds as if you've got something there. And you think this chap may be our Mr. Grey?'

'It had occurred to me,' said Mr. Green modestly. 'Unless you have any better suggestion?'

'He'd certainly fill a long-felt want. We could almost call him the missing link.'

'One of the many missing links,' corrected Mr. Green. 'We shall be able to judge more clearly when we see him again. I have a fancy that it will be very soon. In the meantime, I imagine, we can leave him safely under the supervision of your men?'

'If he manages to give those two boys the slip he's a genius. He'd be more—he'd be the original Invisible Man.' There was a moment's pause, then Waller chuckled. 'For once in a way, Horatio, I must give it to you.'

Mr. Green stiffened. He was all too aware that his Christian name was incongruous. 'I beg your pardon?'

'Come off it, Horatio. I'm paying you a compliment. I was going to tell you that for once in a way you were being really co-operative.'

'You are very kind,' said Mr. Green icily. He replaced the receiver. Really, at times Mr. Waller forgot himself.

He stayed there for a moment, thinking. Then he got out of bed and went over to the tallboy. From the top drawer he took out his camera, an old-fashioned model in a worn leather case. He handled it gingerly, as he handled all mechanical objects; he could never rid himself of a childish complex that they were secretly hostile to humanity and might take it into their heads to explode. There was something uncanny about a camera too, particularly when one had put in a new film and was turning it round to the number "1". He could never see that little black hand creeping in under the red filter, without experiencing a slight tremor.

2

It was shortly before eleven when Mr. Green's telephone rang again. The call came from the lodge; the voice was a stranger's.

'Mr. Green? This is Sergeant Stanley, sir. The party in question left his lodgings an hour ago, and boarded the ten o'clock bus. We followed it. He got off at the top of the hill and made straight for Broome. He's just walked through the gates and should be half way down the drive by now. Any instructions, sir?'

'I think that Mr. Waller wishes you to wait at the entrance,' suggested Mr. Green. 'It is probable that the . . .

er . . . the party will be returning by car, and that I may be accompanying him. When we part company in the village, Mr. Waller feels that it is very important for the . . . er . . . the party to be followed. There are two of you, I gather?'

'Yes, sir. Me and Sergeant Griffin.'

'In that case there will be no possibility of his evading you?'

'None whatever, sir.'

'Good.'

'We'll stand by, sir.'

He rang off. Although Mr. Green had told the sergeant that he would probably be accompanying the mysterious stranger on his return to the village, he had not yet considered how this was to be accomplished. It might prove difficult, unless he were to arouse suspicion. He frowned, reproving himself for his lack of foresight. Then, suddenly, the telephone rang again, and the problem was solved.

Miss Kane was speaking. 'Mr. Green, that dreadful creature's here again. The one in the mackintosh.'

Mr. Green pretended that he did not follow her. 'Mackintosh?' he echoed.

'The one we saw last night,' she retorted impatiently. 'Richard met him at the front door, and they both went straight into the library to talk to Andrew.'

'Indeed?'

'Mr. Green, *do* wake up! I want you to find out what's going on.'

'How would you suggest that I do so?'

There was a hint of irony in her voice as she replied: 'People have been known to listen at doors.'

Mr. Green made no reply to this comment.

'Oh, Mr. Green, don't be offended. But I'm terribly worried. You must admit that it's all very odd. And I've got an awful feeling that it may somehow be mixed up with . . . you know what.'

Mr. Green was inclined to share this feeling, but he saw no reason to tell her so.

'Are you dressed?' he inquired politely.

'I've been dressed for hours.'

'In that case I will come straight down. It would be pleasant to stroll in the box garden, where we shall be unobserved.

'Very well. And I'll send a message to Richard to tell him I've gone down to the village.'

If Miss Kane had expected to be treated to a demonstration of Mr. Green's talents during this brief promenade, she was destined to be disappointed. Mr. Green seemed quite exceptionally uninspired. He made no cryptic remarks, dropped no mysterious hints, and showed no inclination to walk on tiptoe, with his fingers to his lips. He merely plodded backwards and forwards, with his hands behind his back, saying that it was all most puzzling.

'I know it's puzzling,' she retorted. 'but what are we going to *do*?'

He stopped in his tracks. 'I think I have an idea.'

At last, thought Miss Kane, he is going to show his quality! But Mr. Green's "idea" was so commonplace that it was hardly worthy of being called an idea at all. It was simply that when the mysterious young man came out of the library she should intercept him and offer to drive him back to the village.

'If he accepts your offer,' he said, 'and if you engage him in conversation, it is possible that you may learn something about him. One often does.'

'Well, really, if that's all you've got to suggest . . .'

Mr. Green ignored her complaint. 'I shall be happy to accompany you,' he said blandly, 'if you think I can be of any assistance.'

For two pins she would have rejected his offer. However, she had no better notion herself, so she accepted it.

'We'd better go round to the front of the house straight away in case they come out. I'll go and get my car and meet you in the porch.' She hesitated for a moment. 'You're quite sure you don't feel inclined to listen outside the door?'

'Quite,' he replied. 'I doubt whether I should learn anything that I do not know already.'

If he had not spoken in so very flat a voice she might have gained some consolation from this remark; it had a cryptic ring.

3

Some five minutes later she drove up to the porch where Mr. Green was waiting. Miss Kane chose her motor-cars for their colour and their line; she was interested neither in their speed nor their performance; their primary function was to serve as a foil to her frocks, her face and her hair.

Her favourite conveyance at the moment was a scarlet coupé of Italian origin, with seats of pale lemon-coloured leather. It was built in a single, sweeping gesture, very close to the ground.

As soon as Mr. Green saw it his heart sank. Miss Kane observed his expression of dismay and interpreted it correctly.

'You needn't worry,' she said brightly. 'I'm the world's most frightened driver, and I never go over forty.' She opened the door and got out. 'This is what I call my cad's car. It ought to appeal to our young friend.'

She stepped into the porch and was about to sit down when there was the sound of voices at the end of the long gallery.

'Here they come,' she whispered, putting a scarlet-gloved hand on Mr. Green's arm.

Even as she spoke, Lord Richard appeared, followed by the offending young man. Lord Richard looked pale and tense, but the young man appeared to be in high spirits. There was a satisfied smirk on his face, and a glassy stare in his eyes that showed he had been drinking more than was good for him.

Lord Richard started as he saw Miss Kane. 'I thought you'd gone down to the village.'

'No, darling. I was delayed. I'm just off now, with Mr. Green. Can we give a lift to . . . I don't think I know your friend's name?'

'Jones is the name, madam,' replied the young man with an unsteady bow. 'Most kind of you, I'm sure. Charmed to drive with you. Abs'lutely charmed.'

Lord Richard stepped forward. 'I was going to take Mr. Jones along with me.'

The young man pushed Lord Richard aside. 'Now then, Dickie, don' be tactless.' Mr. Green saw Lord Richard wince. 'Charming young lady asks me go for a drive. I accept. That's that. Not a chance that comes every day in a fellah's life. What?'

'So that's settled, then.' Miss Kane spoke in tones which showed that as far as she was concerned there was no need for further argument. They were tones Lord Richard knew all too well.

'See you at lunch, then,' he muttered. 'So long, Jones.' He did not wait for a reply but set off down the drive, with his hands thrust deep in his pockets.

'Good sport, Dickie,' commented Mr. Jones as he lurched towards the car, followed by Mr. Green. 'Rattling good sport. One of the best.'

Miss Kane shuddered but her smile remained fixed. 'Have you known him for long?'

Before he could reply, Mr. Green interrupted. He had taken out his camera, and was blinking up at the sun.

He turned to Miss Kane. 'May I take a picture of you and the car?'

She shifted impatiently in her seat. 'Must you? I look ghastly.'

'On the contrary.' He took her permission for granted and bent over the lens.

Mr. Jones stepped to one side. 'Wait a jiffy! I'll get out of the way.'

Mr. Green looked up. 'I should prefer that you remained,' he said quietly. 'It improves the composition.'

Mr. Jones appeared to hesitate. Then, with a certain reluctance, he stepped back into the picture.

The shutter clicked.

F

'Thank you,' said Mr. Green. 'That will be a very pleasant addition to my little album.'

Miss Kane, who was having some trouble in finding the right ignition key, repeated her question: 'Have you known Lord Richard for long?'

'On and off, you know, on and off. One gets around.' His senses were warmed by alcohol and flattered by her proximity. He began to make what he considered to be polite conversation.

'Fine old place they've got here,' he observed, with a vague gesture through the open window. 'Stately homes of England and all that, what?'

'This is your first visit?' inquired Mr. Green.

'That's right, old boy. Never been here before. Never had what's known as the entray. But hope to come here again. In fact, *shall* come here again. You can count on it.'

'That will be delightful,' observed Mr. Green. He spoke as though an asp were poised before his lips.

Mr. Jones continued to make polite conversation. 'As I was saying, regular stately home. Everything just right. Even the stables over there.' He pointed in the direction of the east wing. 'I suppose they *are* stables?'

'That was their original function,' replied Mr. Green. 'Nowadays they are . . .'

'Never mind about nowadays,' interrupted Mr. Jones. His voice was becoming thicker every minute. 'Live for the past, ignore the present, and forget all you know about the future. Or is that a bit mixed up?'

Mr. Green looked at him with a sudden flicker of interest. Out of a drunken brain had come a strange paradox, with a perverted wisdom.

'As I was saying,' resumed Mr. Jones, 'very pretty stables. Wouldn't mind living in 'em myself. Just the job. Could be very comfy in a place like that. All I'd do would be to cut down a few of those old trees. Not healthy, old trees. And I'd take the chimes out of that damned clock in the tower. Keep me awake, they would . . .'

Mr. Jones had no chance to enlarge upon the further

changes he would make, during his projected residence, for at this moment Miss Kane pressed the starter and the car shot forward with a jerk.

4

In his last analysis of the many factors which contributed to his final solution of the Broome Place mystery, Mr. Green was to attach considerable importance to the conversation that now ensued. And yet, a shorthand transcript of it would have revealed little to excite the suspicion of the average man. Such a transcript would have read as follows:

Sally. So you're selling Lord Richard a car, Mr. Jones?

Jones. Well, you might put it that way.

Sally. I hope it's not going to be a very expensive one?

Jones. Couldn't be, could it? Not if he's as hard up as he says he is.

Sally. Oh! So you've been talking finances already?

Jones. That's right. (With a throaty chuckle.) That's just what we've been doing. Talking finances. But you needn't be afraid I'll sting old Dickie too hard. Much too fond of old Dickie. Always have been. Never know what he's going to get up to next. All those practical jokes of his . . .

Sally. He's given those up.

Jones. Oh no, he hasn't!

Sally. I beg your pardon, but I happen to know he has.

Jones. And I happen to know . . . (suddenly he pauses) . . . I say. Are you sure of this?

Sally. Of course I'm sure. Does it matter?

Jones. I'd say it matters!

Sally. I'm afraid I don't understand.

Jones. No. I don't suppose you do.

A pause, during which Mr. Jones appears to be wrapped in thought. Eventually he turns to Mr. Green.

Jones. Terrible thing, that girl going and shooting herself like that. Shook me no end.

Mr. Green. You were acquainted with Miss Larue?

Jones. I wouldn't say yes and I wouldn't say no. Or would I? Oh well, I'll come clean. Yes, I was acquainted.

Mr. Green. Had you seen her recently?

Jones. (Quickly.) No. Certainly not. Different social circles and all that. Not like the old days in Hampstead.

Mr. Green. Was that where she used to reside?

Jones. Yes. She had a sort of studio place in . . . (he checks himself) . . . oh, somewhere or other. Often used to visit there. Never struck me as the suicide type.

Sally. She was, though. Lady Coniston heard her talking about suicide that very afternoon.

Jones. Who's Lady Coniston when she's at home?

Sally. She's one of the house guests. She's had her face lifted.

Jones. She has, has she? And she heard Margot . . . Miss Larue, I should say . . . threaten suicide? I'd like to meet Lady Coniston one day, if she's no objection.

Mr. Green. (The asp is again poised on his lips.) No doubt she will be delighted.

Jones. Well, well, we live and learn. When was it precisely?

Sally. When was what?

Jones. The suicide. When did she do herself in?

Sally. Just before eleven, wasn't it, Mr. Green?

Mr. Green. So I understand. You will find a fairly full account of the affair in the newspapers.

Jones. I must read it.

Mr. Green. You have not already done so?

Jones. I've glanced at it. But . . . well . . . I think I'll glance again. Second thoughts and all that. What?

At this point, our imaginary transcript may be put away, for Mr. Jones made no further comments that could possibly be regarded as significant, even to Mr. Green. He threw himself with renewed vigour into the art of polite

conversation, and was so obliging as to enlighten Mr. Green
on the charms of the new bungalow settlements which
were springing up, with mushroom rapidity, on the outskirts of the village. The architecture of these bungalows,
he assured Mr. Green, was Tudor, nothing bogus about it,
the real stuff, and in Mr. Jones' opinion there was nothing
like Tudor for a chap with taste, what? Because each of the
bungalows had an inglenook which would be just the job
for the telly set. And if your telly set was in fumed oak, and
if you hung a copper warming-pan above it, you'd got
just the job, what? That's what he liked, Mr. Jones did,
culture and Tudor and old world elegance. None of your
modern stuff. A gentleman of the old school, he was. And
so, he generously admitted, was Mr. Green.

5

Mr. Jones desired to be dropped at the corner of a
quiet road leading to the High Street. When Miss Kane
suggested that he might prefer to be taken to the bus stop—
or to the inn—he replied with some brusqueness that he
knew where he wanted to go, thank you very much. Some
of his alcoholic *bonhomie* seemed to have worn off.

Miss Kane watched him shuffle round the corner—he did
not wave or raise his hat—and then she turned to Mr. Green.

'If that isn't poison,' she exclaimed, 'my name's Annie
Arsenic!'

Mr. Green appeared not to hear her. He had turned his
head, and was staring intently at a black car that was just
coming up to them. As it passed he gave an almost
imperceptible nod.

Miss Kane did not observe the signal. 'Sheer poison!'
she repeated. She scowled at him, for she was a spoilt and
ill-mannered young lady. And yet there was a gleam of
amiability in the scowl—if such a facial paradox is possible.
It was difficult to be really angry with Mr. Green.

'Maestro,' she said severely, 'you've disappointed me.

You left me to do all the cross-examination. And it's got me nowhere. Just plain nowhere.' She tapped her scarlet-gloved fingers impatiently on the even brighter scarlet of the steering wheel. 'What's more, you're not even listening.'

Mr. Green sat up and blinked. 'I beg your pardon. I was thinking.'

'Don't overstrain yourself, maestro. What were you thinking about?'

At long last Mr. Green stepped, for a fleeting moment, into the shoes of Sherlock Holmes. They were too large for him, of course, and for the moment they appeared to lead him to no special destination. But they had the authentic mark of Baker Street.

'I was thinking,' he said, 'about the clock.'

'Which clock?'

'The clock over the stables. Mr. Jones said that if he were ever to take up residence in the stables . . .'

'May the saints preserve us from *that*!'

'Quite. But he said that if he did, he would stop the chiming of the clock, because it would keep him awake at night.'

'So what?'

'The stable clock stopped shortly after midnight on Saturday night. It has not chimed since then.'

She turned to him with such interest that the car nearly swerved into the ditch. Mr. Green put his hand gently but swiftly on to the steering wheel.

'Sorry,' she murmured. 'But I'm fascinated. What does it mean?'

'It means that Mr. Jones was not telling us the truth when he said that he had never been to Broome Place before. I am certain that he has been there before.' He nodded to himself. 'I am even more certain that he will go there again.'

16

DIALOGUE

"ATMOSPHERE", as we know, was not one of Mr. Green's favourite words. At the same time, Mr. Green was a human being and a highly sensitive one, and he was bound to admit that as the hours passed by, and the darkness gathered round Broome Place, the "atmosphere" in the great house became more and more tense. Dinner was a strained, unnatural occasion, with awkward silences and sudden scraps of artificial dialogue. Mr. Green's attention seemed to be wandering, but from time to time phrases caught his ear which caused him, almost imperceptibly, to blink.

Thus, he blinked when the high, affected tone of Cecil Gower-Jones drifted down the table. He was talking to Mrs. Lloyd.

'I do wish you'd find out from that wretched husband of yours whether I ought to buy some of those ghastly oil shares.'

'You had better ask Sir Luke.' Her voice was very cold.

'On the contrary,' retorted Sir Luke, 'our host is the ultimate authority. But he doesn't seem to be talking.'

'All I want to know is whether they are going up or down.' Gower-Jones' voice became quite shrill. 'If I buy them and they go down I shall die; if I don't buy them and they go up I shall *expire*. It really is too tiresome, staying in a house with two financial giants and nobody tells one a *thing*.'

Anybody who had been watching Mr. Green at this moment would have noticed that he had begun to frown, as though in an effort of concentration. The economic motive . . . had he paid sufficient attention to the economic motive? This case was so dark and tangled; there were still so many pieces of the puzzle that refused to fit into place.

His frown faded. He was listening again. It was the drawling voice of Sally, speaking across the table to Lady Coniston.

'It's lucky I was brought up to be a good mixer,' she was saying. 'If you'd only *seen* him! That mackintosh! Those boots! Those cuff-links!'

Lord Richard cut in tersely. 'Don't you think we've had enough of Mr. Jones for one evening, Sally?'

'He's your friend, not mine.'

'I've told you forty times he's not a friend, he's a business acquaintance.'

The conversation wrangled on. Mr. Green was frowning again. Mr. Jones—Mr. Grey—Mr. X—call him what you will—was one of the key pieces of the puzzle. But even Mr. Jones did not fit perfectly.

He felt a gentle pressure on his arm. It was Charlotte, who was sitting next to him.

'Darling,' she said softly, 'it's pineapple.'

Mr. Green blinked and looked down at his plate. The plate was a masterpiece of Meissen, the slice of pineapple was of exceptional opulence, and there by his side was Palmer, with a bowl of Devonshire cream in a Queen Anne porringer.

Mr. Green sighed, and helped himself to the cream. He was already suffering from mental indigestion; he might as well go the whole hog.

2

Mental indigestion?

If Mr. Green was indeed suffering from this complaint, he showed no sign of it after dinner.

He had retired to the deserted drawing-room to think. After all, he had a good deal to think about—among other things, his immediate plans for the future. How long was he expected to remain at Broome Place? He had already been here a week, and although his host had courteously suggested that he would be welcome for an indefinite period, he wondered if the invitation were still as sincere as it had sounded at the time it was delivered.

What were his precise terms of contract? He had been engaged—if so vague and generous an assignment could be called an "engagement"—to inquire into the death of Margot Larue. Was he still bound by that engagement? More important . . . did Andrew Lloyd wish to hold him to it? If he guessed even a fraction of the ugly pattern which Mr. Green had uncovered . . .

But perhaps Lloyd did guess? Or perhaps he was on the point of guessing? Perhaps he might guess this very night?

Even as he asked himself the question, the door opened and Lloyd came into the room.

As always, in the presence of the financier, Mr. Green had the sense that the tempo of life was quickening. Lloyd had an extraordinary economy of movement, of gesture, even of facial expression; the smile with which he entered seemed genuine enough, but it was switched off as soon as it had served his purpose. He walked directly to a chair by Mr. Green's side, and drew it closer with his left hand while he reached for a cigarette box with his right.

'Mr. Green,' he said, 'you are fulfilling all my expectations.'

Mr. Green raised his eyebrows. 'In that case, I fear that your expectations cannot have been very high.'

'On the contrary, I expected charm. I am getting it.'

Mr. Green bowed politely.

'I also expected mystery. And cryptic remarks. And unaccountable behaviour. They have all been supplied in abundance.'

'Has my behaviour been so unaccountable?'

Lloyd smiled. 'There have been several mysterious

excursions to London and maybe elsewhere, or so my spies report.' He held up his hand. 'Oh, please don't think that I am asking you to explain them. I merely wanted you to know that they had not passed unnoticed. I am not entirely unobservant.'

'So it had occurred to me.' Mr. Green's voice was very dry. 'However, there must surely be one respect in which you must be feeling disappointed? Surely you expected some decisive *action*?'

'At this point? Would that not be premature?'

Mr. Green shrugged his shoulders. 'There have been occasions when my employers have expressed impatience if I have not completed my work within twenty-four hours. And I have been here over a week.'

'I hope you will remain for as long as you please.'

'You are sure of that?'

Lloyd looked him straight in the eyes. 'Quite sure, Mr. Green. Not only for your company but also for the sake of appearances.'

'I am not certain that I follow you.'

Lloyd's eyes did not falter. 'It would look very strange, wouldn't it, if I suddenly asked you to suspend your inquiries at this stage?'

'Strange?'

'As though I were afraid that you were on the point of discovering something about the death of Margot Larue—something that might incriminate myself?' He did not raise his voice; he put the question almost indifferently. '*Are* you, Mr. Green?'

'If you wish me to continue to live up to expectations, you can hardly expect me to answer that question.'

'Of course not. In any case, it was in poor taste.'

He threw away his cigarette and rose to his feet. Then he walked over to the chimney-piece and stared up at the picture of the Madonna. His face was in profile, and as Mr. Green watched him he had a sense that Lloyd was staring through the picture, into far distances. He stayed there for several moments in silence.

Then he turned abruptly. 'But there is one question that I hope you will answer for me.'

'Yes?'

'*Is there such a thing as the perfect murder?*'

3

Mr. Green sat up sharply. Something told him that this question, in its context, was of vital importance. True, it was a stock question, a *cliché* of a question; he had been confronted by it time and again, in his encounters with the Press. Always he had parried it with a shrug of the shoulders, or a facile generalization.

But now it was different, and it was the context that made the difference—the setting, the background, the hour and the man himself.

The question had suddenly come to life. He was quite certain that a great deal depended upon his answer. He had very clear ideas about that answer, but until this moment he had never put them into words.

Mr. Green closed his eyes for a moment. He wanted to marshall his thoughts. Then he nodded to himself. Yes, he had it.*

Lloyd. Is there such a thing as the perfect murder!

Mr. Green. I do not think so.

Lloyd. Why do you say that!

Mr. Green. I say it because I find it difficult to associate perfection with evil.

Lloyd. Isn't that a quibble? A play upon words?

Mr. Green. Quite possibly, and as such it is suspect. At the same time, it was my immediate personal reaction to your question.

Lloyd. Can you explain that reaction?

Mr. Green. It is very simple. The phrase . . . "a perfect

Authors Note: The scene that follows is presented in the form of a dialogue, because it was upon this conversation that Mr. Green later modelled his well-known essay "Murder and the Artist". The student of criminology will readily recognize the essentials of the argument.

murder" . . . implies a work of art. As though it were a picture that was impeccable, or a piece of prose that could not be faulted. But this comparison is based on a fallacy.

Lloyd. Why?

Mr. Green. I can best answer you with the old tag from Wordsworth. "Poetry is emotion recollected in tranquillity." I believe that to be profoundly true. Not only of poetry, but of music and of all the arts. (There is a pause of several seconds. Mr. Green resumes.) First comes the inspiration; in the brain of the artist it is a form of ecstasy, in the brain of the murderer it is a form of hatred or of fear. If the ecstasy, or the hatred is strong enough, it creates its own pattern—a pattern of beauty for the artist, a pattern of ugliness for the murderer. In each case, that pattern is the initial sketch, the ground-plan as it were, of the finished work. Do you follow?

Lloyd. I think so.

Mr. Green. Very well. In the case of the artist, he is able to develop this sketch in tranquillity. He has had his ecstasy, in which he has seen his vision or received his message. The ecstasy may have faded, but that does not matter, for the vision has been sketched and the message has been recorded. All that remains for the artist to do is to develop the sketch as faithfully as he can, to record the message in the most fitting words at his command. But in the case of the murderer . . .

Lloyd. Yes?

Mr. Green. The murderer is denied this interlude of tranquillity. He has his moment of passion, true, in which he forms his design. But his "ecstasy" does not cool, there is no chance of that vital period of comparative calm which is so essential to perfection in any work of art. As long as the object of his hatred is alive, his brain is clouded and his hand is inclined to falter.

Lloyd. Then how do you account for such a crime as a cold-blooded murder?

Mr. Green. I do not account for it; I deny it. There is no such thing. The murderer may delude himself that he is cold-blooded, and his actions may be such as to give that impression to the investigator. But the very fact that he murders at all is a proof that the initial passion is still burning intensely. What does this imply? It implies that the pattern—the design—is still fluid, liable to change and therefore to error. In every murder, however carefully planned, there must be an element of improvisation.

Lloyd. Does not that also apply to every work of art?

Mr. Green. To an inferior work of art, maybe, to a perfect work, no—and we are considering the possibility of the perfect murder. I repeat, there can be no such thing. It is a contradiction in terms. To sum up . . . I refer you back to Wordsworth.

4

"Emotion recollected in tranquillity."

Lloyd echoed the words. He seemed to be speaking to himself. 'Yes. I believe the argument is valid, and the distinction holds good.' He gave a sudden smile. 'Though, of course, there is always the exception that proves the rule.'

'I think not.'

'Not even in the case of a man like myself? Supposing that I myself decided to commit the perfect murder— merely as an intellectual amusement. Supposing that I chose as my victim a person against whom I bore no grudge, a person to whom I was quite indifferent. What happens to your argument then? I should not be animated by hatred—*ipso facto*, there would be nothing to cloud my brain, nor cause my hand to falter. Well?'

Mr. Green looked at him thoughtfully. 'Do you really think so?'

'That is no answer to my question.'

'Does it deserve an answer?' Mr. Green rose slowly to his feet. 'That question was hardly worthy of your intelligence, Mr. Lloyd.'

'Why do you say that?'

Mr. Green sighed, and his voice had a tinge of sadness. 'Because you are arguing from a false assumption. You postulate a man who would commit a murder as an intellectual exercise. And you ask me to believe that such a man had no hatred in his heart. You are asking me to believe the impossible.'

'But if he did not even know the victim?'

'I was not thinking of the victim. He would not be animated by hatred of the victim. He would be animated by hatred of someone far more important . . . himself.'

There was a chime from the Louis Seize clock on the wall behind him.

'It is half past eleven,' said Mr. Green abruptly. 'With your permission, I shall retire.'

Lloyd did not seem to hear him. He was staring straight ahead of him. His lips framed the word . . . "himself". Then he came back to earth.

'Of course.' He forced a smile. 'Forgive me. I was trying to find a flaw in your argument.'

'I doubt whether you will find it easy to do so.'

'So do I. However, we shall see.' He walked with Mr. Green to the door. 'In the meantime . . .' He paused, as though searching for words.

'Yes?'

'There may be some action, in the near future?'

'I am afraid I cannot commit myself.'

'Naturally. Good night, Mr. Green.'

Mr. Green walked slowly down the long corridor and up the stairs. From the distance came the tinkle of a harpsichord—Mrs. Lloyd's favourite form of instrumental music. A gramophone record, no doubt. It faded into silence as Mr. Green closed the door of his room.

Mr. Green's forehead was creased in a frown. "There may be some action in the near future?" Lloyd had given those words a note of interrogation. But Mr. Green had the impression that he had spoken them as a statement of fact.

17

A STAB IN THE DARK

AND then, on the following morning, the drama took a new and totally unexpected turn.

It was nearly ten o'clock when Mr. Green, who had been dozing pleasantly in the no-man's-land between sleeping and waking, was roused by a knock on the door.

It was Palmer with his breakfast tray, on which there reposed, among other delicacies, a large bunch of white Muscat grapes.

Palmer set the tray by his side, switched on the electric fire and drew the curtains. Mr. Green saw that the day was grey and misty.

'Mrs. Lloyd told me you were not to be disturbed, sir,' remarked the young man. 'But I thought you'd rather be woken, considering.'

Mr. Green studied the grapes with approval. 'Considering?'

'Considering what's been going on.'

Mr. Green sat up sharply. 'Not another . . .'

'Oh no, sir. Nothing like that. No corpses or anything. But nearly as bad, if you ask me.'

Then the story came out. At half past seven that morning, the first housemaid, who had been into the drawing-room to draw the curtains and light the fire, had come running back into the servants' hall saying that something terrible had happened.

The painting of the Madonna over the fireplace—the masterpiece of the Maître de Reims—had been brutally slashed across its entire surface.

'You could have knocked me down with a feather, sir,' said Palmer. 'At first I thought the girl must be joking—

she's a flighty bit of goods—but it was just as she said. Two great jagged cuts right across the chest, and two great holes dug in the kid's eyes. Fair frightening it was, sir, and no mistake.'

'Has anybody any idea . . .?'

'Whodunnit, sir? No, sir. That's why I woke you, sir.'

'You were quite right. There were no signs of violence? Of forcible entry?'

'Nothing to notice, sir. But then, of course, I'm not an expert.'

'Do the rest of the guests know of this outrage?'

'No, sir. As soon as Mr. Lloyd came down he gave orders for the door to be locked and for nobody to be allowed in. He said you'd like the field to yourself, as it were, sir.'

'That was very thoughtful of him. I imagine that he must be greatly distressed—and Mrs. Lloyd too.'

'You'd think so, sir. But they've both taken it uncommon calm like, if you ask me. However, you never know what Mr. Lloyd's really feeling, nor her either, though perhaps it's not my place to say so. Shall I run your bath, sir? I expect you'll be wanting to get cracking.'

'Thank you. I should be much obliged. When you go down perhaps you would give Mr. Lloyd a message . . .'

'Mr. Lloyd, sir? Oh, he's gone up to London, sir, as usual. A little thing like this wouldn't keep Mr. Lloyd from the City, not when there's money to be made.'

He paused in the doorway to the bathroom. 'By the way, sir, I nearly forgot. Superintendent Waller telephoned at eight o'clock. He is on his way down to see you. That'll brighten things up no end, won't it, sir?'

With a cheerful grin he vanished into the bathroom.

In spite of the urgency of the occasion, Mr. Green did not hurry over his bath. It would indeed have been difficult for any man with sybaritic tendencies—and Mr. Green was not devoid of them—to resist the temptation to linger in so opulent a chamber of ablution. The walls of the bathroom were decorated in a mosaic of mother-of-pearl, the bath itself was sunk into the floor, and the water gushed from a dolphin's head carved in alabaster. Against the cunningly lit triple mirror stood a table laden with every conceivable variety of bath salts and bath essences. An alabaster bowl, on another table, was filled with a peach-coloured powder, surmounted by a powder puff as large as a football. The towels, he noted with approval, were as large as blankets. He noted, with less approval, that they were heavily monogrammed. As he put his small pink foot into the perfumed water he frowned, ever so slightly. It was curious, he thought, that a man of Lloyd's breeding and sensibility should have monograms on his towels. Monograms on towels were ostentatious. Apart from that, they scratched.

Mr. Green lay in the bath and savoured the warmth, and the soft, satiny water. In the flattering hue of the misted wall-lights he looked like a large pink baby, enjoying its tub. But his thoughts were not the thoughts of a baby. They were very grim indeed.

2

The clock over the stable tower struck half past ten. Mr. Green emerged from his bath and dried himself on one of the questionable towels. Five minutes later, looking very neat and spruce, he opened the door of his bedroom and stepped out.

Palmer was waiting for him.

'I've got the drawing-room key, sir. I'll let you in.'

Mr. Green nodded. They walked down the great staircase.

'The house is very quiet,' said Mr. Green.

'It's a big house, sir. It's usually quiet at this time of day.'

'But the other guests?'

'Sir Luke and Lady Coniston went up to London with Mr. Lloyd, sir. So did Lord Richard, in his own car.'

'And Mr. Gower-Jones?'

'Oh, *him*, sir? He went up by train.'

'So we are all alone, apart from Miss Kane and Mrs. Lloyd?'

'Yes, sir.' He chuckled. 'Sounds sort of creepy like, doesn't it, sir, with a maniac round the corner?'

Mr. Green glanced at him sharply. It was a curious phrase. "A maniac round the corner". Some such image had been in his own mind. He wondered how Palmer would answer if he asked him to explain himself.

The face told him nothing; it bore the same cheerful, impersonal grin. He was still grinning when he took out the key and opened the door.

Mr. Green had a sudden urgent desire to be alone.

He turned to Palmer. 'Thank you,' he said. 'I don't think I need detain you any longer.'

A shadow crossed the young man's face.

'You're not detaining me, sir.'

'I expect you have other duties. If I need anything I will ring.'

A moment later Mr. Green's urgent desire was fulfilled. The door was shut behind him, the key was in his pocket, and Palmer was walking away down the long corridor with a look of frustration on his handsome face.

3

The drawing room was hushed and evasive in the sombre light of this misty morning, and Mr. Green, as he walked across it, had a sense that he should tread on tiptoe.

He arrived at the great chimney-piece. For a momen the did not look up at the picture; he stared at the smouldering logs in the fireplace.

The he lifted his head with a jerk. And his small body quivered with a sudden access of pain.

It was as though the picture bled before him. There were two savage slashes running diagonally from corner to corner; one of them passed through the Virgin's breast and the other through the heart of the child. In addition there were two gaping holes where the eyes of the child had been, and the knife had stabbed these with such violence that it had cut into the plaster on the wall behind.

Mr. Green was deeply distressed. As he gazed at these mutilated bodies he felt that he was confronted not merely with an artistic outrage but with a human disaster. His lips moved in mute protest and his fingers, which were trembling, pressed tight across his jacket.

There was the sound of a door opening. He turned and saw Mrs. Lloyd walking towards him. She was in deep black, and her face was very pale, but she looked quite composed.

'At least we can be thankful that it's insured,' she said abruptly.

The callousness of her remark shocked Mr. Green. He made no reply.

'I'm sorry,' she said in a softer voice. 'But what else is there to say? It's finished. It's a part of one's life that's over. The best thing to do is to accept the fact.'

'That is one way of looking at it.'

'It is the only way.'

Mr. Green noticed a curious thing; since she had come into the room she had not even glanced at the picture; she had turned her back on it. He wondered if her action was deliberate.

'There is one part of the picture,' he suggested, pointing to it, 'that is not so badly damaged as the rest.'

'Please do not ask me to look at it.' He saw that her fingers were tightly clenched. Evidently Mrs. Lloyd was not quite so composed as she had seemed.

'I beg your pardon. I can well understand how you must feel about it.'

She made no reply.

'I can also understand,' persisted Mr. Green, 'how much this must have upset your husband.'

'It was not his favourite picture.'

She walked towards the window and threw back one of the heavy velvet curtains which the housemaid had forgotten. A beam of watery sunlight lit up the picture for a moment, making the wounds seem even more cruel. Then it faded again.

She stood looking out of the window. 'Shall we all have to go through another cross-examination?'

'I do not see how it can very well be avoided. Your insurance company would feel obliged to call in the police, even if you yourselves were reluctant to do so.'

'We are not in the least reluctant,' she retorted. 'In fact, my husband has already done so. Your friend, Mr. Waller, is on his way down at the moment. In the meantime, if you want to make any preliminary inquiries . . .'

Mr. Green made a gesture of dissent. 'It is hardly my province.'

'My husband would not agree with you. He never ceases to remind me that you are a genius. And if this tragedy has any connexion with the other, you are obviously the man to find it.'

'Have you any reason to suppose that it has a connexion?'

For a moment she hesitated. 'Yes, I have, but I do not suppose it would impress you. It is a very feminine reason.'

'That is hardly an excuse for rejecting it.'

'Very well. It is simply this. Whatever may have happened last Saturday week—and I still see no reason to disbelieve that poor Margot Larue took her own life— there was certainly a murderer in this house last night.' She pointed in the direction of the picture, though she still averted her eyes from it. 'That was murder, Mr. Green.'

She spoke with an extraordinary intensity, and though her hand was steady, her breathing was unnaturally swift.

'There may have been a crime ten days ago. Or there may not. That is for you to discover. But there was certainly a crime last night, and that crime was murder.' Her hand dropped to her side. She seemed to be speaking to herself. 'Who was it who said that all the worst crimes in the world are committed in the brain? It does not matter. All that matters is that *this* crime was murder. The man—or woman—who did this was not merely destroying a masterpiece. He—or she— was destroying human life.'

Mr. Green nodded. 'I am inclined to agree with you.'

She forced a smile. 'I feel greatly flattered.' Her voice took a lighter note. 'One day I might apply for the job of your assistant.' She glanced at her watch and turned towards the door. 'I must go and order luncheon for Mr. Waller. Is there anything I ought to do before he arrives?'

'I cannot suggest anything. I understand that the door of this room has been kept locked?'

'Yes. Apart from the housemaid and ourselves—and Palmer of course—nobody has been in and nothing has been touched. My husband and three of the gardeners made a thorough examination of the outside windows, immediately after breakfast. They found nothing.

'The other guests have not been informed?'

'I saw no reason to inform them.'

'You yourself heard nothing during the night?'

'Nothing at all.'

'Nor any of the servants?'

'If they had, they would have told me.'

'So we start, as it were, with a blank sheet of paper.'

'Is not that how you would prefer it?'

She lifted her head and regarded him with the faintest of smiles. Mr. Green was puzzled by the expression in her eyes. He seemed to read a challenge there.

She went out. Not once had she looked at the picture.

4

And then Waller walked into the room. Mr. Green turned with a start. The superintendent did not greet him. He was staring at the picture.

'How did it happen?'

'We are completely in the dark.'

Waller stepped nearer, and stretched out his hand as though to touch the wounded canvas. Then he drew back.

'It's murder. That's what it is. What's more, it's the work of a madman. Look at that kid's eyes!' He shook his head. 'Murder. Bloody murder!'

'Mrs. Lloyd had the same reaction as yourself.'

'Have you any line on it at all?'

Mr. Green hesitated. An idea had occurred to him, but it was too fantastic, as yet, to put into words. 'I have made no investigations,' he said.

Waller grunted. He walked over to the window, and for the next few minutes he was busy searching for signs of forcible entry. There were none, in this room at any rate. However, in a house of this size, a lunatic might enter from a hundred places.

When he put this thought to Mr. Green, the little man shook his head. 'According to Palmer, there are no indications that any entry has been made.'

'Palmer? I wouldn't put much trust in him!'

'You have a prejudice against that young man,' said Mr. Green. 'It is not a question of putting trust in him. He was merely reporting the facts. Mr. Lloyd seems to have made a thorough search . . . or rather . . . his gardeners have done so. There is no evidence at all.'

'I'll have to satisfy myself about that.'

'Of course.'

Waller sank into a chair, folded his arms, and stared once more at the picture. 'Bloody murder!' he repeated grimly. 'Those kid's eyes!'

He turned abruptly to Mr. Green. Now let's get down to your friend in the mackintosh.'

'Mr. Grey . . . or should I say Mr. Jones?'

'The name's Grey. Didn't you know?'

'I know nothing about him at all. Or almost nothing.'

'In that case, you had a lucky hunch.' Waller's eyes twinkled as he noticed Mr. Green's faint shudder of disgust. "Lucky hunches" played no part in Mr. Green's technique.

'Grey has a record,' continued the superintendent. 'He's a merchant navy man—on and off. Usually more off than on. And about four years ago—November '52 I think it was—he got three months for breaking into a night-club and walking off with the contents of the cash register.'

Mr. Green looked faintly disappointed. 'Is that all you have against him?'

You'll think it's quite enough when I give you the club's address. It was L'Etoile, 99A Minton Street, Mayfair, which was where Margot Larue had her flat, on the third floor.'

Mr. Green blinked three times in rapid succession.

'Yes,' chuckled Waller. 'I thought that would make you sit up.'

'Did you confront him with these facts?'

'If you mean, did I go for him bald-headed, the answer is no. There were two ways of tackling Mr. Grey; one was to scare the pants off him. I could have done that without any difficulty—in fact they began to slip off as soon as he saw me. I soon put a stop to that. I played the stupid policeman, blundering along in the dark. . . you know the sort of act.'

'I am very familiar with it.'

Waller glanced at him sharply. But Mr. Green's face was expressionless. 'Anyway, we've got him eating out of our hand.'

'But did he make any admissions?'

'Not intentionally.' Waller flicked open his notebook. 'Let's see. First, he sticks to the car story. When I told him we'd have to check that with Lord Richard, he said "Go ahead, that's O.K. with me." '

'Did you bring up the question of his having visited Broome Place before?'

'Yes. As casually as possible. I suggested that Sunday morning was his first visit, and he said "Of course." I need hardly say that I didn't bring up the question of his staying at the Red Dragon. By the way, we'll have to fix up some way for that woman to identify him without his suspecting.'

'That will not be difficult,' observed Mr. Green. He felt in his waistcoat pocket and produced a roll of film. 'I am not an expert photographer but I usually obtain a good likeness. This was taken yesterday.'

Waller grinned. 'Thanks. That's saved me a lot of trouble. Well, then we came to the affair of the cash register at L'Etoile. That shook him for a moment, until I patted him on the back and told him that we'd let bygones be bygones.'

'Did you mention the coincidence of Margot Larue's flat in the same building?'

'Was I born yesterday? No, I didn't mention it. I tell you, we've got to kid him along, and we shan't do that by scaring him. I left him with the very firm impression that we knew nothing about it at all. If it comes to that, we never should have known, if Lloyd hadn't told us.'

'It occurs to me that one might pay a visit to L'Etoile.'

'Do you think it didn't occur to me, too? I paid it a visit; it's gone, vanished into thin air, and everybody connected with it. You know what these little dives are. Their average life-span is about a couple of years. They're usually dependent on one or two attractive regulars, and maybe an obliging pianist and a new line in interior decorations. Then the place gets shabby, and the regulars drift away, and the thing cracks up. That's what happened with L'Etoile. For all that's left of it, there might never have been such a place.'

Mr. Green sighed. The contemplation of such institutions as L'Etoile depressed him.

'Well,' said Waller briskly, 'I wonder where we go from here?'

Mr. Green merely shrugged his shoulders.

'Not that I'm asking for advice.' His voice was somewhat less brisk.

'Of course not.'

'Come off it, Horatio. Let's have one of your hunches.'

'There are times, Waller, when you are quite deliberately provoking.'

Waller grinned. Then he leant forward and held out his large hand. 'Offended?'

Mr. Green, after a moment's embarrassment, shook the proffered fist. 'Not offended. Merely bewildered.'

'By what?'

Mr. Green frowned. How was he to answer the question? He was bewildered by the increasing complexity of the puzzle. In most of his cases, as they progressed, the design became simpler. The main outline of the landscape slowly emerged, the figures solidified. But here, as each piece of the puzzle was fitted into place, the design became more grotesque. There could only be one explanation, and—as yet—he dared not face it.

'So for the moment,' he said, 'it's merely a question of keeping Mr. Grey under observation? And waiting for him to walk into whatever trap you may have set?'

'Unless you've got any better idea.'

Mr. Green shook his head. He seemed suddenly to forget about Mr. Grey. His eyes had again strayed to the picture, with its tragic wounds.

Waller grunted impatiently. 'Well, at any rate he can't have had anything to do with *that*.' Mr. Green made no comment. 'Or can he?'

'One would have thought not. However . . .'

He turned to Waller. 'They say that every picture tells a story,' he said quietly. 'I believe that this picture has a story to tell, perhaps the strangest story of all. And I fancy that it will not be long before I am able to tell that story to you.'

He checked himself abruptly. Whenever he began to talk like that, there was a danger that he might fancy himself playing the role of Sherlock Holmes. And this was a temptation which he felt bound to resist. For though Mr. Green's heart was large, it was also very humble.

18

THE STORY OF A MASTERPIECE

THE establishment of Messrs. Voss and Kauffman at 114B Old Bond Street was famous among connoisseurs the world over. To the casual passer-by there was nothing to distinguish it—merely a small window, framed in faded crimson velvet, in which there stood a single picture. It was always a good picture, but never a very important one—a gouache by Guardi maybe, or a flower-piece by Fantin Latour. Mr. Kauffman did not believe in displaying his masterpieces to all and sundry. In order to inspect these it was necessary to walk up the narrow staircase and ring the bell, when—if you had an appointment—you would be admitted into a gallery of surprising dimensions. There you would see some of the greatest pictures in the world, pictures which could only be purchased by the richest governments or—to Mr. Kauffman's regret—the most successful tycoons of Texas.

It was to this establishment, on the same afternoon, that Mr. Green directed his footsteps, having previously ascertained from Mr. Kauffman that it would be possible to have a word with him in private. Mr. Kauffman had readily agreed. The two men were old friends, and it was not the first time that Mr. Green—in the gentlest possible manner—had picked Mr. Kauffman's brains.

As Mr. Green told him the story of the outrage at Broome Place, Mr. Kauffman's pale face reflected an expression so agonizing that a knife might have been pressing against his own heart.

'But no!' he wailed. 'But no! It is not true!'

'I am afraid that it is all too true.'

'Le Maître de Reims! It is to make one weep!' There were indeed tears in Mr. Kauffman's eyes.

'The act of a barbarian,' concurred Mr. Green.

'Right across the whole picture, you say? It will be impossible to repair. One could try, of course, one *must* try . . . but the magic will have gone. It will be dead.' He clasped his hand to his forehead and stared wildly at Mr. Green. 'This is murder,' he cried. 'This is nothing but murder. Who could have done such a thing?'

'That is what one hopes one will be able to find out.'

Mr. Kauffman seized Mr. Green's hands impulsively. '*You* will bring him to book. You will punish him, as he should be punished.'

'It would be gratifying if that were the case. But I shall need some assistance.'

'Anything in the world, my friend! Show him to me and I will throttle him with my own hands!'

The obvious intensity of Mr. Kauffman's emotion caused Mr. Green to check the smile which was lurking on his lips.

'I do not imagine,' he said drily, 'that any physical action will be called for, from either of us . . . at any rate for the time being.'

Mr. Kauffman threw out his arms. 'How could one restrain oneself?'

'All I need,' persisted Mr. Green, 'is a little information.'

'But anything, my friend. Anything. What are we waiting for?'

If Mr. Green had given a truthful answer to that question he would have replied that he was waiting for Mr. Kauffman to descend from boiling point to a reasonable simmer. So he suggested that perhaps they might sit down. Having sat down he produced his ancient silver case, and offered Mr. Kauffman one of those cigarettes to which he sometimes treated himself in moments of emotional stress. They were loosely packed in coffee-coloured paper, and they were of the variety known as "herbal". Mr. Kauffman took one look at them and hastily declined. He remembered those cigarettes. They seemed to bring him suddenly to his senses. He rose to his feet, making an excuse to open the window. Then he resumed his seat, on Mr. Green's windward side.

2

'What would you know about the picture, my friend —its pedigree?'

'I should prefer to know something about the artist.'

'You are not the only person who would like to know that. All we can say for certain is that he was at the height of his powers at the beginning of the seventeenth century, and that he died at Rheims.'

'It is not much to build upon.'

'No. But there is the legend.'

'What is that?'

'You do not know it? It is a strange legend, but it is a beautiful one. You remember the picture well? Then you will recall that the figure of the infant Christ is . . . how shall we say . . .?'

'Grotesque,' suggested Mr. Green.

'That is *le mot juste*. One cannot say that it is "ugly", because the *maître* could not have drawn an ugly line. But it is quite definitely deformed. If you study it carefully . . .'

'I have done so.'

'Then I need not tell you that there is a very clear indication that the child's spine is twisted. Also, the head is too large for the body . . .'

'And there is a tragic vacancy in the eyes. Or perhaps I should say there *was* a tragic vacancy, for the eyes have gone.'

'In short, the child was what today we would call mentally deficient.'

Mr. Green sighed. 'And yet, in spite of all this, it was a picture of the greatest beauty and tenderness; it did not shock, it aroused our pity.'

'But that is not surprising, my friend. You see, the

child was the artist's own son. And the Madonna was his wife.'

Mr. Green sat up sharply. 'You are sure of that?'

'You can be sure of nothing, with the Maître de Reims. But that is the legend, and it has lasted for three and a half centuries. I see no reason for disbelieving it.'

Mr. Green pressed out his cigarette and stared straight ahead of him. 'It is a strange picture for a man like Lloyd to have chosen.'

'He did not choose it. Mrs. Lloyd chose it. In fact, there was quite a scene about it.'

'Indeed?'

'Yes. She came in one day and saw the picture, which had just arrived from Vienna. It made an immediate impact on her. That same afternoon she brought her husband to see it. His reaction was hostile, to put it mildly—so hostile that he walked out of the gallery in a huff, leaving Mrs. Lloyd alone with me. She was in tears.'

'And then?'

Mr. Kauffman smiled. 'He sent his cheque for the picture on the following morning.'

'Can you account for this hostility?'

Mr. Kauffman frowned. He appeared to be considering his answer very carefully. 'I have often asked myself that question. It puzzled me greatly. Mr. Lloyd's taste, one would have thought, would have responded instantly to a picture of this quality. Apart from that, he trusted my judgement. It would not have been the first picture he had bought from me simply because I advised him to buy it. He might not care for it at the moment, I would tell him, but if he lived with it he would come to love it. But in the case of this picture . . .' Mr. Kauffman shook his head in bewilderment.

'Surely you formed *some* conclusion?'

'Yes. But I fear that you may think it far-fetched. I believe that he hated it because he is a perfectionist. For example, if there was the smallest chip in a piece of porcelain, even if it was a museum piece, he would not have it

in the house. If there was the slightest blemish in the
veneer of a piece of Queen Anne walnut he would send it
back to the sale room. I remember that Mrs. Lloyd once
complained to me that though he had given her many
beautiful jewels, he would never give her the jewel she
loved most—an emerald. Why? Simply because he could
never find an emerald of the right size and quality which
had not a flaw.'

'But surely this picture was flawless?'

'In execution, yes. In design and colour, assuredly.
But in subject, no. The figure of the child . . .'

Mr. Green interrupted him with a gesture of annoyance.
'I have been incredibly obtuse' he exclaimed.

'You see what I mean?'

'I should have seen it long ago. The child offended him
because it was not perfect. He regarded it in the same way
that he would have regarded a Chippendale chair with a
damaged back.'

'Precisely. I warned you that my theory was far-fetched.'

Mr. Green sighed. 'Sometimes the truest theories are
those that are the furthest fetched, even if they have to be
fetched from very unpleasant places.'

Mr. Kauffman had no opportunity to ask him to explain
this cryptic remark, for as he spoke Mr. Green rose to his
feet, observing that he must already have outstayed his
welcome. It was in vain that Mr. Kauffman pleaded with
him to stay—to refresh himself, if only for a few minutes,
with the contemplation of a Joachim Patinir which he had
recently acquired—such a superb picture, with the bluest
and most miraculous sky that even Patinir had ever painted,
a sky of real magic. Mr. Green was investigating another
kind of magic. And its colour was not blue.

19

GOLD, STUDDED WITH SAPPHIRES

THE chimes of Big Ben were striking six o'clock when Waller arrived back at the Yard. He had spent a busy day, but it was not over yet. As he opened the door of his office Sergeant Bates rose smartly from his desk.

'I'm glad you've come, sir.' There was a gleam of excitement in his eye. 'There's been a development in the Larue case.'

'Another?' Waller's voice was not very enthusiastic. Most of the developments, to date, had proved barren enough.

'Yes, sir. Involving one of the guests at the party, Mr. Cecil Gower-Jones.'

'That's new at any rate. What's he been up to?'

'His flat was burgled this afternoon. They caught the thief, about an hour ago. And some of the stuff he had on him will be pretty difficult for Mr. Gower-Jones to explain.'

Waller's interest quickened, and he listened attentively while Bates told the story. Mr. Gower-Jones, it seemed, had left his flat in the King's Road, Chelsea, shortly after luncheon, to attend a concert at the Festival Hall. The performance had not come up to his expectations, and he had left after the first interval. On reaching home at a quarter to four he was met by his daily woman, who had arrived only just before his return, to find that the door of the flat had been forced, and that the place had been ransacked. She had naturally telephoned for the police.

'This is where things get interesting, sir,' continued Bates. 'The nearest station is Yeoman's Row, and the sergeant on duty was young Stubbs.'

'I know him. A bright lad.'

'Yes, sir. Well, Stubbs was along in the space of five minutes, and he found Mr. Gower-Jones giving this woman hell for calling in the police at all. What's more, he turned on Stubbs and told him that he wasn't wanted. He said that he couldn't afford the publicity, and that in any case nothing of any value had been stolen—only a couple of shirts and an old suit. Well, Stubbs would have known how to deal with that sort of situation, but before he could say anything, Mr. Gower-Jones had run upstairs and slammed the door in his face, and was calling out through the door that he had nothing further to say, and that if the police wanted to get into the flat they'd have to produce a search warrant.'

Waller nodded. 'The public,' he observed, 'grow more co-operative every day. Go on.'

'I'll cut a long story short, sir. It was a piece of cake for Stubbs, sir, because the thief was still in the building, in the backyard, to be precise, where Stubbs had gone to have a routine check-up. It was laid out on a plate for him, sir. He walked out to the back-yard, and there was this chap— one of the Chelsea regulars—quietly putting a leather bag into the dustbin, with the idea of calling for it later on. There wasn't any rough stuff, there wasn't even an argument. The chap just said it was a fair cop and held out his hands. And Stubbs took him back to the station. And when they opened the bag, what d'you think they found, sir?'

'You're supposed to be a policeman, Bates, not a writer of whodunnits.' Waller's voice was gruff, but good humoured.

Bates grinned. 'Thank you, sir. I've got the list here.' He took up a piece of paper lying by his side. 'There are a good many items, but there's only one that concerns us. This is how Stubbs describes it: One lady's vanity case, in eighteen carat gold, $3\frac{1}{2}$ inches by $2\frac{1}{2}$ inches, with a border of diamonds. In the centre an elaborate monogram, carried out in emeralds. The letters M.L.'

2

Waller sat up with a jerk.

'Does Gower-Jones know they've got the thief?'

'No, sir. Stubbs thought he'd have a word with you first.'

'Good lad. I'll speak to him.' He lifted the receiver, then put it down again. 'Wait a minute; I think I'll have a word with Lloyd first. In the meantime you can get hold of Stubbs from your own room.'

'Very good, sir.'

'Tell him to contact Gower-Jones urgently. Tell him to lay on the heat. Tell him to say that if he isn't at Yeoman's Row in record time to identify his stuff, it'll be just too bad. Tell him to ring back as soon as he's got him, and I'll be down.'

'Very good, sir.' Bates went out.

A minute later Waller was speaking to Andrew Lloyd. The financier's voice came through against a background of ticker-tape. 'Superintendent Waller?'

'Yes, sir. Sorry to disturb you, sir, but it's a matter of Miss Larue's jewellery.'

'What about it?'

'Do you remember a gold vanity case with her initials in emeralds?'

'Certainly. I gave it to her.'

'What would you estimate its value to be?'

Without an instant's hesitation he replied: 'The price of the gold case at Cartier's was four hundred guineas. It was second-hand, and was therefore not liable to purchase tax. The cost of adding the monogram was three hundred guineas. The emeralds are not valuable in themselves, but the work is expensive. The border of diamonds was nine hundred guineas. They are not large stones but they are of first-rate quality. The total cost of the case was therefore sixteen hundred guineas, which is £1680. I would estimate its break-up value at slightly over a thousand pounds.'

'Can you tell me when you last saw her use this case?

'Yes. On the night of her death.'

'You are sure of that?'

'Quite. I never cared for the case. It was her taste, not mine. And I remember telling her that it was a great deal too ostentatious to use in a country house. Why are you asking me these questions?'

Waller hesitated. He saw no reason to take Lloyd completely into his confidence, as yet. 'I'd rather not give the reason on the telephone, sir.'

'As you wish. Is that all?'

'One last question, sir. This case—was Miss Larue attached to it? I mean, would it be the sort of thing she would be inclined to give away?'

A short laugh answered him. 'Miss Larue was greatly attached to anything in eighteen carat gold. And she never gave anything away. Not even herself.'

The receiver clicked and the conversation ended.

There was a knock on the door and Bates entered.

'They've contacted Gower-Jones, sir. He's on his way down.'

'Good.' Waller rose from his desk. 'We'll go and meet him.'

3

Even if Waller had not been well acquainted with the geography of the police station at Yeoman's Row he would have had no difficulty in finding his way to the interrogation room, by the sound of the angry voice of Mr. Cecil Gower-Jones echoing down the corridor. 'How many more times have I got to tell you?' he was saying. 'How often does one have to say the same thing?'

'Once is usually enough, sir.' Waller spoke as he pushed open the door.

Gower-Jones turned with a start. 'Oh—it's you!' he snapped.

'Good evening, sir.' Waller nodded at Stubbs, and glanced at a collection of objects ranged on the table in front of him. 'Is this the stuff?'

'Yes, sir. The gentleman's indentified it all.'

For a moment there was a pause, while Waller bent over the table. With one exception it was not a very distinguished haul—some cuff-links, an old watch, a pearl tie-pin, a camera, and various silver trinkets. But the exception was sufficiently remarkable to make Waller raise his eyebrows. In the hard glare of the ceiling light the vanity case flashed and sparkled with a shameless arrogance. Lloyd had been right to call it ostentatious.

Gower-Jones' petulant voice broke the silence. 'I suppose you're looking at that wretched case.'

Waller nodded and picked it up. It was very heavy. 'A valuable object, sir,' he said.

'So what?'

'May I ask how it came into your possession?'

'I've told this young man at least a dozen times. It was given to me.'

'By Miss Larue?'

'Yes. And I don't see what business it is of yours.'

'Anything that concerns the death of Miss Larue is my business.'

'Why do you imagine that it concerns her death?'

Waller ignored this question. 'It's rather an unusual object, wouldn't you say, for a lady to give to a gentleman?'

Gower-Jones shrugged his shoulders. 'Perhaps Miss Larue may have taken a liking to me. It is possible, you know.' In spite of his obvious agitation there was a faint smirk of complacency on his face. It faded under Waller's cold stare.

'Was there any particular reason for this . . . gift?'

'What do you mean . . . reason? I was hard up, that was all.'

'And she gave it to you on the understanding that you would sell it?'

'Naturally.'

'And retain the proceeds?'

'Yes . . . yes.' His voice was shrill with impatience. 'I really do think these questions are quite gratuitously unpleasant.'

'Do you remember when she gave it to you?'

'It was one evening when we were drinking champagne cocktails.'

'Was she quite sober at the time?'

Mr. Gower-Jones drew himself up to his full height of five feet two inches. 'Are you suggesting that I would take advantage . . .'

'I'm not suggesting anything, sir. I'm only trying to get the facts. Do you remember the exact date of the gift?'

'I never remember dates.'

'But it was some days before her death?'

'Oh yes. Two or three, I should think.'

Waller paused. 'I suppose you know that she was using this case on the night she died?'

Gower-Jones looked up sharply. There was a light of fear in his eyes. He did not reply.

'Can you explain that?' insisted Waller.

The young man collected himself with an effort. 'We agreed that it would be better that way,' he said.

'I see. You thought it would be better if she continued using it—to avoid rousing comment?'

'That's right,' he agreed eagerly. 'To avoid rousing comment.'

'You've no means of corroborating this story, I suppose?'

'I don't see that it needs any corroboration. It's perfectly true.'

Waller nodded. 'All the same, sir, I think it would be better if you left this with us for a while.'

Gower-Jones gulped, and his hand moved towards the table in an involuntary gesture.

'Very much better, sir' insisted Waller.

The little man stared at the glittering object on the table. He was like a child reaching for a toy. Then he dropped his hand.

'Very well.' He forced a shrill laugh. 'I'm sure I don't want the wretched thing at the moment, not if it's going to cause any trouble. But as soon as all this fuss and bother is finished, I shall expect to have it back. Is that clearly understood?'

For reply Waller picked up the case and handed it to Stubbs. 'This can go in the safe,' he said.

'Is that clearly understood?' repeated Gower-Jones, in rather fainter tones.

Waller still ignored the question. 'This business will come up in about three weeks, sir,' he said. 'You'll be needed in court to identify the stolen objects. I think we can arrange that the vanity case will not be included in the list.' He turned to Stubbs. 'You'll attend to that?'

'I'll see to it, sir.'

'And the case?' Gower-Jones' voice had sunk to a whisper.

'It will come to no harm, sir.'

4

Back at his office, Waller sat down at his desk and drew out once again the plan of Broome Place which Andrew Lloyd had given him, showing the position of the various characters in the drama at the moment when Margot Larue had met her death.

He pin-pointed the cross marked G-J. It was placed half-way down the corridor leading to the dead woman's room. And yet Gower-Jones' own bedroom was on the other side of the house.

He opened the file of evidence; he wanted to refresh his memory on the explanation that Gower-Jones had given for his presence in the corridor.

Here it was: *I went up to my bedroom to fetch a handkerchief. Broome Place is such a vast house that I forgot the precise location of my room. I heard the shot just as I realized that I was walking*

*in the wrong direction. I turned back, to meet Mr. and Mrs.
Lloyd walking up the staircase.*

At the time Waller had taken down this statement, it
had seemed straightforward enough. There had been
nothing to connect Gower-Jones with the tragedy of
Margot Larue; he had been merely a super, hovering in
the wings.

But now?

Had Mr. Gower-Jones really taken the wrong turning?
Was it so very likely? He was an intelligent man; he was
not a heavy drinker; and he had been a guest in the house
for several days.

But if he had deliberately gone to Margot Larue's
room—or at least, in its direction—why? Even if there
were some romantic connexion, which seemed in the
highest degree improbable, the woman was drunk. Wait
a minute! Supposing that he had said to himself . . . 'This
woman's drunk. She's got something that I could sell for
a thousand pounds. I could tiptoe into her room . . .'

Waller frowned and shook his head. The idea was
grotesque . . . this flimsy little man, committing the ultimate
crime merely to gain possession of a vanity case. And yet,
he was too old a hand to dismiss an idea merely because it
was grotesque. He had seen the face of humanity distorted
into too many fantastic grimaces to be surprised by any
expression that it might assume.

He pushed the plan away from him with a sigh. He
stared at the blank wall opposite him. That was all he saw
at the moment, a blank wall, shadowed by many faces—
faces that seemed to be mocking him.

20

A WALK IN THE GARDEN

BROOME PLACE, thought Mr. Green, had never looked more beautiful than on the following morning. The wind had risen during the night and as he drew his curtains and stared down into the valley, the crimsons and the yellows of blowing branches seemed a vast, shifting tapestry of colour.

After breakfast he sat down at his desk. He spread out a sheet of paper and a piece of india-rubber, and sharpened a pencil. He intended to sketch a little picture. He had some talent for drawing, and in his long-distant undergraduate days he had produced several modest water-colours which were pleasing enough to hang on the walls of the country vicarage where he had spent his long vacations.

This picture, he reflected with a sigh, would not be so pleasing. But it had to be done, if only to clarify his thoughts. Sometimes, when the pattern of a story was befogged with words, the only way to make it clear, to bring out the essential design, was to draw it.

This Mr. Green proceeded to do.

But the design which slowly emerged from his plump, patient fingers was so strange that the casual observer might have wondered if Mr. Green had lost his reason.

In the centre of the drawing he sketched the body of a baby. A thin starveling creature. He drew a line through the baby's body, and by the side he sketched another baby— a fat bouncing cherub of a boy. Over this he placed a mark of interrogation. And then he drew yet another baby . . . but this time he traced the outlines in dots.

He paused and put down his pencil. Then he nodded. So far so good. At the top of the picture, Mr. Green sketched the rough outline of a woman's face, a woman whose eyes were closed. Underneath he wrote . . . Margot Larue, deceased.

At the bottom of the picture he drew the figures of five men and three women, very roughly, in a few lines. He placed these figures in two straight rows. Underneath he wrote their names . . . Lloyd, Sir Luke, Lord Richard, Gower-Jones, Grey (alias Jones), Mrs. Lloyd, Lady Coniston, Miss Kane.

In the third row he placed a solitary figure. He did not indicate whether it was a man or a woman. Underneath he wrote a single letter . . .X.

And then he proceeded to link these various figures . . . the dead women, the babies, the *dramatis personae* at the foot of the page . . . with a complicated series of lines, weaving in and out, until his picture looked like some archaic family tree. Some of the lines touched each other once, some several times, some of them not at all. But all of them linked, directly or indirectly, with the single figure X.

Mr. Green laid down his pencil and studied his little picture. Yes—they all fitted in. All except one line. And that, he felt, he would be able to draw before the day was out.

It was then that the telephone rang.

2

Waller brought him back to the immediate present.

'If I told you that Gower-Jones had jumped to top favourite in the list of suspects, what would you say?'

Mr. Green stared at the receiver for a moment, and then glanced at his picture.

Before he could reply the superintendent went on: 'No—that's an over-statement. But when you hear what's happened, you'll agree that he's got a good deal of explaining to do.'

Waller proceeded to tell the story of the discovery of the vanity case. Mr. Green listened to it with no apparent emotion. From time to time he tapped his picture with the point of his pencil. But he made no alteration in the main design.

When Waller had finished, Mr. Green made a very strange remark. He said: 'I must remember to speak to the housemaid.'

'What's that?' Waller's voice was very gruff.

'I beg your pardon. I was thinking aloud.'

'Well, if you can't think any better than that, I shan't tell you the next development.'

'What is that?'

'Your Mr. Jones has been on the telephone. What's more, he's asking for help.'

And now Mr. Green sat up very sharply indeed. 'Jones? Help?' he echoed.

'Perhaps I should say he's offering to give it.'

'Please be more explicit.'

'He rang me half an hour ago to tell me to "stand by" tonight. Sounded pretty cock-a-hoop. I'm not used to getting orders to "stand by", particularly from young gentlemen like your Mr. Jones, but since we're kidding him along I said O.K.'

'Where does he want you?'

'At Broome Place. At seven sharp.'

'Did he give you any reason?'

'Yes. He said he might have something of interest to tell me about the death of Margot Larue.'

Mr. Green frowned. 'Did he use those precise words? I mean, did he say he *might* have something to tell you? Or that he *would* have something?'

'He said "might". In fact, he emphasized it.'

'I see.' Mr. Green nodded to himself.

'Well?' Waller sounded impatient. 'I suppose you're going to tell me that I'll be coming down on a wild goose chase?'

'On the contrary. I think you will be coming down for

the last act of the most absorbing drama we have ever witnessed together.'

'Aren't you a bit of an optimist if you think it's the last act?'

'I am always an optimist.' He sighed, so deeply that he seemed to belie this statement. 'Seven o'clock, you say?'

'That's right. Still no comments?'

'None. Except that I trust you will be punctual.'

There was a sharp click as Waller hung up.

Mr. Green walked to the window and stared out. The wind was still rising; the coloured tapestry of leaves and branches was blowing more richly than ever. He had a sudden urge to go out, and walk.

He went downstairs. As he stepped into the cloak-room to find his overcoat he heard a voice round the corner. It was Mrs. Lloyd, speaking into the hall telephone. Her voice was calm and soothing.

'Of course, darling,' she was saying. 'I shall be here. And please do not say things like that.' There was a moment's silence. Then she spoke again . . . and now, though her voice was still calm, it had a note of conviction, almost of command.

'This is not the end,' she said, 'it is the beginning.'

Mr. Green stepped out of the cloak-room, tucking in his scarf.

Mrs. Lloyd turned quickly.

'You are going for a walk?' Her face still bore a happy smile. 'May I come with you?'

'I should be delighted.'

She stretched out her hand for a fur that lay on the chest beside her. The fur was of exquisite silver mink, but she slipped it over her shoulder's as though it were a peasant's scarf.

'We might go down and see the polymorphums.'

'That had been my intention.'

With an impulsive gesture she linked her arm in his. 'There may not be another chance to see them.'

Mr. Green turned his head. He wondered if he had understood.

'The frosts are on the way. And the last leaves will soon have fallen.'

'Quite,' said Mr. Green. The word was terse, but he said it gently.

They walked across the terrace and took the main azalea walk that led towards the lakes. At every twist and turn the fabulous garden revealed fresh beauties—a pool of purple colchicums round the steps of a Palladian temple —a sudden scarlet flash of Kaffir lilies in the shelter of a grotto—a glade of silver birches in which the rare *sternbergea* . . . the so-called winter daffodil . . . was flowering as freely as the crocuses of spring.

'I think that this must be the most beautiful garden in the world,' she said quietly.

'I know of none other more beautiful.'

'Thank you. Even when I was a child I thought it was very near to heaven.'

'You knew it as a child?'

'But of course. Before my uncle was obliged to sell it, Broome had been in my family for generations. It's in my blood.' She gave a light laugh. 'I am surprised that you should be unaware of that, Mr. Green. I thought you had been delving rather thoroughly into our pasts.'

He made no reply.

'But perhaps you have been too preoccupied with the events of the last three weeks.'

They walked on in silence.

'Yes,' she said at length. 'It is the most beautiful garden in the world. I only hope it will not break Andrew's heart to leave it.'

'But has he ever shown any wish to leave it?'

'It is not a question of wishing. It is a question of necessity.' She turned to him with a little smile. 'Surely you know that we are ruined?'

Mr. Green stared at her in astonishment. Before he could reply she went on: 'You surprise me again, Mr.

Green. How is it possible that you have failed to discover such a very obvious fact?'

'I assure you that I had no idea. I am deeply . . .' He paused, at a loss for words.

Once again she linked her arm in his. 'I was being unfair. There was no reason why you should have known it. There is only one other person in the world knows it, apart from myself.'

'Sir Luke Coniston?'

'Of course.'

'Then it concerns the shares in Wild Range Oil?'

'Among other things. Sir Luke was shrewder than we imagined. Besides, he had one great advantage which was denied to Andrew. He could read Andrew's mind—through Margot Larue. We now know that he had been doing so for over a year.'

Mr. Green was frowning. Once again he was asking himself the question which had troubled him before—had he underrated the economic motive? Apart from that, he was personally distressed by the thought of the dilemma of the woman beside him. And he was unhappy at the thought of these enchanted gardens falling into hands that might destroy them.

'But surely,' he said at length, 'the situation may not be so desperate as you suggest?' He glanced in the direction of the house. 'Surely your husband has assets of immense value, apart from his interests in the City? The pictures alone . . .'

She laughed lightly. 'Would you like some facts and figures? Andrew is a financial genius, but he is a self-made man; he has had to build up his own capital, and that takes time, particularly when you live at the rate of a thousand pounds a week. You talk of assets. Let us see what they are. This estate is worth perhaps £100,000, if one could find a buyer for it. I would value the pictures and the furniture at approximately half a million. My own jewels are comparatively negligible. Let us say £80,000. You see, Mr. Green, it is all very small beer, when one is involved in operations which show a loss of nearly two million pounds.'

Mr. Green sighed. "Small beer" would not have been his own description of such figures. He realized, however, that there was no irony in her observation; like her husband, she had the habit of thinking in millions.

It was in the same spirit that she continued: 'I am afraid you may have been misled by the façade, Mr. Green. It is a very prosperous façade, is it not? And as I told you, it costs us approximately a thousand pounds a week. That has never disturbed Andrew. He has always had a casual conviction that he could make £50,000 between luncheon and dinner, any day of the week, if he set his mind to it. Perhaps he might have done . . . if it had not been for Sir Luke.'

They had reached the great lake. Its surface was angrily rippled by the rising wind; the last of the water-lilies seemed to be straining at their roots and the branches of the weeping willows were streaking the water as though in some futile lamentation.

She let go of his arm and stared across the water. 'It would be very pleasant,' she said, 'to think that one day I might be able to pay back Sir Luke in his own coin. Yes, it would be very pleasant to pay him back, at compound interest.'

She spoke quietly, but in her voice was a note of venom so bitter that Mr. Green found himself shuddering.

She turned to him quickly. 'It is cold standing here,' she said. 'And you have only a light overcoat. Let us go back to the house.'

21

INTO THE ABYSS

MR. GREEN sat at the window of his bedroom, listening to the wind. This had always been one of his favourite occupations, and Broome Place, on this wild November evening, was an ideal situation in which to indulge it. The old house flung back a thousand answers to the wind's assaults, shrill protests in the high chimneys, long-drawn sighs in the gables, and many threats and whispers in the dark arches of the courtyard.

To the clamour of the house was added the dark chorus of the forest trees that shadowed it. He had a fancy that these trees were crying out to one another, sending messages in a language that he could nearly, but not quite, understand. The leaders of the chorus were the giant pines immediately outside his window; their voices had a fierce urgency that sometimes rose almost to a scream. For a moment they would die down, as though waiting for an answer, and then the answer would come from far and wide, from the silver cypresses at the end of the terrace, from the ancient beeches on the slopes above, even from the harsh clatter of the magnolias on the wall. But the pines were never satisfied; again and again they returned to the assault, as though they were demanding not merely assent but action. As Mr. Green leant forward and stared into the night, he had a fleeting impression that the giants were actually on the move, that they were drawing closer to the house.

Mr. Green continued to listen to the wind, trying to interpret its language. If you had asked him what he was doing, at this moment, you would have received precisely this reply, and he would have expected it to be literally interpreted. He believed that the wind had a language, with a vocabulary of infinite subtlety, to be read in the lisp of leaves and the sigh of branches; he believed that this language was capable of interpretation, if only a man were wise enough and clean enough to learn its roots and its syntax.

And then Mr. Green sat up with a start. The turbulent, sighing chorus of the trees was suddenly interrupted by another sound. It was as though a soaring orchestral passage for strings and woodwind had been cut short by a staccato beat on a kettledrum. And another . . . and another.

The sound was in a language that Mr. Green understood all too well. It was the sound of a revolver shot. Of three revolver shots.

He sighed, and rose to his feet. He moved quickly, but not hurriedly. As he opened the door, he did not forget to switch out the light. Even in moments of crisis, Mr. Green remembered the smaller economies.

2

Mr. Green paused at the top of the staircase. Here the sound of the wind was muted, and the various sounds of the house, the ticking of clocks, the rustle of curtains, proclaimed themselves. He had expected to hear other sounds—doors slamming, voices raised in anger or alarm. There were none. Then he remembered. There had been *three* shots. He caught his breath, and hurried downstairs.

He reached the bottom step. As he did so the door of the library was flung open, and Nancy Lloyd appeared. At the same moment Palmer came running down the long gallery. When he saw his mistress he paused.

'I thought I heard . . .' he began.

'There has been an accident,' she interrupted.

'Mr. Lloyd?'

'No. Not Mr. Lloyd. You had better go in there and see what you can do.'

'What about getting the doctor, madam?'

She looked at him with a curious expression. 'I will see to that.'

'Very good, madam.' He went towards the open door.

For a moment she stayed there, looking straight in front of her. She had not noticed Mr. Green. Then she began to walk swiftly in the direction of the main entrance. The rustle of her silk dress echoed down the long gallery, which seemed to be wrapped in a strange silence.

Mr. Green emerged. She started, and stared at him. Her lips twisted into the ghost of a smile.

'Mr. Green!' Her voice was very faint. 'One can always rely on you being here when you are wanted.'

'Or when I am not wanted?' he said gently.

She was very pale, but she held herself erect, and she was not trembling.

'There has been an accident,' she repeated.

'So I gather.'

'A . . . a friend of my husband's. I am afraid he is seriously hurt. Perhaps . . . perhaps you would go and see if there is anything you could do.'

'Of course.' But he did not move.

'Is there . . . is there anything you want to ask me?'

'I think not.'

'You are looking at me so strangely.'

Mr. Green blinked. 'I beg your pardon. I am afraid my wits were wandering. I will go at once.'

'That is very kind of you.'

She turned and walked away from him. She did not look back. But Mr. Green looked back. He saw her turn the corner. A few moments later a chill gust of wind swept down the gallery, blowing out the heavy curtains. Mr. Green put his hand over his eyes, and his lips moved as though he were saying a prayer.

Then he pushed open the door and stood there, blinking. He had a sudden feeling that the whole great room was bathed in red. There were only two lights burning; one of them spot-lit the scarlet cloak of the Patinir madonna, the other threw a lurid pool over the crimson velvet of the

Knole settee. But the most vivid patch of red was seeping from a wound in the side of the man who was lying back on the cushions, with Lloyd kneeling by him.

Mr. Green walked across and bent down. Without saying a word he lifted the man's wrist and felt the pulse.

Lloyd looked up. His eyes were dazed and his voice was hoarse. 'Is he going to die?'

Mr. Green did not seem to hear the question. Very gently he let go of the man's wrist. Then he knelt down and put his hand on the handkerchief which Lloyd was pressing over the wound. He lifted it and frowned. Then he pressed it back again.

He turned to Palmer, who was standing behind him, very white about the gills.

'You will find a first-aid case in the cupboard of my room,' he said. 'Will you run and fetch it at once, please?'

'Yes, sir.' Palmer turned to go.

'One moment. Before you do that, you had better telephone for the doctor.'

'Mrs. Lloyd is attending to that, sir.'

Mr. Green did not address his reply to Palmer. He was looking straight at Lloyd.

'I think you will find that Mrs. Lloyd has forgotten to do so,' he said quietly.

'Very good, sir.'

He hurried out. Mr. Green was still staring at Lloyd. Then he lowered his eyes. A few inches from Lloyd's knees lay a revolver.

'Is he going to die?' Lloyd spoke in a whisper.

'I think he has a chance.'

'Thank God! You realize that I shot him in self defence?'

'Yes?'

'I swear it. He was trying to blackmail me."

'I see.'

'He threatened me with this damned thing. It was frightening Nancy and I tried to take it from him. There was a struggle . . . and it went off.'

'Quite.'

'Don't you believe me?'

Mr. Green did not reply. He was watching the wounded man. His eyelids had fluttered open, and his lips were moving.

'Lie still,' he said quietly.

The man groaned and turned his head.

'Quite still,' repeated Mr. Green. 'Quite, quite still. It is your best chance.'

The eyelids flickered back again.

'Isn't there something I can get? Some brandy or something?'

'Not for the moment.'

Lloyd struggled to his feet. 'Palmer's taking a hell of a time,' he muttered.

The seconds ticked by. Suddenly Mr. Green looked towards the door.

'I think I heard the sound of a car,' he said.

'Good God! I'd forgotten. That'll be Waller.'

'Did you send for him?'

'No.' Lloyd glanced at the wounded man. 'He did.'

'With what object?'

'It was part of his little scheme. You'll understand shortly.'

As he spoke Palmer hurried through the door, carrying a heavy wooden box.

'Over here, please,' said Mr. Green.

Palmer set the box on the floor. 'The doctor's on his way, sir,' he panted. 'And there's a car just drawn up outside. I think it's the superintendent, sir.'

Lloyd went to the door. 'I'll go and meet him.' He turned to Mr. Green. 'You'll be all right for a minute or two?'

Mr. Green nodded. The two men left him alone.

Mr. Green opened his first-aid box and set to work. There was nothing very drastic to be done until the doctor came. But at least he knew how to administer a sedative, how to clean the wound and check the bleeding. Judging from the steadiness of the man's pulse, no vital organ had been affected. If he could be kept completely still he had a good chance.

Meanwhile, at the end of the long gallery, Lloyd faced the superintendent. He was so agitated that he had forgotten to close the heavy door of the portico, so that the wind swept in, billowing the tapestries.

Waller's face was grim as he listened to the story, but he made no comment. He let Lloyd talk. The only time he interrupted was when Lloyd mentioned that Mr. Green was attending to the wounded man.

'What's Mr. Green say about him?'

'He thinks he'll pull through.'

'That's good enough for me.'

Lloyd finished his story. It was more detailed than the one he had told Mr. Green, but in essence it was the same.

Then Waller spoke. 'How soon do you expect Mrs. Lloyd to return, sir?'

Lloyd stared at him. 'Return?' he echoed.

'She is a vital witness. I'd like to see her as soon as possible.'

'But of course. I'll fetch her at once.'

'I'm afraid that's impossible for the moment, sir. Mrs. Lloyd is not in the house.'

'What do you mean?'

'She has gone out.'

'Out. Where?'

'Her car nearly collided with mine at the entrance.'

'But I don't understand. Why should she go out on a night like this, without telling me?' Lloyd flicked his fingers nervously. Then his face cleared. 'Wait a minute! Perhaps she went for the doctor.'

'I don't think so, sir.'

'Why not? Did she tell you so?'

'She didn't stop, sir. She was driving at a very high speed. A very dangerous speed, if you ask me. Particularly on that narrow road.'

'The road isn't so narrow as that.'

'I beg your pardon, sir. The road to the valley is very narrow indeed.'

Lloyd started, and took a step forward. 'The road to the valley!' His fingers went on twitching automatically, and then were still. Suddenly he cried 'No!' And again, in a voice of intolerable anguish . . . 'No—no!'

He stood there, his face twisted and tortured. Then without a word, he ran through the door into the night.

Waller followed. There were fitful gleams of moonlight through the racing clouds, and he saw that Lloyd was heading for the stable buildings. For a moment he lost sight of him, and took the wrong turning. Then he doubled back into the courtyard, just as Lloyd was flinging open the doors of the furthest garage.

The car was already gliding forward as Waller jumped in. It was a powerful Italian model, open to the winds, and it leapt up the drive with a snarl and a splutter, like an angry beast.

'Your lights, sir!' shouted Waller. They were driving in the dark.

Lloyd turned the switch. The yellow beam flared against the trunks of the trees, flashing past them at an unholy pace. There was a scream of brakes as they passed the gates of the lodge. And another scream of brakes as they swerved left into the road to the valley.

And now Waller resigned himself to the nightmare. There was nothing else he could do. He was deafened by the roaring of the wind, half blinded by the glare of the lights. The road grew narrower and narrower, and from time to time the overhanging branch of a tree shot out from the darkness, like a giant hand seeking to arrest them. He had a sense that he was driving with a devil . . . but a devil who had luck on his side. Lloyd flung the great car down these dark perilous corridors with an uncanny skill.

He glanced at the luminous dial of his watch. They had been driving for seven minutes. They must be near the end of the road. Eight minutes, nine minutes. The lane twisted and shot upwards They seemed to be going up the side of a mountain. Suddenly the trunks of the trees around him were lit by a red glow. Somewhere out there, in the darkness, something was on fire.

The car stopped . . . on the edge of infinity. The glow on the trunks of the trees grew brighter. Lloyd had run to the edge and was standing there, shading his eyes with his hands. He looked strangely small and shrunken. Waller followed him. He came to his side and stared down into the depths of the quarry.

There was a twisted lump of metal from which flames were leaping. The wind played with the flames, and giant shadows swept across the cliffs.

Lloyd turned and spoke. His voice was quite calm.

'I would like to go down,' he said. 'And I would prefer to be alone.'

22

MR. GREEN BEGINS

THE storm died, and a mist came creeping up from the lakes in the valley, cloaking the great house in a veil of sadness. Because of this veil, the events of these last few hours had, for Mr. Green, a strange unreality—the cars that came and went seemed to be drifting out of nowhere, the voices that echoed down the long gallery whispered like the voices of ghosts.

Mr Green had luncheon with Charlotte in his room. Apart from a grim and brief encounter on the previous night, he had not seen Andrew Lloyd; nor had Waller and Bates put in an appearance. His only contact with the outside world had been through Palmer, who appeared from time to time with miscellaneous items of information. Perhaps the most important of these was that the wounded man was making steady progress, and was now off the danger list.

Charlotte touched his hand. 'Darling . . . couldn't we go now? This very minute?'

'No, my dear. I may still be needed.'

'I suppose that means that you will have to tire yourself out as usual—explaining to Waller and everybody what really happened?'

'I do not know what really happened.'

She stared at him in astonishment. 'But darling, you *always* know!'

'Perhaps I am growing old.'

He sighed. There was a knock on the door. It was Palmer, bearing a note from Andrew Lloyd. He opened it and read:

Dear Mr. Green,

You must forgive me for my neglect; the events of last night have involved me in a considerable amount of business. I hope, however, to have dealt with the more urgent matters by late afternoon.

I have no doubt that you have by now unravelled the tangled web of circumstances which culminated in the death of my wife, and that you will have come to certain definite conclusions. I am told by Mr. Waller that you might be persuaded to explain to us the various steps which led you to these conclusions. If so, I should feel honoured if you would allow me to be present at your exposition.

May we meet at five o'clock, in the library? My presence need cause you no embarrassment. I am aware of my own follies and weaknesses, and it is a matter of indifference to me if they are exposed.

Yours sincerely,
Andrew Lloyd.

Mr. Green looked up from the letter. 'Would you inform Mr. Lloyd that I shall be pleased to see him at five o'clock?'

2

The Louis Seize clock on the chimney-piece struck five. Mr. Green, at a table near the fire, tapped his fingers and cleared his throat. For the first time in his life, he was feeling nervous. He had not been exaggerating when he had informed Charlotte that he did not know all the facts. Certain vital points were still escaping him.

There was another cause of this nervousness—the presence of Andrew Lloyd. However, Lloyd had asked for it.

He took a last look round the room. Waller and Bates occupied the sofa immediately opposite him. Charlotte was in the armchair on the left. She gave him a smile of reassurance.

Lloyd sat bolt upright in a Tudor chair, staring into the fire, with his back towards Mr. Green. Without turning his head he spoke.

'If you are ready, Mr. Green?'

'Thank you. I am quite ready.'

He began.

'Since Mr. Lloyd is a newcomer to these expositions—the rest of you will excuse me if I remind him of the main principles which guide me in any inquiry. They are all variations of one central principle . . . the reconciliation of action with character. In other words, I attach the greatest possible importance to any action, by any of the participants in the drama, which seems *out* of character.'

'Let me give one very simple example. Almost my first clue in this case was provided by a gramophone record. This record was lying on the turn-table, where it lay on the night of Miss Larue's death. It was a piece of modern jazz by a coloured trumpeter called Blue Joseph. In order to create the atmosphere of that last night, I played it—or rather, began to play it, for after a couple of minutes I could endure no more. For me, it was the musical equivalent of Pandora's box.

'Yet it was Mrs. Lloyd who had purchased this record—Mrs. Lloyd who loved the music of Couperin and Scarlatti. If ever there was an action out of character it was the purchase of this record. For the moment, I will not tell you where it led me. I am merely citing it as an example of general principle.

'Let us regroup the players in the positions that they were occupying when the shot was fired. Thanks to Mr. Lloyd, we can do this with some precision. I have here a copy of the chart that he prepared for Mr. Waller. Several people are shown in this chart who might have entered Miss Larue's room, on the assumption that she met her death by some hand other than her own. The only persons who most certainly could *not* have entered her room were Mr. and Mrs. Lloyd themselves.

'I propose to deal with these persons one by one, in

the hope that we may be able to eliminate some of them from suspicion.

'Let us begin with Miss Kane. What do we know about her? We know that she was immensely rich, and accustomed to having her own way. Also, that she was exceedingly superstitious. Perhaps most of all, that she had a very bad complexion, of which she was almost morbidly self-conscious.

'That was not much to go on. But there was one awkward fact to be explained—from Miss Kane's point of view. On the morning after the tragedy, the key of one of the doors in her bedroom was missing, and it was the key that led directly into Miss Larue's bathroom.

'Nor is that all.' Here Mr. Green paused and glanced in the direction of the superintendent. 'Perhaps Mr. Waller will agree that I have a somewhat highly developed sense of smell.'

'Somewhat!' grunted Waller.

'Thank you.' Mr. Green gave a short sharp sniff. 'I can assure you that it does not always add to the pleasures or existence, though it sometimes enhances the faculties or perception. And in this case it informed me that Miss Kane had, in fact, entered Miss Larue's room on or about the moment that the shot was fired. My grounds for making this statement are purely olfactory. You will recollect that the broken fragments of a scent bottle were found scattered in Miss Larue's bathroom. The scent was curious, exotic, and exclusive to Miss Larue. But it was the same scent that I detected on the dress that Miss Kane was wearing three nights later. And that was the dress that she wore on the night of the tragedy.

'With which,' he concluded, 'for the moment, we will leave Miss Kane.'

3

'Let us turn to another character, Mr. Cecil Gower-Jones. What do we know about him? We know that he was a brilliant critic of music and of ballet. But what about his private life?

'Firstly, he was an amorist, with highly inflated notions of his own powers of physical attraction. It is a type that is not rare in the young male intellectual. In spite of the most unpromising exterior, Gower-Jones was invested, in his own imagination, with the powers of a Don Juan. You may think it is of small importance that even on the morning after the tragedy, within a few yards of the door of the room in which Miss Larue's body was lying, he made impertinent advances to one of the housemaids. But if you consider this behaviour, you may not perhaps find it so incongruous if I suggest to you that he also made advances to Miss Larue herself.

'What else did we know about Mr. Gower-Jones? Thanks to Mr. Waller's investigations we know that he was desperately hard-up. I have no doubt that he intended, during the course of the week-end, to ask Mr. Lloyd to lend him some money. He did not do so, for the very good reason that he obtained it by other means—by the gold vanity case.

'Are we then to assume that Mr. Gower-Jones shot Miss Larue for the sake of a gold vanity case? We have only to ask the question to perceive its absurdity. He was not only a weakling but a coward. Such an action would not only have been out of character, it would have been unthinkable.

'And now,' said Mr. Green, 'I am going to make a departure from my usual procedure; I am going to tell you what occurred, without giving you every detail of the deductive process. I do so for the sake of economy; we are dealing with two minor figures and you will be impatient to arrive at the more important actors.

'These, then, were the movements of Mr. Gower-Jones and Miss Kane at ten-forty on the night of October the thirteenth. I may as well tell you that both parties have fully—if reluctantly—endorsed the accuracy of my reconstruction. Let us take the man first. As soon as Mr. Gower-

Jones saw the jewelled case which Miss Larue had left by the side of the gramophone, he realized that here was a golden opportunity. For a moment the idea of theft did not occur to him. Don Juan was uppermost. He decided that he would use the case as an excuse for paying Miss Larue a visit.

'Mr. Gower-Jones went upstairs.

'And so, at almost the same moment, did Miss Kane, using the smaller staircase opposite the flower-room. But Miss Kane was animated by very different motives. It is now that we reach one of the few moments of comedy in our drama. You will find the clue to it in a single sentence in Miss Kane's original deposition. Speaking of Miss Larue, Miss Kane observed: "She was so mean that she wouldn't even lend you a pot of cold cream."

'That phrase suggested an actual grievance in Miss Kane's mind. It was not long before I was able to locate this grievance. She had quarrelled with Miss Larue, over a certain cream which—according to Miss Larue—had almost magical properties. It appears that she was deliberately taunting Miss Kane. This grievance smouldered through the whole day, and then, after Miss Larue had retired, Miss Kane decided to follow her, to tiptoe into her bathroom— you will remember that she had the key—and to steal this coveted prize which, to her small, superstitious brain, was worth its weight in gold.

'So there we have these two figures of comedy, against a tragic background, poised in their strategic positions at the crucial moment. Miss Kane is in the bathroom, stretching out her fingers towards the shelf. Mr. Gower-Jones is in the corridor, stretching out his fingers towards the handle. The door is shut against him. He raises his arm and knocks. Miss Kane hears the knock and takes fright; in her confusion she pushed over a bottle of scent, which breaks on the floor. She darts back to her room, locks the door and— in a panic—throws the key out of the window. Mr. Gower-Jones prepares to knock again, and then there is the sound of a shot. He too takes fright. What has happened? At all costs he must not be involved. He starts to walk back along the corridor. He is saying to himself . . . "I must have an excuse—I will tell them that I have lost my way." Which, as we know, was what he did say—with his hand in his pocket, resting on the jewelled case.'

Mr. Green tapped the silver ink-stand. 'I said that this was a scene of comedy. Now that I have re-enacted it, I wonder if that is true?'

He was suddenly conscious of a movement by the fire. Andrew Lloyd had turned and was staring at him. His face was set in a fixed smile.

'But of course it is true, Mr. Green,' he said softly. 'It is all highly diverting. Will you not continue?'

4

'We are now approaching the major figures in the drama. Perhaps we shall be able to eliminate them, perhaps not. One thing is common to these people; they all gave false evidence on vital points.

'Let us begin with Lady Coniston. There were two crucial matters to which she was a witness. The first was that Margot Larue had constantly threatened to commit suicide. In this statement she was supported by Mrs. Lloyd. Both women were emphatic about this point.

'Now this struck me as very curious. No other member of the house-party had heard these threats of suicide. From their knowledge of Miss Larue she was the last person to talk about suicide, still less to commit it. She was the least introspective of women, she was in perfect health, she was young, prospering, full of *joie de vivre*.

'However, there was an even more vital piece of evidence, to which there was only one witness—Lady Coniston herself. I refer, of course, to the direction of the shot. Lady Coniston stated that it came from the next room to her own. There seemed no reason to question her statement.

'But there was another curious detail about this part

of the evidence. When the various guests ran upstairs, Mrs. Lloyd paused at Lady Coniston's room, opened the door and spoke to her. According to her statement she said to her "You heard the shot?" Or words to that effect. She explained her action by saying that she had thought the sound of the shot to have come from Lady Coniston's room. She may of course have done so. The fact remains that for the second time, on a point of vital importance, we had to rely only on the word of Lady Coniston, backed up by the word of Mrs. Lloyd.

'I was therefore obliged to consider the possibility that there might be some sort of conspiracy between these two women. But the more I considered it, the less happy I felt about it. And yet I was convinced that both of them were giving false evidence. What was I to do about it?'

Mr. Green turned to the superintendent. 'You read detective stories, Mr. Waller. What is your feeling about red herrings?'

'They annoy me.'

'They annoy me also. But I suppose they are a necessary evil. However, if the red herrings were to be laid by the detective himself . . .?

'I'd say the author ought to be shot.'

'I was afraid that you might feel like that.' Mr. Green heaved a sigh. 'Because in order to clear up this matter I laid one of the most shameless red herrings that can ever have been contrived, either in fiction or in fact.

'It was on the day of the first performance of the revue. And it was entirely due to a casual remark that I made to Lady Coniston at luncheon. She happened to look up at one of the pictures on the opposite wall. I turned to her and said: "I believe it is uncertain whether that picture is by Brueghel the Elder or the Younger". She started, and replied: "I'm sure you merely say that to be polite." Then, in some confusion, she began to talk of the performance that night. I was so mystified by her answer that afterwards I went out into the garden, to do some hard thinking. Suddenly I understood. And I laid my little trap.'

He smiled across at Bates. 'You will remember that your brother was on duty in the neighbourhood of the theatre that evening. I gave him a simple task. All he had to do was to telephone an anonymous message containing a complicated number, 839766041.'

'Had that number any particular meaning?' demanded Waller.

'None whatever. I merely wanted to be sure that Lady Coniston would be obliged to copy it.'

Charlotte tapped her foot impatiently. 'But *why*?'

'I wanted to observe her in the act of writing.'

'Was she left-handed or something?'

'No, my dear. But you are getting warm. I stood near the telephone and watched her. She lifted the receiver with her right hand, and put it to her right ear. But when she wished to make a note of the number, she was obliged to keep the receiver at her right ear and support it with her left hand.'

Waller leant forward. 'You mean . . .'

'*I mean that—in her left ear—Lady Coniston was stone deaf.*'

The superintendent gave a low whistle. 'So that was it!'

'Precisely. And you will be the first to realize the implications.'

Waller nodded. 'For one thing, it invalidates the evidence of the direction of the shot.'

Charlotte interrupted. 'Was that why you produced that quite appalling sneeze, during the performance?'

'I'm afraid it was, my dear. I could not wait to see how she reacted.'

'But she didn't react at all.'

'Which, of course, was the whole point,' retorted Mr. Green.

Waller spoke again. He appeared to be thinking aloud. 'A person who is deaf in one ear has no sense of direction. If I were deaf in the left ear, and if a shot was fired in the next room, I should be unable to tell you whether it came from the left or the right.'

'Or above or below. Think it out.'

Waller shook his head. 'Above or below? No, I give it up. But there's something else. Why was she so determined that the shot *did* come from Margot Larue's room?'

'Have you forgotten the curious incident of Mrs. Lloyd opening her door, and asking her if she had heard the shot?'

'What's that got to do with it?'

'Supposing that Mrs. Lloyd's actual words had been . . . "Did you hear the shot *next door*?" What would Lady Coniston have replied? Think of her psychology. She was the vainest of women. She had a phobia about her deafness. If she were asked if she had heard anything, her instant reaction was to say yes.

'The same applies to the evidence of suicide. Supposing that Mrs. Lloyd had said to Lady Coniston . . . "Of course, you will remember how Margot Larue talked about suicide"? Once again, the immediate reaction of Lady Coniston would be to say yes. Anything rather than admit her deafness.'

'But why *should* Mrs. Lloyd . . .'

It was Charlotte who had begun to speak. But Andrew Lloyd interrupted her. 'Will Mr. Green allow me to say a word?'

'By all means.'

'Thank you. You have eliminated three characters—Miss Kane, Mr. Gower-Jones and Lady Coniston. For the sake of economy, may we also eliminate a fourth—Sir Luke?'

Mr. Green glanced at the superintendent. 'If Mr. Waller has no objection?'

Waller hunched his great shoulders. 'We've no evidence against him. Lord knows it isn't for lack of trying.'

Lloyd's lips twisted into a smile. 'For which I am much obliged. It would have given me a good deal of personal pleasure to have caused Sir Luke some discomfort. In the meantime, Mr. Green will agree with me that Sir Luke had no part in the actual death of Miss Larue?'

'That is so.'

Lloyd nodded. 'So the stage is emptying,' he said.

'There are only a few characters left.' His voice, of a sudden, had a curious veiled quality, as though he were speaking to himself. 'I feel as though I were waiting in the wings of a theatre, preparing to play a part of which I had not learned all the lines. It is an exhilarating sensation. Mr. Green, will you not continue?'

23

MR. GREEN CONTINUES

PERHAPS Andrew Lloyd's use of the theatrical metaphor made Mr. Green feel that the tension in the great room had subtly increased. He resumed at a heightened pace.

'Yes,' he said, 'the stage is emptying. But at the same time there are other figures who are beginning to make their appearance. By far the most important of these newcomers is the man upstairs—the wounded man whom we know by the name of Jones.'

He stared up to the ceiling as though he were listening for something, then he looked down again.

'And the man Jones,' he continued, 'must be coupled with another major figure, Lord Richard Marwood, for it is through Lord Richard that he comes into the picture at all.

'I will deal with Lord Richard first.

'From the beginning I was forced to the conclusion that Lord Richard was far more deeply involved in this tragedy than he cared to admit. My first suspicion arose from the coincidence of his arrival at the house within a few seconds of the firing of the shot. There is no doubt that he was, in fact, standing in the portico, ringing the bell, within the space of those few seconds. And those few seconds would have been quite inadequate for him to have returned from Miss Larue's room, assuming that he even entered it. It seemed, therefore, that Lord Richard was exonerated by the ticking of those few seconds.

'But I was not satisfied.

'It was on the Monday morning that my suspicions were confirmed, beyond any doubt, by a certain scrap of paper. It was a garage receipt for fifteen gallons of petrol, bearing the address of a garage in Mayfair. I discovered that it had been handed to Lord Richard at four o'clock on the Saturday afternoon. About ten minutes later he telephoned to Miss Kane telling her that his car had broken down. This, of course, was untrue. He then disappears from the picture for six hours.

'What had Lord Richard been doing in those six hours? I can tell you one thing he had *not* been doing. He had not been standing still. He had driven nearly two hundred and fifty miles. Where he had driven is not important; knowing Lord Richard's passion for speed we should probably be justified in assuming that he took to the open road, without any precise objective. What matters is that he lied about his breakdown, and that when he arrived at Broome, his petrol tank was nearly empty.

'Why?

'But there is another question, of the greatest importance. Why had nobody noticed his arrival until he rang the bell? The lodge-keeper was waiting up for him, waiting to close the gates as soon as he had driven through. It is difficult to believe that he could have failed to notice a car like Lord Richard's passing within a few yards of his window. It has particularly brilliant lights and an open exhaust which can be heard from a distance of a mile. And as we know, this is the only entrance; the West Lodge entrance is never used, and the gates are heavily padlocked.

'There was only one assumption that seemed to answer this question—namely that Lord Richard had stopped his car on the brow of the hill, had extinguished his lights and switched off his engine, and had free-wheeled the entire distance down the drive. This assumption, as it transpires, was correct.

'But why this extraordinary conduct?'

'Before we can answer that question we must turn our attention to Mr. Jones—who may still be described as the man upstairs, for that is all, at the moment, that we seem to know about him.'

2

'I happened to be among those present when Lord Richard encountered Mr. Jones for the first time, after the premiere of the review. There was no doubt that it *was* a first encounter. Lord Richard was obviously bewildered, and a few moments later he was equally obviously intimidated.

'On the very next day, Mr. Jones arrived at Broome Place, and was received by Lord Richard and Mr. Lloyd in the library. What transpired at their meeting Mr. Lloyd can tell you. I cannot. I am therefore obliged to rely on assumption. My assumption is that Mr. Jones was attempting to blackmail Lord Richard on a matter which also concerned Mr. Lloyd.' Mr. Green paused. 'And since Mr. Lloyd does not correct this assumption, we may conclude that it is correct.

'After Mr. Jones' interview, I was a passenger in the car in which Miss Kane drove him down to West Greenstead. During the journey I learned several things about Mr. Jones which increased my interest in him. And the most important of these was that Mr. Jones had been at Broome Place before.'

He turned to the superintendent. 'You remember glancing at the stable clock, on our first meeting?'

'Yes. It had stopped.'

'Quite. I discovered that it had stopped at midnight, a few hours after Miss Larue's death. Yet Mr. Jones referred to its chiming. When had he heard it? Not during the daytime; he had never been invited to the house. Besides, he had only arrived in the neighbourhood on the day before. I therefore assumed that he had heard it on the night of the tragedy.

'Let us try to fit these few pieces of the puzzle together. What do we see? We see the figure of Lord Richard, arriving secretly. We see the figure of Mr. Jones, standing in the shadows. We are forced to conclude that Mr. Jones witnessed some action of Lord Richard's which enabled him to threaten Lord Richard with exposure.

'But how? And why?'

Mr. Green glanced at the superintendent. 'Mr. Waller has sometimes accused me of taking leaps in the dark. He is right. At this point I decided to take such a leap. The vital question was . . . who *was* Mr. Jones? That he had some connection with Miss Larue, and that he was in a position to damage her, I had no doubt. But who *was* he? A relation? There was no sort of physical resemblance. A lover? All the facts suggested otherwise. There was one other possible connection. A husband.'

Mr. Green took a deep breath. The moment of climax had arrived. He waited for Andrew Lloyd to speak—waited for the contradiction.

It did not come.

Mr. Green had a sudden sense of relief. From now on his story would be easier to tell.

'There,' he said, 'we will leave Lord Richard and Mr. Jones. Before we return to them, I believe that we shall have learned enough about the remaining characters to be able to establish the nature of the hidden bond between them.'

3

'There are two main figures left on the stage. One of them is with us at this moment.

'I should have preferred to tell this story on different circumstances. It is bound to be extremely painful for Mr. Lloyd.'

'Pain is a relative expression.' Lloyd's voice was cool and indifferent. 'Which episode is this?'

'The burning of the school books.'

'I imagine you obtained that from Palmer. I am sure he gave you a highly coloured account. But I cannot see how you interpret it.'

'I will try to show you.'

Mr. Green proceeded to recall the conversation in which Palmer had described how Lloyd had made a bonfire of the souvenirs of his schooldays. When he had finished this description, he continued: 'I have told that story simply: we are not concerned with its drama but with its significance. I concluded that this lay in the remarkable contrast between Mr. Lloyd's behaviour when he first began to take a revived interest in his old school and when —only a month later—this interest suddenly turned to hatred.

'Consider the dates. At the end of last March Mr. Lloyd instructed Palmer to bring his school things down from the box-rooms. For six weeks he occupied himself in sorting them out.

'In May came this sudden change. It was not merely a slow dying away of interest, it was a violent reversal of emotion. What did it mean?

'To me it could only mean one thing. A man like Mr. Lloyd is not swept off his feet by a sentimental whim. He must have some compelling reason for such conduct. I concluded that the reason for Mr. Lloyd's conduct was deeply personal. I decided that his first mood of exaltation was due to the fact that he was planning the future of *his own son.*'

A deep sigh came from the figure by the fireplace, but Lloyd did not speak.

'And that for some reason which still evaded me, this future had suddenly been shattered.

'How was I to put these conclusions to the test? When I tell you the method I adopted, I may be accused of yet another leap in the dark. I do not think the accusation would be justified. Mr. Lloyd's conduct suggested that he was projecting himself into the future of his own son, reliving his schooldays in his son's image. The most natural conclusion was that he would ensure that future by entering his son's name for the school at the earliest opportunity. The waiting list for some of our great schools is so long that many parents enter their son's names within a few days of their birth.

'Here I had a stroke of luck. Marlbourne College happens to be not only Mr. Lloyd's old school but my own. I therefore decided to pay a visit to Marlbourne. The Bursar is an old friend of mine. My visit confirmed my assumptions to the full. Mr. Lloyd will correct me if I am wrong.

'On March 31st last, Mr. Lloyd made a formal application to the Bursar of Marlbourne College for the entry of his son. The description of the boy was "Andrew Lawrence Lloyd, aged five years."

'On May 18th the Bursar received a further letter from Mr. Lloyd. He showed it to me. It was so brief that I memorized it. It ran: "Sir, kindly ignore my previous letter regarding the child described to you as Andrew Lawrence Lloyd. My application was made in error and is hereby cancelled."

'In the light of our previous assumptions, this letter told a very clear story. The first point it established was that the child Andrew Lawrence Lloyd was still alive. It is inconceivable that a man who had *lost* his son would use such a phrase as "my application was made in error". Not only would it be inhuman, it would be meaningless. The second point was that Mr. Lloyd had suddenly discovered that the child was not his at all. The normal phrase to have used would have been "my son". There is a sort of hostility, a deliberate rejection, about the words "the child described to you as Andrew Lawrence Lloyd."

'These are, perhaps, steps in the dark. But I do not think these can be regarded as *leaps* in the dark. Consider the dates on these two letters. The first was written on the 31st March, only a few days after Mr. Lloyd had installed Miss Larue in her new home at Elvira Place. Are we justified in attaching any significance to this coincidence of dates? I believe that we are. Here is a man, who has an illicit association with a woman for a period of five years. He has been quite content that it should be conducted in modest circumstances.

'Suddenly he instals her in a luxurious house, and engages a staff. He does this at a time when he is in a state of exaltation, having discovered that he is the father of a son. Is it unreasonable to suppose that Miss Larue was the son's mother?'

'There is only one flaw in this assumption. If Mr. Lloyd's liaison with Miss Larue had been continuous over a period of five years, how could he have been previously unaware of the existence of this son?'

The financier half turned, so that his face was in profile. There was a faint smile on his lips.

'But surely, Mr. Green, you know the answer to that?'

'Am I right in assuming that your association with Miss Larue had not, in fact, been continuous?'

'Quite right.'

'Had there been a lapse of some years between your first meeting with her and the time of her reappearance?'

'There had.'

'She was, indeed, a voice from the past?'

'She was.'

'And one of the reasons why you listened to that voice was because . . .'

'You are very clever, Mr. Green.' The financier's voice was harsh and abrupt. 'But is it fair to exercise your cleverness at the cost of my humiliation?'

He rose to his feet, and then sank back in his chair.

'Forgive me; that was a quite unwarranted outburst.' He put his hand over his eyes. 'The whole theme of this story, as you well know, centres round my humiliation. You might as well tell it to the full.'

Mr. Green glanced at him covertly; he was acquainted with the symptoms of hysteria; he wondered how long Lloyd would be able to keep a grip on himself.

'But I cannot tell it to the full, Mr. Lloyd, as you are well aware. I have nearly reached the point where you will have to fill in the gaps.'

Lloyd nodded. 'When you reach that point . . . we will see.'

4

'The rest of my story,' resumed Mr. Green, can be told by a picture. Or rather, by two pictures.'

'The first is a rough sketch of a cherub which was scribbled by Mr. Lloyd on the plan which he drew up to illustrate the position of the guests on the night of the tragedy.' He turned to Waller. 'You remember it?'

'I remember it all right. It was damned ugly.'

'Quite. And the ugliness was deliberate.'

'So what?'

'Does it not strike you as a curious thing for Mr. Lloyd to have drawn? A cherub with a hump and a squint? Does it not occur to you that the man who drew that might have some form of obsession?'

'Maybe. But I don't see where it takes us.'

'It takes us to the picture over the mantlepiece. The picture that was stabbed to the heart. I am going to tell you the story of that picture. When I have done so . . .' His eyes flicked for a moment in the direction of the financier. He received no response. He went on:

'The picture was purchased from the firm of Voss and Kauffman on November the twelfth 1953. I would ask you to remember that date. Mr. Kauffman happens to be an old friend of mine. I called to see him, and discovered two facts of primary importance.

'The first fact related to the legend of the picture itself. It claims that the model for the Virgin was the artist's own wife, and the model for the child—his own son. The second fact was that the purchase of the picture was the occasion of a violent argument between Mr. and Mrs. Lloyd. Mr. Lloyd stamped out of the gallery in a towering rage, leaving Mrs. Lloyd in tears.'

'Why was Mr. Lloyd so extremely hostile to this picture? Mr. Kauffman's explanation was interesting, but to my mind it did not meet all the facts. He suggested that it was because Lloyd was a perfectionist. The smallest crack in a piece of porcelain, the least blemish on the veneer of a table, and he would not even consider it for his collection. In Kauffman's opinion Lloyd projected this perfectionism to the picture. The child in the picture was deformed, so he would have none of it. A plausible theory in its way, but it underrated Lloyd's intelligence. A man of taste does not reject a work of art because the subject-matter is displeasing; if he were to do so how would he reconcile himself to Rembrandt's warts, or Holbein's wrinkles, or for that matter, some of the most powerful works of Hogarth?'

'But if . . .' and here Mr. Green spoke very slowly, emphasizing his words with the tap of his small plump forefinger . . . 'if the picture portrayed some object which was personally intolerable to him—if, every time he looked at it, he suffered an agony of the soul . . .'

He did not finish the sentence, for Waller had clapped his great fists together. 'Good Lord!' he cried. 'I believe I understand at last! The drawing of the cherub on the plan . . .'

'Quite. It was a drawing of the same child, and it was always in his subconscious.'

'And the picture itself? It reminded him of a real child—his own child—*their* child?'

'That was my assumption.'

Slowly they all turned in the direction of Andrew Lloyd. His eyes were closed and his face was set in a mask.

He heaved a deep sigh.

At last, he began to speak.

ANDREW LLOYD'S STORY

'WE were married in November 1950. I was thirty-one, she was twenty-three. We had everything in the world that two people could want. We were very much in love, but it was not primarily a physical love; it was rather an exquisite identity of interests, made all the stronger by the fact that it had a material foundation. We both—quite unashamedly—liked money. I believe that we spent it with some intelligence; Broome is a proof of that. But we also liked money for its own sake, and for the sense of power that it gave us.

'There was only one thing lacking—a son. In the early Spring of 1953 Nancy told me that she was going to have a child. I shall always remember that moment. It was a brilliant morning in March. We were walking through the woods. I looked up to the sky and I said to her: "We neither of us really believe in God . . . but just as a long chance, a sort of covering bet . . . suppose we say thank You?" And we both said thank You.

'Maybe God heard us. Maybe He was waiting to strike two people who were having rather more than their share of His bounty. But whether it was God, or Fate, or the person Thomas Hardy described as "The President of the Immortals," He struck.

'It was midsummer—the twentieth of June to be precise. I had come home earlier than usual; it was a golden evening and I wanted to see the sun setting on the lakes. After dinner we sat on the terrace. I noticed that Nancy was looking a little pale, and I suggested that we should go for a drive in the cool of the evening. She smiled and nodded and went in to get a scarf.

'I chose a new car which had just been delivered—a Bugatti sports model. I had never driven it before, and I wanted to test it on the open road. I knew that Nancy would enjoy this too; that was another thing we had in common—a love of speed. I shall always remember the remark she made when she climbed in by my side. She turned to me and said: "Is it really true what they say about this car? Is it really true that it's becalmed at eighty?"

' "We'll see," I said.'

Lloyd hesitated. Almost in a whisper he muttered . . . 'And we saw.'

'I have lived over that moment so many hundreds of times that I could probably describe the accident to you without undue emotion. It has become like a tragedy that has grown meaningless to me by constant repetition. We crashed over Blackstone Quarry. When they picked us up, Nancy's child had been born, and by some miracle it was alive. I had been more seriously injured than my wife, and it was not till nearly a month later that I saw my son for the first time, when I went to visit Nancy in hospital. It was not a pretty sight. The spine was hopelessly twisted. There was little hope that he would ever see or hear. For all practical purposes, the child was an idiot. I hated it. And my hatred was made all the more bitter when they told me that Nancy would never bear a child again.'

2

'We can pass quickly over the next two and a half years, and move the clock forward to last January. As I said, I hated the little twisted thing that was my son, and I never saw it again. I put it out of my mind. I concentrated on the one thing that might help me to forget—making money—more and more money.

'And then, suddenly Margot came back into my life, and everything was changed. The precise date was January the eighth. It was a Sunday, and that morning the *Sunday*

Mail printed a sensational front page story about the millions I had been making on the Stock Exchange. I was none too pleased; I have always tried to avoid publicity. I particularly resented the photograph of me, which was spread across three columns. It was six years old, and showed me as I had been when my association with Margot came to an end.

'This was the photograph that Margot saw and recognized, and this was the story that she read. You can imagine the effect it had on her. We had parted amicably when I married, and she had not seen me for over five years. Nor had she made any effort to do so; she did not even know my real name, and though I had been reasonably generous, she had no idea that I was a very rich man.

'But now it was a different matter. I was a millionaire. So she sat down and wrote me a letter, and in the letter she told me that she had been searching desperately for me, for I was the father of her son. And she asked me what I was going to do about it.

'Any normal man, on reading such a letter, would have taken one of two courses. He would have thrown it into the waste-paper basket or he would have sent it to his solicitor. Here was a woman whom I had not seen for over five years. She was not, in the strict sense of the word, a prostitute, but she was quite openly . . . shall we say "supported" . . . by several men, of whom I was only one.

'Any normal man, therefore, would have treated such a letter with contempt. But I was not a normal man. I was a man who longed, above all things, for a son. If I had any doubts, I stifled them. It must be true; it *had* to be true.

'I saw Margot that same evening. She played her part with great intelligence. She showed me the birth certificate of the boy, who had been christened Andrew Larue. The date on the certificate tallied with her story. She did not ask for money for herself, she only pleaded with me to help him. As if I needed any encouragement! And then she took me to see him.'

'I won't attempt to describe that first meeting with my

"son". If there is such a thing as paternal instinct it was obviously lacking in my case. He was being looked after by a grim-looking woman who kept a dubious boarding-house near King's Cross. He bore no sort of resemblance to myself; he had rather coarse features, and he looked young for a child of nearly five. But I accepted him unreservedly. For a little while, I walked on air.'

3

Lloyd suddenly rose to his feet.

'The room is growing chilly,' he muttered. He stepped to the fireplace and threw some logs on the dying fire.

'All these things,' he resumed, 'are implicit in Mr. Green's deduction. But there is one fact that he could never have known, unless he were a thought-reader. It concerns Marlbourne College.

'Mr. Green has told you of his visit to my old school, and his discovery that I had entered my "son" as a future pupil. That was a brilliant piece of deduction. What he did not know was that it was a letter from the Bursar of Marlbourne which began the whole chain of events that ended in last night's tragedy.

'This letter—it was merely a formal acceptance of my application—I carried about with me. You may tell me that this was madness; no doubt it was; but that letter meant more than any love-letter.

'And one day, Nancy found it. Palmer, who usually valets me, was ill; she went into my bedroom to hang up my clothes; and she found it in the pocket of my coat. It was as simple, as crude as that. But there was nothing very simple or crude about the scene that followed. If it had been played on the stage it would probably have been described as excessively sophisticated. We were both quite calm. I told her the facts. There was no need for me to interpret them for her. She knew, only too well, what it would mean to me to be the father of a son. I told her that I proposed to adopt him legally, and to make him with her, my joint heir.

'If I had not been utterly blind, I should have been warned by her reaction. She was incredibly restrained. She had been stabbed to the heart. It was not only a question of wounded pride, of jealousy, of all the normal reactions. There was more to it than that . . . there was Broome. Broome meant even more to Nancy than to myself; she was brought up here as a child; it had been in her family for generations; and though they had been obliged to sell it, she had always dreamed, even as a little girl, of coming home again. When she married me she told me, quite frankly, that one of her reasons for accepting me was that I was rich enough to buy Broome; indeed, she made it a condition of the marriage.

'And yet, at this moment when—without a moment's warning, remember—she was suddenly informed that Broome would one day pass into the hands of another woman's son . . . she scarcely raised her eyebrows. She merely asked me, quite quietly, how I could be sure that it was my son. I replied that I was sure, and that was an end of it. She looked at me, with a little smile, and then she went out of the room—as she said, "to think things over".

'Nancy had one of the quickest brains I have ever known, and she must have made her plan of campaign in the next couple of minutes. The first part of that plan was to prove that the boy was not my son at all. In order to do that, she must have access to him. When she came back into the room, she gave me the impression that she had accepted the situation. I was deeply grateful, and I readily allowed her to visit the boy. She showed not the smallest interest in Margot. She said that she was not jealous of such women, who were merely physical conveniences. And the following day she went to see my "son". She went, at her own insistence, alone.

'To this day I do not know the full story of her inquiries in the next four weeks; all I need tell you is that at last she succeeded in her purpose. It was a question—as you will probably have guessed—of a blood test. She knew that I belonged to the group known as AB. She obtained a test of the boy. He belonged to group O. It was genetically impossible that I could have been the father.

'She confronted me with this evidence. She showed no sign of exhilaration; she did not even raise her voice; she might have been giving an opinion—as she often did—on a speculative investment.

'It was then that I said something to her for which I shall never forgive myself. I looked at her and I said: "You have ruined my life."

'Even then, she did not reproach me. She merely asked me: "What are you going to do?"

'I told her: "I am going to have another son."

'She said: "By Margot Larue?"

'I told her . . . yes.

'She nodded. I suppose that nod was Margot's death sentence.'

4

Lloyd paused and turned to Charlotte. 'Would you think me discourteous if I asked you, at this point, to leave the room?'

Charlotte flushed, and glanced at her uncle.

'There are some things,' insisted the financier, 'that I should find it difficult to say in front of a young lady.'

'I understand.' She rose to her feet and left them.

'And one of those things,' he continued, as soon as she had closed the door, 'concerns what one might call the chemistry of sex.

'I am not a highly physical man.' He frowned and half closed his eyes, as though arguing a point with himself. 'Perhaps, if I had not been working at top speed all my life, I might have been different. Even so, I doubt whether I should have been the conventional pursuer of women; it is more likely that I should have drifted into some form of abnormality.' He shrugged his shoulders. 'However,

that is by the way. All that need concern us is that—
outside my marriage—Margot Larue was the only woman
for whom I felt anything that could be described as a strong
physical attraction. To put it bluntly, it was highly improbable that I should have been able to consummate a physical
union with anyone else.'

He paused and glanced at the superintendent, who had
nodded to himself. 'I expect that Mr. Waller's experience
has taught him that men like myself are not so rare as may
be generally imagined.

'So the scene was set. I telephoned to Margot and
arranged to see her that night. She was by now installed
in the house at Hampstead. I arrived at about six o'clock.
I had spent a stormy day, but by then I was again master
of myself. I confronted her with the evidence and—after
a moment's hesitation—she accepted it. Perhaps that is
an overstatement; it would be truer to say that she did not
contest it. Margot had a genius for reflecting a man's mood;
my own mood at the moment was completely cold-blooded;
very well . . . she would be cold-blooded too. She realized
that I did not even feel any great resentment against her.
The fact that she had deceived me once did not mean that
she could deceive me again. I merely regarded her as a
necessary partner in a business of vital personal importance.
I had no doubt whatever that if there were any difficulties
they could be resolved by the only god in whom I had
any trust—money.

'But first, I had to know the facts. And some of them
were stranger than even I had imagined.'

The financier turned towards Mr. Green. 'You have
told us that a large part of this story has evaded you. That
is unduly modest. Only a very small part of it has evaded
you. You have deduced the beginning, you have interpreted
almost all of the middle, and you know the ending—which
I hope you will shortly be explaining to us. But there was
one fact that you could not possibly know, because there
were only two people who could have told you—Margot,
who is dead, and myself.'

Mr. Green sat up sharply and began to blink.

'And that fact is that there was not only one child . . . but two.'

Mr. Green ceased to blink and gave a gentle nod.

Lloyd allowed himself a fleeting smile. 'If Mr. Green had already discovered that fact, of his own accord, he is even more of a genius than I imagined. For the benefit of the rest of you I will merely state that the child "Andrew Larue", whose birth certificate she showed me, had lived for only a few weeks. The second child—the child whom I had accepted as my "son"—was born over a year later. It was to this child, when she decided on her plan of deception, that she attached the birth certificate of "Andrew Larue".

'And as we now know, though she did not tell me at the time, the father was Stephen Grey, her husband . . . the man upstairs.'

5

Lloyd glanced towards the ceiling. Then he heaved a deep sigh.

'I have nearly done. When I have finished, perhaps you will realize why I asked our young friend Charlotte to leave the room.

'It may seem inconceivable to you that after these revelations I could possibly have any feelings for Margot but contempt and mistrust. I do not remember that I had either of these feelings. Indeed, the fact that she had duped me increased my admiration for her. The woman who could get the better of Andrew Lloyd was no fool, and I did not desire a fool for the mother of my son. As for mistrust . . . why should I mistrust her when I had a proposition to make which it was so overwhelmingly in her interest to accept?

'I made the proposition there and then. I made it over a candle-lit dinner table, to the accompaniment of an excellent Alsatian wine. (For a woman, she had exceptional taste in wine.) I told her that she was to bear me a child, and I made the conditions as plain and watertight as the most impeccable prospectus. I warned her that I should take out—as it were—an insurance on her fidelity. Her movements would be watched by a private detective. If and when the child was born there would be exhaustive medical tests. If these were satisfactory, the child would be mine, and she would be a rich woman for life.

'All this I told her . . . quite coldly and calmly . . . in the candle-light. Perhaps it was the candle-light that saved my words from sounding so inhuman that I—even I— might have been appalled by them.

'I stayed with her that night.

'That night my son was conceived. My son who was never born.'

Waller suddenly sprang to his feet. 'But Mr. Lloyd,' he cried, 'there's something here that I don't understand. Surely you are aware . . .'

Before he could finish, Mr. Green had interrupted him. He too sprang to his feet with surprising agility. 'I think I know what you are about to say, my friend,' he said. 'And I am quite certain that it would be better if you did not say it.'

'How do you know what I was about to say?'

'I should have thought it was obvious.' He hesitated for a moment. 'But if you doubt me, I will give you a hint. I can best express it by saying that I believe you are concerned by a matter of routine procedure.'

Waller nodded. 'You've hit it,' he said.

'What is all this about?' It was Lloyd speaking.

'It's just something that bears on your story, sir,' he said. 'A matter of common custom.'

'I don't understand.'

'Mr. Waller says it is a matter of common custom.' Mr. Green spoke very gently. 'I should prefer to call it a matter of common kindness.'

'I still don't understand.'

'No. But I hope Mr. Waller does.'

The two men stared at each other across the room. They made a grotesque picture in the flickering firelight— the bald dumpy detective with the shining forehead, and the giant superintendent with the deep shadows under his eyes.

Slowly Waller's face broke into a smile. 'O.K. You win.' He turned to Lloyd. 'Sorry I interrupted, sir. Perhaps you'll go on with your story?'

6

'And now the last, the crucial date . . . September the third.

'This was the day when I came home in a state of almost unbearable tension, because I had seen Margot that afternoon, and had learned that she was going to have a child. This time I was in no doubt that the child would be mine. Apart from the fact that my detectives had been keeping her under constant surveillance, she had every motive of self-interest for wishing to be the mother of my child. She knew enough about me, by then, to realize that as such she could make any demands she chose.

'There was only one problem that concerned me—the attitude of Nancy. However strange it may seem, she was still the most important woman in my life; indeed, she was the only woman in my life. Would I be able to convince her of this? When the child was born, and when she was persuaded that it was in fact my child, would she bring herself to accept the situation? Or would there be a final break? If there were . . . but that was unthinkable. I *must* convince her.

'Once again we sat on the terrace; once again it was a golden evening. I think that Nancy knew what I was going to tell her before I even began to speak. She heard me in silence. She turned to me, and put her hand on mine, and smiled. Then she looked out over the terrace, and her eyes wandered down the valley, towards the lakes, and up to the temple on the hill. And she said, very quietly: "So one day, all this will go to a son of yours."

'The tension was unbearable. I tried to break it with a laugh. I said: "We don't know that it will be a son. It might be a girl."

' "What does it matter, so long as it is a child of yours?" She looked away from me when she said that. I understand why, now. We knew each other so well that there were some lies that could not be said between us. They would reveal themselves in the eyes.

'I could scarcely speak. I was filled with such an over-whelming happiness that I was very near to tears. I managed to stammer out some sort of banal question—something like "Do you really mean that?" And then she said it again: "What does it matter, so long as it is a child of yours?" '

Lloyd's face twisted to a grim smile. 'She must have been rehearsing that line for weeks.

'In fact, the whole of the scene that she proceeded to play—now that we can view it in retrospect—must have been rehearsed down to the last detail. It could not possibly have been improvised; it was too intricate, too smoothly constructed. Look at it from Nancy's point of view. She had decided that no other woman's son should ever inherit Broome. That, I am convinced, was the deciding factor . . . Broome. Therefore, Margot must be eliminated. Having come to this decision, she proceeded to make her plans. It is possible that she had several alternative plans; she was a woman of great resource; what is certain is that the success of any plan would depend, firstly, on disarming my own suspicion, and secondly, on having constant access to Margot herself.

'So she played her little scene, beginning with the cue line . . . "What does it matter, so long as it is a child of yours?" She developed that theme very convincingly. She persuaded me that when the child was born she would forget the mother and remember only the father. "After all," she said, "I might have adopted a child and I might have come to love it, even though I had no ties with it at all."

'That was part one of her act. Part two was more difficult to put across; I remember that even in my unnatural state of exaltation I could hardly believe that any woman could have been capable of such generosity, such self-sacrifice, as she was now showing. From now on, she declared, Margot must become one of the family. We must do all in our power to make her feel at home. We must do this for the sake of her unborn child. We must see to it, of course, that she had the best possible medical attention; but we must do more than that . . . we must set her mind at rest, we must see to it that she had no anxieties, we must make her feel that our friends were her friends.

'As she talked, I sat and listened, and marvelled, and rejoiced. A situation of infinite complexity and delicacy seemed suddenly to have resolved itself . . . thanks to Nancy. The shadow of losing her seemed to have vanished for ever.

' "We must ask her to Broome for as long as she may care to stay," she said. "I insist on it. And you must leave everything to me." She rose to her feet, saying that there was no time to be lost, and that she wished to make some rearrangement in the guest rooms. Then she bent down and kissed me. She whispered that it would all come right in the end.

'For a moment she stood there in the fading sunlight, looking out across the valley. Her eyes were shining very brightly, as though she had found a new purpose in life.

'Suddenly she laughed, quite lightly and gaily. She said: "It's all rather a joke, isn't it?" Then she ran into the house.'

Lloyd nodded to himself. 'It's all rather a joke,' he repeated. 'Maybe that was the moment when she thought of it. Or perhaps she had already made up her mind. It is of no consequence. But if I had understood that remark, if I had been able to interpret it, she would be alive today.'

He turned to Mr. Green. 'Perhaps you will be good enough to interpret it for us?'

'If you insist,' said Mr. Green.

MR. GREEN CONCLUDES

'A Joke' repeated Mr. Green, staring into the fire.

The superintendent stirred uneasily. 'If this is your idea of humour . . .'

'No, Waller. It is not. But it was still a joke, even if it was the grimmest joke that was ever played.'

Lloyd turned his head. 'Perhaps Mr. Green had better tell his story in his own way.'

'There is so little to tell,' demurred Mr. Green. 'And I am afraid that after the very moving story to which we have just listened, it will come as an anti-climax. However . . .

'I will preface these last few words with a general observation. The man or woman who intends to commit a murder, particularly a murder in which a number of other people are involved—a murder, as it were, on a crowded stage—must make the best of the human material at hand. He must take advantage of every human weakness that he sees around him, he must exploit every human folly.

'Mrs. Lloyd was well aware of this, and I have no doubt whatever that she timed her plan with these considerations in mind. The week-end of October the thirteenth gave her a special opportunity, because two of the guests had peculiarities which could be used to her advantage.

'The first of these guests, of course, was Lord Richard Marwood, the practical joker. Mr Lloyd has told you of the conversation on the terrace, at the end of which his wife used the surprising words . . . "It's all rather a joke, isn't it?" He has suggested that Mrs. Lloyd's plan may have been born at that very moment. That is possible. What seems certain is that from the outset she decided that Lord Richard was to be an unwitting accomplice.'

'But how? There are endless varieties of practical jokes, and many of them have an element of danger. We have all read stories of the joke that ended in tragedy. But Mrs. Lloyd, if she considered them at all, must have rejected them as too crude and too obvious. What she wanted was a joke with the simplicity of genius. And she found it.'

He turned to Waller. 'Here then is the end of the story. Anything that follows must necessarily be only in the nature of a tidying up.'

Deliberately the little man paused. He gave the superintendent a quizzical smile. Then he said:

'There was not one shot only. There were two.'

Waller stared at him.

'The shot that the guests heard, at a quarter to eleven—the shot that sent them speeding upstairs—was not the shot that killed Margot Larue. It was fired outside, into the air, by Lord Richard.'

Waller gave a long, low whistle.

'You will remember my remarking on the strange fact that nobody—not even the lodge-keeper—had noticed his arrival, and my assumption that he must have switched off his lights and his engine, and free-wheeled down the drive. Lord Richard has since confirmed this assumption. He also confirmed the assumption—which followed automatically—that he stayed outside in the dark, waiting. Thanks to Mr. Lloyd, we know what he was waiting for.'

The financier looked up sharply. 'Thanks to me?'

Mr. Green smiled.

'Do you not remember telling me that just before the sound of the shot was heard, Mrs. Lloyd stepped across the gallery, drew the curtains, and looked out?'

'Did I tell you that? I had forgotten. It seemed such a trivial detail.'

'It was anything but trivial. It was the signal for the shot to be fired.'

Waller lurched forward in his chair. 'But what in heaven's name did Lord Richard imagine he was *doing*?'

It was Lloyd who answered the question. 'Lord Richard

was not in the habit of imagining.' His voice was curt and bitter. 'He has the mind of a schoolboy. He thought it was all part of a joke to enliven a dull week-end. For all I know, he still does.'

Mr. Green spoke gently. 'I think that is hardly fair to the young man.'

'Forgive me. I will not interrupt again.'

Mr. Green turned to Waller. 'At the time Lord Richard fired his shot, Margot Larue had been dead for nearly an hour. She was shot within a few seconds of entering her room—as soon as she had lain down on her bed. She was killed with an icy deliberation. I do not think that the adjective is excessive. Every second counted, and every second was used. Only one shot was needed. A moment later, Mrs. Lloyd locked the door of the bedroom from the inside. She went out by the door of the bathroom, locking it from the outside and taking the key with her. She presumably intended to replace this key when she returned with the rest of the guests an hour later—after the "dummy" shot, fired by Lord Richard. Something must have prevented her, so . . .'

'So that was why the key was lying on the carpet?'

'Precisely. It was one of the few occasions when luck was against her. Not that luck played any great part in her calculations. They were dovetailed with almost perfect precision. They all fitted in.

'Consider the gramophone record, which I described as my first "clue" . . . to use a word of which I am not over fond. From the outset, that record disturbed me. It was like a question mark. It was a gross and ugly thing which had been bought by a woman of exquisite taste. Why? We can now answer that question. She bought it because she was contemplating a gross and ugly deed. And she needed noise—strident, ugly noise—to cover the evidence of that deed. Margot Larue's bedroom was a long way from the music room, in a quiet corner of the house. She had made sure of that. With all the guests assembled downstairs and the servants in their own rooms on the other side of the house, it was improbable that the sound of a shot would be heard at all. But she wanted to make doubly sure. Hence the record. It was what might be described as "a clue of sound". Lady Coniston's deafness might also be described as "a clue of sound"—or rather, the lack of sound. The connexion between these two clues was not immediately apparent to me, but that there was some connexion I was convinced.

'One final question remains. How could she be sure that Lord Richard would not betray her? But surely, that is not a very intelligent question? From the moment she had persuaded him to co-operate, she had nothing to fear. An innocent and harmless action on his part had suddenly become invested with an extraordinary menace. Even though he may have been bewildered by the course of events, it was overwhelmingly in his interest to remain silent. You may also ask . . . was it not "out of character" that Mrs. Lloyd should ask Lord Richard to run this risk for her? Apart from her determination to eliminate Margot Larue, she was an honourable woman, and she had a fondness for young Lord Richard. But *was* she asking him to run a risk? I do not think so. Her plan was timed so carefully that Lord Richard could not possibly be involved in it. And if it had not been for the presence of Stephen Grey—the man upstairs—hiding in the shadows, he never would have been involved at all.'

2

Mr. Green glanced up to the ceiling. 'The man upstairs—Stephen Grey, alias Mr. Jones. It is curious how one has come to think of him as merely "the man upstairs", as though he were someone anonymous, some figure lurking in the shadows.

'Thanks to Mr. Waller, who has a genius for extracting bedside confessions, we now know rather more about Mr. Grey than we knew before. There is not, indeed, very much to know; his is a small and squalid story which need not long detain us. His marriage to Margot Larue took place five years ago; it was apparently the aftermath of some drunken party. Grey was, and still is, a merchant seaman; no doubt he gave his bride an exaggerated account of his circumstances, and no doubt she concealed from him her true way of life; it seems highly unlikely that two such people would have contemplated a permanent union, if they had known all the facts about each other. The marriage was a casual affair, and we may assume that even the birth of a son did little to cement it; if Grey had felt any natural affection for his son he would hardly have allowed him to be "farmed out". They would probably have drifted apart altogether, but last January, when Grey returned from a long trip, he discovered that his wife had left her old apartment. He became suspicious and made inquiries. She seemed to have vanished without trace, but eventually he tracked her to Hampstead, where she refused to see him. Grey was not angered by this refusal; on the contrary. He had discovered his wife living in a luxurious house under the name of "Mrs. Stanwyck". The obvious assumption was that she had contracted a bigamous marriage.

'That is all that need concern us about Mr. Grey. He is not a very interesting person, and his subsequent career follows well-worn lines. At first reading, his blackmailing letter to his wife has a sinister ring; it is couched in bombastic terms. In fact, it was a simple demand for money. Let me remind you of it.'

Mr. Green reached for a piece of paper by his side and adjusted his glasses. '*Dear Margot, So you are determined to play the Sphinx. Very well. If it isn't in my hands by Saturday night there will be a showdown. And I don't mean merely a little matter of social embarrassment.*'

He paused. There was a faint wrinkling of his nose. 'I said a moment ago that this letter told us nothing beyond the fact that it was a demand for money. Perhaps I was wrong. Is it unduly fanciful to suggest that it also tells us something of the character of the writer? It is improper

not only legally but socially. The word "show-down",
for example, is hardly a phrase that would be used by a
gentleman. Nor are the words "a little matter of social
embarrassment".

'The really important thing about this letter, from our
point of view, is that it was Mrs. Lloyd's second stroke of
bad luck, and by far the more serious one. If it had been
destroyed, it is highly improbable that Mr. Waller would
be sitting here today. Even if it had not been destroyed,
Mrs. Lloyd's secret might never have been discovered,
provided that the answer had arrived in time.

'But the answer did not arrive in time. For that, Palmer
was to blame. Miss Larue, as we know from Palmer's
evidence, received the note by the second post on Friday.
She did not answer it at once. On the following day, the
day of her death, she must have felt that she should have
answered it. The threat of "a little matter of social embarrassment" may have worried her. She scribbled her reply, and
gave it to Palmer to deliver by hand. But Palmer did not
deliver it. He posted it.

'And so, there was Mr. Grey, waiting in the Red
Dragon Inn for a letter that never arrived. And when the
time of his ultimatum had expired—ten o'clock on Saturday
night—he came to Broome. Perhaps the size of the house
intimidated him, perhaps he was afraid of approaching the
great portico and ringing the bell and confronting the
butler. Perhaps he was merely a little drunk. Whatever the
reason, he hesitated and stepped into the shadows. Then
he saw Lord Richard and heard the shot, and was a silent
witness to the commotion. And his sharp little brain told
him that perhaps there were even greater prospects ahead
than he had expected, if he bided his time.

'From this moment onwards his behaviour follows the
classic pattern of all blackmailers. *L'appetit vient en mangeant*
was certainly true of Stephen Grey. His original demands
would probably have been modest enough. But after the
death of his wife . . . although he was wise enough to lie
low till he knew the result of the inquest . . . he realized

that if he played his cards properly, he was in a position to make any demands he chose. The trouble was, he played his cards too well. He was so sure of himself that he was ruthless. He was so ruthless that he compelled Lord Richard, in sheer desperation, to take Mr. Lloyd into his confidence. And that started a chain of events of which the end was inevitable tragedy. It compelled Mr. Lloyd to challenge his wife, and it compelled her to confess to him.'

Mr. Green turned to the financier. 'Am I right in suggesting that your immediate reaction to her confession was not shock at the crime itself, nor concern for Margot Larue, but grief for the unborn child?'

Lloyd gave a bitter laugh. 'Grief would be a mild word for it. It was a murderous resentment. For a few hours I was not quite sane. That is why I came down in the middle of the night and stabbed the picture. I was saying to myself . . . "She has killed my child; very well, I will kill hers." As soon as that act was accomplished, all those feelings left me.'

'And you became her ally?'

'As far as it was possible. But there was not much one could do.'

Mr. Green nodded. 'No. There was not much. Mr. Grey saw to that. If he had not been so implacable . . . But then, we must remember, he felt sure of himself. He had no doubt whatever that his demands would be met. That is why, yesterday morning, he telephoned to Mr. Waller and asked him to stand by. It was the final act of intimidation . . . the act of a dictator. It left Mrs. Lloyd with no alternative. To kill herself, after she had first killed him. I have no doubt whatever that she thought she had done this, when she went to her death.'

Mr. Green turned to Lloyd with a sad little smile. 'I think she was acting to save the two great loves of her life—yourself, and Broome. You would be set free, and your secrets would be safe. And one day, perhaps, you would be able to fight back, and rebuild your fortune, so that the time would come when the old house would belong to you again, and through you . . . to her.'

There was silence. Lloyd stared into Mr. Green's eyes. It was as though he were trying to read some message in them. Then he nodded and rose slowly to his feet.

At the doorway he paused. He said one word, very softly . . . 'Thank you." Then he went out.

Waller walked over to the fireplace, and kicked a dying log with his great boot.

'I'm glad you stopped me,' he said. 'You were referring to the inquest, of course, and the fact that there was no trace of pregnancy.'

'Yes.'

'I'd have thought that a man like Lloyd would have known that in cases of female suicide an examination for that sort of thing was automatic.'

'That is because you are a policeman.'

'Maybe.' Waller sighed. 'Thank God you reminded me that I'm also a man.'

Mr. Green stared into the fire. 'If we had spoken,' he said, 'if we had told him that she had lied, that his hopes had been groundless, that the death of his wife had been totally unnecessary, I think it would have destroyed him. As it is . . .'

He glanced towards the door. From the end of the long gallery came the soft echo of music. Mr. Green's face softened.

'As it is,' he said, 'while there is life, and Mozart, there is hope.'

POSTSCRIPT

MAYBE Broome, one day, will again belong to Andrew Lloyd. Even in these times, a man who has lost a fortune can still make another, if money is his god.

Meanwhile, the great house lies empty and deserted. Perhaps you saw the photographs of it in *Country Life*, when it was advertised for sale. "The finest residential estate in the South of England," they called it. The price was £100,000—"or near offer". There were, indeed, several prospective buyers. There was a Canadian carpet king. There was a French wine merchant and a German ship owner. There was a motor manufacturer, a Lancashire cotton millionaire, a newspaper magnate, and even a Spanish royal duke. All these important persons, with their secretaries, their wives and their advisers, were greatly impressed. Here, they agreed, one could live *en prince*. Many were the hours they spent, wandering through the great rooms, exploring the incomparable gardens, standing by the temple on the lake.

And yet, for some reason which none of them could quite explain, nobody made an offer. There was something not quite—not quite "suitable"—about it. This discovery, curiously enough, they all seemed to make towards the end of their inspections, when dusk was falling, and the mists were creeping up from the valley. The wife of the Canadian carpet king, for example, standing in the twilit music-room. suddenly announced, in a strained and unnatural voice, that "this was no place for children". And though one would have thought that it was, indeed, a paradise for children, her husband quickly agreed with her.

Perhaps it was the small daughter of the German ship owner who hit the nail on the head. She had wandered off by herself on to the terrace while her father was inspecting some of the conservatories. When he returned, he found her sitting on the balustrade, staring out on to the darkening valley. She seemed to be listening for something.

Whe she turned to him, her little face was troubled. She put her hand in his. '*Warum singt hier Kein Vogel?*' she whispered.

Why does no bird sing at Broome? Perhaps you know the answer.